Hi Nickie:
Enjoy the's
Buckeyes thrilling

Denny Hausker
MSU class of 1969

SECRETS

IN A CORRUPTED SOCIETY

DENNIS K. HAUSKER

Copyright © 2021 Dennis K. Hausker
All rights reserved
First Edition

PAGE PUBLISHING, INC.
Conneaut Lake, PA

First originally published by Page Publishing 2021

ISBN 978-1-6624-6419-5 (pbk)
ISBN 978-1-6624-6420-1 (digital)

Printed in the United States of America

CHAPTER 1

Mentally distracted by her concerns, Lily stared blankly at her reflection in the vanity mirror as her mind was elsewhere, pondering job issues. Living dual lives had always been challenging, but recently it was becoming more difficult. Outside her bedroom door, she heard her children arguing.

Like living examples of sibling rivalry gone to extreme, Tommy at eight and Cathy at seven sparred constantly over virtually anything and everything. It brought Lily out of her stupor. Fluffing her long dark hair one last time, she arose to head out of the bedroom to start her day. Standing for a moment, she adjusted her dark-blue wool dress, or at least she tried. Static caused it to cling too tightly nonetheless. Regardless, it was a cold winter day, which in her case meant dressing in wool.

Stepping into the hallway, her kids quieted, looking at her unsympathetic facial expression.

"Enough, I'm not in the mood for it today."

"But—" Tommy started to complain.

"Shhh!" She pointed her finger at him, her face with a stern look.

The children were cowed. "I'm hungry, Mom," Cathy whispered.

She nodded. "Okay…so let's go eat, folks."

In the kitchen, three bowls, three spoons, and three juice glasses later, Lily put out the OJ, milk carton, and cereal boxes.

"Eat up. The bus will be coming soon."

Tommy had her husband Jack's brown hair, while Cathy had Lily's long black hair. She looked like a miniature Lily. However, her hair could often be askew.

"Cathy, did you comb your hair?"

Cathy answered, "Yes."

Tommy added, "No."

It started another argument. Lily simmered and replied too angrily.

"Stop! Cathy, go comb your hair again, and, Tommy, mind your own business."

Later, after shooing them out the door, Lily watched them through the window joining the other neighborhood children waiting for the school bus. It always tugged at her heart watching her babies get on the bus to go out into the world. Lily saw the world much differently than the other neighborhood moms.

Jack was still away on his overseas business trip until the weekend. It always bothered Lily when no parent was available during the day.

"Oh well," she muttered reflectively. "Time to jump back into it, Lily."

Grabbing her gym bag, she walked into the garage.

Opening the garage door, she backed her new black Ford Mustang out onto the street and drove away toward her office.

The weather was overcast and gloomy, like her mood. It started misting as she drove along, so she turned on her windshield wipers, setting it on intermittent.

Turning on her radio, she listened to the news, which always seemed to be problematic these days. Idling along in a traffic backup on the expressway, her thoughts raced again. The taillights of the cars ahead looked like a long winding glowing red snake.

She mused, *There is so much to do and so little time. I wonder if the report is in yet?*

Speculating was risky in her line of work; hence she needed facts. That field report was a way she got those critical facts.

After an hour on the road, she finally reached her exit and headed onto side streets to the office parking structure. Pulling into her unofficial parking space, Lily got out and walked toward the elevator door. Pushing the button on her key fob, she heard the chirp from locking her car, but as a habit, she always looked backed anyway to see the doors lock.

Three colleagues were waiting there, waiting for the elevator door to open.

"Hi, Lily," said Nancy Mitchell.

"Hi, Nancy. Hey, Carrie, Marnie."

"You dressed up today. What's up, Lily? I'm not sure I've ever seen you in a dress before."

"I've got that meeting I'm not ready for."

"There's nothing you're not ready for, darling." Nancy punched her playfully on the shoulder.

Lily smiled while her friends laughed.

"We'll see about that. This is a delegation from Washington, DC. I doubt they're coming to exchange pleasantries."

"You'll be fine."

"I repeat, we'll see."

They rode upward to the tenth floor, where the friends went to their clerical desks, while Lily went to her office.

Her phone was ringing.

"Hello?"

"Are you here yet?"

Lily chuckled. "Obviously. I just answered your call, didn't I, Wesley."

"I called because I heard some of my British friends will be coming to our meeting."

"That sounds worrisome. Do you have any idea what this is about?"

"I do not. However I'm going to let you do all of the talking."

"That's not going to happen. You're in this as much as I am, whatever 'this' is."

Lily glanced to her door as her boss, Ray Stager, loomed.

"I've got to go, Wesley. Yes, sir, what can I do for you?"

"The meeting has been moved up. Our visitors should be here soon."

"Okay. Do we have any idea—"

"No, we don't. At this point, we respond to whatever they say." He cut her off tersely.

"That's pretty nebulous."

"It is what it is." He scowled before walking away.

His unusual mood for a mild-mannered guy left her puzzled. For a rare time, Lily felt anxiety.

Sifting through her new mail, she immersed into it to take her mind off her tension. That didn't completely work as her roiling tummy remained.

It seemed like no time had passed before Wesley came to her office.

"They're here. Are you ready?"

"Probably not."

They walked to the large conference room, which was filling rapidly. Among the visiting delegation were numerous military uniforms. Lily recognized some SEAL team acquaintances. Donna Smith, a light-skinned Black woman from Detroit; Joe Gilson, a Biloxi, Mississippi, sharp shooter; and Andy Rieger, a "Boston Strong" former police officer. All three were in superb physical condition and confident in their demeanor.

They walked over to her.

"Hey, Lily."

"Donna, what are you doing hanging out with these two reprobates?"

Donna laughed. "Joe and Andy are like gum stuck to my shoes that I can't get off."

Lily noted, in spite of the banter, both guys had serious expressions.

"Are you guys okay? You look pretty grim."

Before they could respond, her boss spoke. "Everybody, go find a seat. We've got a lot to cover."

It took only moments for everybody to sit down.

"First, I'd like to welcome our friends from MI-6. Also, we have Ari Goldstein from Mossad and Hassan Aboud from Egyptian intelligence. Everything that is said in this meeting is classified, so repeat it to no one, no exceptions. Understood?"

"Yes, sir," everyone spoke in unison.

"I also want to point out we have Bill Barton from the FBI, Cal Greer from NSA, Captain Patty Baymill from the US Navy. As you can see, she brought three friends, all SEALs. You all know John Jakes from the White House staff and Megan McCoin, also from the White House staff. You already know the CIA agents in the room. I called back more folks, but they're away on overseas assignments currently. They'll be back as needed. We do have Lily Carson here, Ron Gray, Steve Sawyer, and Grace Bailey. You overseas folk know Lily very well."

"Oxford University hasn't been the same since she left England with her master's degree," Wesley Bromwell joked.

The room laughed.

She tried to smile, as all eyes were suddenly on her, to cover her annoyance. Attention was not something she ever sought. For her, it was something unsolicited that always landed on her going all the way back to elementary school and had followed her all the way through college and into her current life. Beauty had always seemed a curse for a person who chose to ignore the trappings. Equally, she attended office social gatherings only when required.

"The reason we have some visitors like the FBI here in this room is that we're unsure what this operation is going to involve. There could be both foreign and domestic situations to deal with. I can only say you didn't get advanced warning because we didn't know anything before yesterday."

He looked around the room at many confused faces.

Before he could explain, the door opened.

"Admiral Billings, I didn't know you would be attending." Ray had a look of surprise. "As you all know, the admiral is chairman of the Joint Chiefs. Welcome, sir."

"I didn't know I was coming here either, Ray. The president asked me to sit in to brief him directly right away after we're done."

"Certainly, sir. I…eh…let me start by explaining we have covert operations ongoing in numerous hot spots, and recently, some disturbing chatter has surfaced that points to a very dangerous situation. What's different is the same rumors are being heard in locations all across the globe. As you know, some radical movements are multinational, but in this case, we suspect they are banding together to hatch some serious trouble outside of their own regions. If that is true, you can see why they have our attention. The what, when, and where is something we need to know right now. We're directing our staff to reach out to our local contacts to shake the tree and see what falls down. Once we get a preliminary idea of what we're dealing with, we can dispatch assets to address the issues we find. In a sense, we're mirroring their idea of combining forces, which is why Mossad and Egyptian intelligence are sitting side by side. There will be other international partnerships included, but with such short notice, we couldn't get everybody here this quickly."

He paused to take a swallow of water. Lily noticed the Poland Springs brand name on the plastic bottle. It brought back a pleasant memory of vacationing in Maine, coincidentally, near one of their bottling plants.

"Admiral, would you like to add anything?"

"Thanks, Ray. I'd like to emphasize the urgency of this mission. You're all consummate pros, so I realize I'm preaching to the choir, but there could be a great deal more jeopardy here than we've ever faced before. I have faith in you. With whatever you find, I want to say good hunting."

"Thank you, sir. Next, I want to discuss some other data we're wrestling with. As concerning as the international threat seems to be, there's also some rumblings of domestic discord, possibly in league with these terrorist plots. Hence, we need the FBI working with us. I know that irks you all that any Americans can be working to attack our great country. It's despicable but a challenge we need to be ready for nonetheless."

"Lily, I'm going to ask a lot of you. You're our most experienced field operative, and you have contacts virtually anywhere on the planet. We may need an extended stay out of country. With the short notice, is that something you can accommodate?"

"Sir, I'll do whatever is required. Depending on the assignment, some things are going to be more difficult than others. What kind of cover story do you have in mind for my family?"

"Depending on the circumstances, we may read-in your husband."

"You realize he has no idea about my job. I told him I work for the government as an agricultural liaison traveling to third world countries."

"I understand, but there could be some lengthy trips abroad. We'd fill him in as needed."

"He knows I have a concealed weapon permit, but supposedly it's just for personal protection. He doesn't know that I actually fire it. He hates weapons and hasn't touched one since his army days."

"Duly noted. After we go through some specific regional issues, I want you guys all to eat lunch together in the cafeteria to get to know one another. We need to quickly build teamwork like never before."

Several hours later after the meeting ended, they headed over to get some food. Lily drew a lot of attention and new friends. When she sat down, Hassan Aboud was to her left and Ari Goldstein to her right.

"Hassan, it's nice to meet you. I've heard a lot about you over the years."

"Is that good?"

They chuckled. "Yes, it's good, Hassan. Our governments don't always agree, but at our level, we appreciate what our peers in the craft accomplish. I think you're principled, a good man."

"Thank you, that means a great deal coming from a legend such as yourself."

"Legend…" She laughed. "That's a stretch."

"If you say I have a reputation, I reply you have an unmatched record. If there is a prototype spy, it would be you."

Ari piped in, "I agree with my esteemed colleague. Mossad would love for you to join our ranks."

Out of the corner of her eye, Lily noticed Grace Bailey staring at her.

"What?"

Grace smiled wryly. "You're widely respected, Lily. Just accept it and move on."

Lily shrugged. "Yes, ma'am."

"Are you up for an afternoon workout?" Turning her head at the voice, she saw Donna Smith smiling like a Cheshire cat. Tough looking, athletic, and aggressive, Donna intimidated most people, as SEALs tend to do. Having the respect of her male comrades spoke for itself.

"Sure, Donna. I've got some mail to finish processing, but maybe in an hour?"

"That works for me." Donna flexed her arms. Lily laughed.

The idea gained steam quickly, and soon the entire group of field folk decided to go to the gym. An hour later, they jogged on the track to warm up before squaring off on the mats.

Donna grinned with confidence.

"You should know, SEAL training is tough sledding, princess."

The gathered onlookers guffawed and chuckled.

"Princess?" Lily responded. She gestured for Donna to make her move.

Donna attacked immediately, trying to overwhelm Lily before the fight could even start. Lily fought off the initial strikes, pivoting often to avoid heavy strikes from Donna's gloved fists.

"Careful, ladies," said Ray. "Remember, we're on the same side."

"No worries," Donna muttered and then started an even stronger strike. Lily dodged the worst of the swings, but Donna landed a couple of body blows with loud smacks.

Lily huffed as the thuds knocked the wind out of her lungs. The other SEALs cheered on their mate, as if Lily was an enemy combatant.

Suddenly as Donna launched into another attack meant to take down Lily, she got a savage counterattack instead. Lily drilled her both to the gut and then a smack to the cheek. Donna staggered back a step.

Lily stopped, merely watching her. Donna glowered and attacked again. Both women landed stiff blows this time. Before they could draw blood, Ray stepped in to break up the bout.

"Enough, ladies! This is supposed to a friendly bout."

Rather than the simmering hatred he expected, both women took off the gloves, smiled, and slapped hands.

"You're pretty good, Donna."

"I'm better than pretty good. I'm surprised you're still standing."

"The SEALs aren't the only units that get strong training."

"I'll admit you're deceptive. You look like this dainty cheerleader type, but you do pack a punch. You move well."

"Thank you. I grew up as a tomboy playing with the boys, not with dolls."

"Did you, I wouldn't have thought that. I wasn't into dolls either. Earning the respect of my SEAL comrades, that's validation enough for me."

"You've added me as a fan too."

"I appreciate that, Lily."

"Let's jog again for our cooldown."

"Okay."

The two women were joined by Grace Bailey and Patty Baymill in taking more laps. This time the pace was much stiffer. The others of the group went through their own sparring episodes in the meantime.

The women showered together afterward in the group shower.

"Patty, do you have any inkling about this threat beyond what was said in the meeting?" asked Grace.

"Not really. As they said, we're all picking up on chatter because there is so much of it happening now. There are no specific plans or targets we can distill out…yet. We're going to get a handle on it, believe me."

Donna spoke, glancing at Lily's torso. "Did I give you some boo-boos? You've got a couple of nice welts."

Lily looked back with a smirk. "I've had boo-boos before. I'm fine. I seem to have tagged you too. How many of those marks did I give you?"

"Most of these are old damage. SEALs have a very physical life. I'm fine also. You can see that Patty has been gored too. Rank doesn't protect you in the SEALs."

Patty laughed.

"I'll take your word for that. Have I validated myself?"

"We'll let you live, for the moment. Can you shoot?"

"Is that our next contest?"

"Why not keep sharp, I always say."

"It will have to be tomorrow. I've got a couple of things to wrap up before I go home to feed my brood."

"You've got kids?"

"I do, a son and a daughter. Is that a problem?"

"Well, in the field, that could be an issue if enemies can leverage that against you."

"We don't broadcast our personal lives."

"You know as well as I do the other side can get our secrets whether we take measures or not."

Lily didn't respond. It was a troubling possibility she'd thought about a great deal over the years as international politics eroded.

"I'm not trying to yank your chain, Lily. That's one reason I never sought a marriage."

"I'm aware of the danger. What are your other reasons?"

"I never found the right person, I guess. Maybe I'm too picky."

"I will say marriage with the right person is great. With the wrong person…well, I would agree with you. Before I met my husband, I had a relationship with a guy that soured over time. His true nature came out, and I didn't like what I saw. I'm not a person to be owned, controlled, and belittled. He did love himself. You get the picture."

"I've known some of them. Those relationships of mine I had resulted in some painful conclusions, for them."

Lily chuckled. "So you were a badass from day one? Perhaps I was too immature back then in college. He was an athlete with all of the baggage that goes with it. Egocentric and a misogynist, feeling entitled, demanding, insistent, I was probably too dazzled by good looks and star status. It took me a couple of years before the drawbacks chafed enough that I started to come to my senses. When I cut the cord, he did not handle it well. Actually, he didn't handle it at all. That was the start of my road to toughening up to defending myself. I never wanted to be abused and helpless again. He was a painful lesson. The next day I signed up for a self-defense course, and I've never looked back."

"I had my own version of growing pains and hard lessons, different than yours, but no less mortifying. I also was forced to toughen up. Those grim memories stick with you."

"They certainly do."

"I gather there was…stuff, Lily. Did you report him?"

"I was ashamed and young. Hindsight is so tough because we're our own worst critics. I blamed myself then and I honestly can't remember why. God help the guy that tries to mess with my daughter. Both of my kids are enrolled in self-defense courses. I started them early."

Patty eyed her thoughtfully, lost in her own memories and issues, while Grace had an enigmatic look.

The women got dressed and parted ways for the evening to wrap up personal affairs.

Lily returned to her office to find a large manila envelope sitting on her desk. Inside was the long-awaited field report. Though it took time, she read the entire document. Before she started reading, she'd called her neighbor. "Hey, it's me. I've got some work to do at the office. Would you mind watching my kids until I get home? You know I never leave them alone."

"Sure, Lily, no problem."

The report was as frightening as she anticipated. She couldn't put it down as she read it in total, and that was not a good sign.

TOP SECRET

Credible sources have confirmed rumors of an international plot dwarfing anything we've ever faced. The alleged players are both foreign and domestic. How this could come about seems

13

impossible, yet it appears true. Radical sects throughout the Middle East, Asia, Europe, Africa, and both Americas are pooling resources and plans for some great event, or events, that threaten stability anywhere on the globe.

Possible scenarios include triggering existing antagonistic rivalries causing global powers into conventional warfare. That doesn't mean nuclear conflict wouldn't occur too as an off-shoot. As traditional treaties have been eroded by toxic politics, inherent weakness remains, making individual countries highly vulnerable. This we will discuss later.

A second theory is both more and less credible. It says the amassing enemy forces are intent on anarchy breaking down all existing governments and social structure. Set free of competent authorities to deal with national crisis, what are seen as outlier groups would be free to practice their extreme measures and take revenge on whoever they might choose. The obvious examples are the Taliban reimposing their onus on the peoples in Afghanistan, all-out war between Sunni and Shiite sects in nearly every Islamic country, India facing shooting war with Pakistan, Russia and China facing internal Islamic uprisings, the African continent also facing whole scale insurgencies. The same would be true in South America, Central America, and the Caribbean. Criminal gangs, drug cartels, antigovernment militias, they all seem to be moving with a common purpose.

In the USA, there is no lack of groups who would like a different country more to their liking. Hate groups fostering intolerance and prejudice, criminal enterprises looking to break down legal and moral standards to ease their illegal operations and avoid consequences, corrupt officials from local all the way up to national figures, it's staggering the potential scope of the threat. Certainly, it's unprecedented in our experiences. The absence of civility, good character, and respect for law enforcement we found was appalling. Overt disturbing incidents are sharply on the rise. Below are the details from our findings.

Lily read intently every single page and some pages multiple times. It took several hours before she put it down and left the building.

Driving home, feeling dread like she never had before, she mused, *What are they already doing? We're too far behind the eight ball on this one.*

She parked in her garage and then went next door to retrieve her children. Ringing the doorbell, Nancy Green answered the door.

"Hi, Nancy, I'm sorry to impose on you with such short notice."

"No problem, Lily. Things happen. Your kids are great and my kids love them. It kept them occupied, so for me it was a few moments of peace."

Both women chuckled.

The children came out the door, Tommy and Cathy, along with James and Sadie.

"Hi, Mom."

"Let's leave the Greens in peace. What do you want for supper?"

"Pizza."

"Okay, this once, but only because I'm so late."

Going into their house, she ordered the food, got the delivery a little later, and then her children went to their rooms after eating the meal.

Lily heard her cell phone ringing.

"Hello."

"Lily, it's Donna. We just got word to prepare for an assignment. I think we're all going, so you may be getting a call too."

"I had a feeling something was up. Thanks for the heads-up."

Once she hung up, her phone rang again almost immediately.

"Lily, it's Ray. I'm sorry to spring this on you with no notice, but you're going overseas. You'll get the details tomorrow. Can you make rapid arrangements? We're going to call your husband. We'll see if he can cut short his trip. Otherwise, we can make arrangements for placing somebody in your house overnights until your husband gets back."

"I'll talk to my neighbor. She's very helpful. Do you have any idea how long we'll be gone?"

"No. It will depend on how things develop."

"That doesn't sound good."

"You speak Farsi and Urdu, correct?"

"I do. I studied abroad for a year after college."

"Good. It may come in handy."

"Is that a hint about where we're going?"

He didn't reply. He merely hung up.

Lily pondered for a moment before dialing next door. "Nancy, I'm sorry to ask, but I need another favor, maybe a big one."

"How can I help?"

"I'm heading out of town unexpectedly, and Jack isn't back from his trip. Can I impose on you to watch the kids?"

"Sure."

"Jack might be back early, but if he can't break away..."

"I understand, dear. No worries."

"You are a peach. I owe you big time. I will find a way to repay your kindness. I'm probably the worst neighbor in history."

Nancy laughed. "No, you're not. It's no big deal. It will keep my kids out of my hair."

"Thank you again. Tomorrow I'll tell the kids to go to your house after school. There may be somebody from my work showing up to stay the night in my house with them tomorrow."

"Okay, whatever you need."

Lily went to bed early, but sleep was elusive. Her mind wouldn't shut down as she worked through various scenarios, most of them very troubling.

The alarm rang in the morning seemingly too early. Her shower and plenty of coffee helped to an extent.

"Kids, I've got to go on a trip."

"Mom, no," Cathy complained.

"You go next door after school. If Dad can come back early, he'll be here for you. Otherwise, my office will send somebody to stay with you."

"I don't like it either," Tommy added.

"I'm sorry, kids, I don't like it, but life isn't always fair."

"How long?"

"I don't know when I'll be back. I need to assess some things where I'm going."

Both children stared at her.

"Do you want some coffee?" Lily smirked.

Everybody laughed. "Mom, you know we don't drink coffee," Cathy replied, snickering.

"I know, honey. Listen, I've got to get to the office. You guys go next door and wait with your friends to go to the bus."

She firmly hugged them and kissed each on the top of their heads.

Hauling her luggage from the bedroom, she loaded her car and drove away. Lily couldn't escape a feeling of foreboding. She pondered, *Something is different this time. Something is off actually.*

The drive to the office on this day went surprisingly well. She arrived fifteen minutes earlier than usual.

Going up to her office, she hauled her luggage with her.

Ray walked in. Handing her a folder, he waited while she glanced at it briefly. Turning her face, she spoke. "Can this be right?"

"Sadly, it seems to be."

"I've never seen anything remotely like this. From the prelims, we all felt a little skeptical, but this…"

"We're getting new data constantly. Leave your cell on. You'll get a stream of updates on your flight overseas. I'll leave it to you to absorb the material and then prepare your team accordingly. We're going to be making decisions and adjustments on the fly. I suspect you'll do a lot of coping out there, but I know you can handle it."

"Understood, sir."

"When you land at your final destination, we need to hit the ground on the run."

"This doesn't look like a short trip. My family?"

"Carrie Grimes is going to your house tonight. We had local assets sit down with your husband in England to fill him in. He can't leave early, so Carrie will be there with your kids until Saturday evening when he walks in the door."

"Thank you."

"Eh…one other thing, Carrie will be armed. You understand why."

"I do. I assume there will be protection after she leaves. As I said, my husband doesn't like weapons. He hasn't touched one since he left the Army."

"We've advised we're providing him with a military-style weapons, and he agrees. We're going to be spread pretty thin, but we'll do what we can. Your unit is going to be configured as we envisioned. Patty and her three SEALs, Donna, Joe, and Andy, Ari from Mossad, Hassan from Egyptian intelligence, Wesley from MI-6, and a few more you'll meet over there. Pakistan is donating two agents from ISI as well as Afghanistan supposedly giving us two of their best. Although these picks initially are based on that region, any operations developing anywhere else in the world will bring all of them with you. Do you see the issues? The Arab members are both Sunni and Shia, along with an Israeli in the mix."

"Any other good news?"

"I'm sorry to put this on you. We have our reasons."

She sighed and shook her head. "I'll do what I can."

"That is all we can ask. Much of the rush is based on rapidly deteriorating circumstances. We have no time to diddle around."

CHAPTER 2

As if to certify Ray's prediction, events left Lily no time to dwell on her challenges. Within an hour, she was riding in a car traveling to the nearby US Air Force base. Upon arriving, she saw her team members were waiting together talking softly. When they saw her emerge from the government car, they started ambling toward her as she approached.

"Lily, what's with the bum's rush? Did something new happen we should know about?" Donna eyed her darkly.

"I don't know. I worry we're in a need-to-know situation, and somebody thinks we don't need to know."

"That's not good. Can I still get out of this mission?"

Lily snickered. "I don't think so. Suck it up, princess."

Donna laughed heartily. "That'll be the day that I'm a princess."

Retrieving their gear, they headed for the C130 transport plane. The first thing they all noticed was the equipment already stowed on the plane.

Andy and Joe smiled. Joe spoke. "We've got some serious weaponry here. Ari, Hassan, can you guys shoot straight?"

They chuckled, not bothering to respond to the inane banter.

Patty Baymill walked onto the plane. "Sorry, guys, I was suddenly pulled out of a meeting and told to get on this plane."

Wesley Bromwell nodded in greeting. "Hey, Patty, welcome to the party. I saved you a seat."

"Without knowing I would be on this flight? How did that happen?"

"I'm always prepared."

"Right. I'm thinking there is more to the story behind the scene."

Wesley merely smiled.

Andy Reiger looked at Hassan. "What's the name of your agency?"

"I could give the long name in Arabic, but what's easiest for you is Mukabarat."

"Got it."

They eyed each other for a moment. Hassan chuckled and replied, "I doubt it."

Lily muttered softly to Donna. "Possibly trust is going to be an issue for this mixed group."

"It's easy to understand. Some of the people we're supposed to work with now are often adversaries. You realize Andy knows the name of all the security services."

"I do realize that."

"Reading between the lines, he's telling Hassan we're going to have an eye on him. We all have long memories for past indignities."

The plane ascended into the sky shortly afterward for the long flight toward the Middle East.

Lily tried to settle in, but the seats weren't built with comfort in mind.

"Donna, have you read Hassan's file?"

"Not really. I glanced at a couple of things."

"He went to college at Georgetown, and he was an honor student there."

"Good to know."

There was a chirp as the pilot spoke over the speaker. "We've reached cruising altitude, folks, so relax and enjoy the flight. Skies will be clear for a while, but there is a storm front ahead we can't avoid. Select of you will have access to your cell phones as I was told there will be critical messages coming our way."

As if on cue, Lily received a text message. Pulling it up, she read it with concern.

"That doesn't look good," Donna muttered. "What's up?"

"I'm going to need to talk to everybody." She paused a moment to collect herself.

"Listen, everybody. Now that we're in the air, I can tell you Ray showed me a file that was the latest appraisal and projection about this situation we're wading into. In addition, he told me I'd get prompt updates of new events and projections from the analysts. That was the text I just got. As incredible as it seemed about our foes banding together, it does seem they're doing exactly that. What's startling to me is they don't seem concerned about keeping it secret. Chatter has reached an all-time high to the point it feels like they're waving a big red flag at us purposely. What this text indicated was our best and brightest have discovered some disturbing new aspect in the dark web, one they haven't been able to crack. If it's a means for the enemy to have real-time secure communications or secret financial transactions or a myriad of other bad possibilities, we don't know. If they're able to ramp up plans and operations outside of our ability to intercept, there could be serious attacks very soon, which could occur anywhere in the world."

Lily paused a moment, glancing at the silent, grim faces.

"The implications and ramifications are pretty obvious. We can't spread resources everywhere to cover all possible targets."

Again, no one said a word.

"Any questions?"

Wesley spoke. "Are we going to stop in England? I was hoping to see my mom."

"I don't believe so. I think we're heading to Ramstein AFB in Germany for a stopover. After that, I suspect we're headed somewhere in the Middle East. I haven't been told that, but it's my gut feeling."

Joe Gilson spoke. "Judging by the firepower in these crates, I'd say an active war zone is a high probability."

"I can't disagree, Joe."

Andy Reiger added, "I'm not sure why, but I've got a bad feeling about this trip."

"That's probably one too many beers last night talking," Joe replied, causing the group to chuckle.

"Go ahead and laugh. I trust my gut feelings. They're never wrong."

There were no further smirks. The worried look on his face dampened the mood among the whole group.

Lily decided to speak. "Okay, guys. What I just received was news of a significant attack in Afghanistan in Kabul, simultaneously at a number of different foreign embassies. I'm talking about attacks in force. By the time military forces could arrive on scene, the troops guarding each of the buildings had been overwhelmed, and security was breached. They were brutal once inside the buildings, killing and capturing embassy staff and local employees. Apparently, they filmed the entire incidents and posted it on the internet, including some beheadings. Our US ambassador was one of the casualties as well as the small Marine detachment. Wesley, I'm sorry to say the British ambassador is missing and assumed to be in their hands. What they would do to a captive Western woman, we don't know yet. Beheading her…well, it's hard to conceive of people doing that, but… Anyway, they've made no demands yet. Honestly, it's hard for me to get my head around such a potential atrocity. You're right, Andy, this will be a serious challenge, no matter where we end up."

Now as Lily glanced around the group, uniformly she saw intense anger.

"Bastards," Joe muttered. He gripped his weapon.

The aircraft passed through a patch of severe turbulence, like it was an omen of bad things to come. Lily was bounced into Donna, who grabbed her to avoid a fall off her seat.

"Sorry, Donna."

"No worries. I'm here for you, babe."

Lily snickered. "First you call me princess and now babe?"

"I don't mean any disrespect. I'm showing you're worthy of my attention. With most people I just ignore and let them fall on their asses. You earned my respect, and believe me, that's not easy to do."

Andy piped in. "Believe her, Lily. Joe and I are still on the outside looking in with her."

Donna grinned. "That's because you two are blockheads that get on my nerves most of the time."

Lily replied, "Well, thank you, Donna. I appreciate the high compliment. I have the same great respect for you and your prowess."

Ari asked, "Lily, do you think this will become a rescue mission going after the British ambassador? I'm not sure my government would sanction my presence in such a mission. No offense, Wesley."

"None taken, Ari."

Lily answered, "I can't say at this point, but I think not. Of course, that will be a critical mission to answer that challenge, but our little group wasn't intended for that sort of action. At least that's my opinion going in. I can't even say that Kabul is a destination for our travels. I think I'm being kept apprised of worldwide events so we're ready for anything."

"I'm ready to go. That attack is sickening. Their kind of war doing what they do, it needs an answer and sooner rather than later."

Everybody looked at Hassan. It wasn't what they expected from an Egyptian intelligence officer.

"I'm on your side, remember." He looked annoyed. "Do you think any rational person agrees with such horrors? I'm as angry as you. Islamic folk are just as subject terrorist attacks as non-Muslims. As Lily said before, we need to trust each other."

"They wouldn't behead the British ambassador, would they?" asked Wesley. "She's…a mom." His voice cracked with angry emotion.

"I can't speak for them," Hassan replied sadly. "There are demented people among their adherents. Who knows what things they would stoop to for shock value?"

"I remember in a prior war in Iraq, I think, or maybe Syria, there was that butcher that always aired his crimes on the internet beheading victims. I think he may have been born in England in a Muslim community but then came over to the Middle East to join ISIS. He had his face covered but made a chilling threat about going to Western nations to behead our children. That image haunts me to this day. He ended up getting killed, but I understand your statement about the demented being among our enemies. They need to be sent straight to hell. I, for one, want to say, I trust you, Hassan."

"Thank you, that means a great deal to me, my friend."

Lily received another beep. She pulled up the message with the same grim facial expression.

"They just sent a video to display Amanda Torry as their captive. She's still alive, but their threats were nauseating. She was terrified, and it appeared she hasn't been treated well. They held a big knife to her neck and laughed at the end but didn't kill her. I think they've possibly done other things to humiliate her though."

She looked at Wesley, who was seething with rage for his fellow Brit.

"I swear they will pay for this," Wesley hissed.

"That's exactly what they want," Lily opined. "They'd love to cause reactions that are pure rage and revenge but not well planned out. It plays into their false narrative of them as Allah's invincible instruments, inspired and guided from above, no matter how heinous their actions."

Patty Baymill whispered to Joe and Andy. Lily couldn't hear what she said, but watching the reaction of the two men, she could surmise the gist of the message.

"What did she say?" Lily whispered to Donna.

"It's team stuff. We're kind of like a family."

They looked at each other.

Donna continued. "The guys are determined not to let her down in whatever we do. That's something of a simplification of the moment, but you get the idea."

Lily noted her intense look staring at her SEAL teammates.

"You guys are really good at your focus."

"It's part of the DNA of the SEALs. It has to be with the type of missions we handle. Dealing with tense, high stress environments, it can take a toll. If you're not dedicated to your jobs, there can be some very bad endings."

"Do you mean in your personal life?"

"That's part of it. I've avoided it to an extent by not having a personal life, other than family. I realize I can't go on forever this way, but for the short term, it's my choice."

"I'm sorry about that, Donna."

"We don't get do-overs. Our mistakes are splashed all over the headlines."

"That's true for me also."

"This is stirring me up. I'm going to try to nap. I need to calm down."

Lily closed her eyes too, but her thoughts were back home. Again, she had to shift duties onto her husband for school functions for the kids. As the mom, missing parent-teacher conferences was becoming too frequent.

"You're a godsend, honey," she whispered. "I'm not much of a marriage partner these days."

Before she could doze off, she received another message.

Everybody looked at her.

"Well, they made a demand, but it is senseless. They want the entire Western world to apologize for our actions, forever, including the crusades. We must acknowledge being infidels and renounce every religion other than Islam. Women must assume subservient roles and can no longer be educated. All women in authority must resign immediately and agree to submit to male governance. All non-Muslim nations must pay a penance in money to the mullahs and…"

"What?" asked Donna.

"It's just idiotic ravings, like the fantasies of adolescents. This is no real demand. It's their way of saying we've got her, and there is nothing you can do about it."

"What else did it say?"

"It was some sick things not worth mentioning."

"Like killing her?" Wesley asked.

"No. If she's dead, they lose her as a pawn to taunt us."

Wesley seemed to realize what she wasn't saying. The hatred returned to his facial expression.

The plane banked as they approached Ramstein. Upon landing, they were greeted by a German soldier.

"Guten tag, komen zie hier."

They were escorted to a building into a conference room. The local American command staff was waiting.

"Please take seats, folks."

Cups of coffee were provided, and the general began to speak.

"I'm sure you're aware of what happened in Afghanistan. In addition to that large assault on foreign government facilities and staff, there have been numerous actions across the country that is pressing the Afghan forces to their limit. Basically, too many incidents for them to cover. I've just gotten an assessment from our intelligence services that this might be a trial run for a strategy of disruption for use elsewhere. If successful, it can cause chaos and instability too numerous to cope with. Any questions?"

No one said anything initially. Eventually, Wesley spoke.

"Sir, is there a plan in action to recover her?"

"I wish I could say yes, but at this point we don't know where they're keeping her. I suspect that options will develop soon, but in the meantime, we're helpless. I think we're starting with closely analyzing the broadcasts to narrow down where they originate. It's a start."

Wesley stared at the general grimly.

"Listen, we all know what you're feeling, Wesley. We feel it too, but there's a bigger picture threat we cannot ignore."

"Yes, sir,"

Lily turned to him sitting beside her and squeezed his hand in sympathy. It softened his glare.

"I'm okay," he whispered to her.

"We'll get them."

The general resumed. "In addition to that matter, there are more rumblings in virtually every country in the world. Those dark web communications are ramping up. So far, we've been unable to break through the encryptions."

"Do we have any idea about an end game? What are they trying to accomplish?"

"That same agency analyst of ours floated a theory about anarchy, worldwide destruction of governments and authorities. That would leave them free to do whatever they wish and what they wish. Obviously it would vary from region to region."

"Like imposing strict Sharia Islamic control like the Taliban want?"

"That's one example but on a universal scale. Wherever there are Muslim populations imposing Sharia law worldwide."

"Wow, that's ambitious in a diabolical way. Do you think the Muslim masses would accept that?"

"It seems an irrational aspiration, I agree. It's possible attacking in Afghanistan is meant to embolden like-minded forces around the world. This is our greatest fear at this point. Dangling the vulnerable British ambassador as bait is a way of saying, 'Look, they're helpless against us. We can do this in your country too.'"

"Can you tell us our next destination?"

"We don't have a decision yet. It isn't a matter of keeping it a secret. I think they haven't decided yet. There are multiple places that need prompt attention. I suspect they're assembling other quick-strike teams like you for deployment. I guess you should settle in with us for the short term. We'll get you bunked in and get some chow in you."

"Can we call home?"

"As long as you don't divulge anything about your location or the mission."

Lily followed Donna to share a room. She immediately dialed home. Carrie Grimes answered the phone.

"Hi, Carrie, I gather my husband isn't home yet."

"There was a delay in his flight. No worries, I can stay here as long as necessary. I met your neighbor, who is very nice."

"Good. I'm not sure when we leave here. We've got a temporary lull, but that could change in a hurry. I want to talk to the kids."

"Sure, they're in their rooms. Hold on a second while I get them."

Tommy came on the line first. "Mom?"

"Hi, son, how are you?"

"Fine."

"Did you have a good day in school?"

"Yes, ma'am."

"I'm thinking about you."

"I like Carrie. She's nice."

"Good, she is a very nice person. She'll stay until Dad gets home."

"Can we play with our friends?"

"Not until Dad is there."

"He got delayed. We're fighting hard in karate class, Cathy and me. We'll be ready to help you when you get home."

"Thank you. I'm sure Dad will be home soon. Can you put your sister on the phone?"

Cathy spoke softly. "Mommy?"

"Yes, baby, I'm here."

"When are you coming home?"

"I don't know yet."

"We really miss you."

She felt a lump in her throat as her maternal emotions punished her. "I wish I could be there, but this is my job. I'm sorry, honey. I'll come home as soon as I can."

"I don't like it when you go away."

"I know."

Her phone beeped with an incoming message. "I'm sorry, Cathy, I have another message coming in, so I've got to go. I love you guys so much."

"Bye."

For a moment, she had to pause to control her feelings.

"Are you okay?" Donna asked.

Lily took a deep breath and accessed the text message.

"We're leaving tomorrow but won't know our destination until we're in the air. We're picking up the other unit members, so I suspect it's somewhere in the Middle East."

"It must be hard dealing with separations from your family."

"You have no idea. Children don't understand. It's hard on them. Sometimes they get funny ideas, like Mommy keeps leaving because she doesn't like them. It sounds silly, but little minds can go in unexpected directions."

"I can see how hard it is on you. In a way, I'm envious. Having children who care about you, it's—"

28

Lily's phone rang.

"Hello."

"Lily, it's Ray. I'm sorry you're stuck in limbo in Germany. I know you want to get after the mission so you can come home. You've probably surmised we're looking at a number of problem areas to see where best to utilize your talents and that of your team. We don't want to play whack-a-mole and end up accomplishing nothing."

"Yes, sir."

"Carrie is still at your house. There is a problem of civilian airport threats all across Europe. If need be, we'll pick up your husband and put him on a military flight to get him back to your children. We've got you covered."

"Any word on the rescue of the British ambassador yet? I shudder to think about what she's going through."

"Significant resources have been brought into play. The Brits have dispatched their special forces units to join the recovery effort. We can't be sure she's still in Afghanistan. There are a number of surrounding countries that could sympathize with extreme terrorist causes. For example, if she was taken to Iran or Pakistan, it would be a delicate matter trying to get in and out before their forces took defensive action."

"I didn't think of that. I assumed our logical targets would be in established hot spots where we already have troops."

"Open your mind to all possibilities, no matter how improbable they might seem."

"I got a message we fly out tomorrow."

"That may not happen. Reports are coming in so fast now we nearly can't keep up. Keep your bags packed though because a departure call might come at any time, including at night."

"We'll be ready."

"I know you will, Lily. Of all the missions I've sent you on, this one bothers me the most. You be very careful out there."

"I will, and I know what you're saying. Many of us have a bad feeling about what's coming. For the first time, I wish it was over before it even starts. I'd appreciate your efforts at getting my husband back on US soil."

"We're working on it."

"Thank you, sir, I truly appreciate that."

After hanging up, she stared at the wall, lost in her thoughts.

"You don't need to explain," Donna said. "I got the gist of it. So I guess we really do settle in for the moment."

"Jack is still stranded as all airports in Europe have had serious threats. Ray said they're trying to get him onto a military flight home."

"That would be good for your peace of mind."

"Carrie is still at my house, but you're right. I want him home safe."

"It seems we have some time. What would you like to do, Lily?"

"I'll pass on having another fight. I don't need any more boo-boos."

Donna chuckled.

They heard a tap on their door. Andy and Joe came into the room.

Andy smiled. "I figured you probably miss us, so here we are."

"In your dreams," Donna retorted.

"What do you say, boss?" asked Joe. He smirked at Lily.

"Nothing. We're still waiting on Langley."

"I thought maybe…" He winked at her playfully.

"I won't bother answering that. You guys need to get different hobbies."

Everybody laughed.

The guys sat down on the beds with the ladies.

Joe looked at Lily. "I'm thinking we're going to Kabul, no matter whatever they're dithering about back home. I doubt they'd send these Pakistani and Afghan teammates to meet us out of their region. Their benefit to us, if there is one, is in those two countries."

"I tend to agree with you. Don't sell them short. Hassan is a man I trust. I'm sure they've been fully vetted."

"We're betting our lives on that vetting. How many infiltrators have taken out our troops over the years? I'm going to reserve judgement and keep my weapons close at hand."

"You do that," Lily replied.

"So you trust them, sight unseen?"

"I didn't say I won't be cautious. There has to be a reason for this alliance."

"Trusting ISI is a bad judgment call, in my opinion. Who is it at the agency, ignoring their past actions, that they could sign off on this?"

"I guess we sort it out later. Give them a chance. Don't throw out the baby with the bathwater, as they say."

"By the way, there's a rumor you dated Wesley?"

"That was in college before I met my husband. Why do you ask?"

"Inquiring minds want to know such things."

Donna replied. "Joe, you've bumped your head too many times. That's personal for her."

Lily eyed his continuing smirk and shook her head dismissively.

He added, "Lily, macho isn't such a bad thing." He flexed his large arm muscles.

She held up her wedding ring. "That's not going to change, dude."

There was another tap on the door.

Wesley came in and eyed the amused expression on their faces. "Am I missing something?"

"You missed nothing at all, believe me," Donna replied.

"Okay, I wanted to say, I saw our supplies are being loaded onto a private jet. This next leg will be in comfort at least."

Lily opined, "It seems somebody made a decision. That's good. I really don't want to sit around here. Let's get this over with."

Another tap on the door was expected, and it came.

"Ma'am, it's wheels up in two hours." The messenger was a young-looking woman, seemingly. She was barely old enough to be in the service.

"Thank you."

Lily turned to her comrades. "Let's gather our things and get on board the aircraft. Wesley, can you tell our other teammates?"

"Sure, Lily."

Later, when they boarded the plane, they were shocked to be on such a luxurious aircraft. Also, the fact they were joined by Patty Baymill and Lily's CIA fellow agents Grace Bailey, Steve Sawyer, and Ron Gray seemed to verify Lily's ideas about what was ahead.

Lily sat down beside Patty. "We have more CIA operatives added?"

"I think there might be more units formed up for joint operations. This remains a developing story. I think there may be additional staffing wherever we go."

"What's the latest on the ambassador?"

"I've heard nothing. I think they'd contact you first, Lily. You're still in charge."

"I'm surprised they'd send an officer of your rank into harm's way."

"They have their reasons."

Joe piped in, "Patty, what's with the luxury plane? Are we suddenly drug lords?"

Andy spoke. "No, this is like the last supper."

People laughed, but for Lily, she felt a chill of foreboding.

"It's good to see Ari and Hassan getting along well. They act like old friends now," Patty muttered.

"That is good." Lily smiled at Donna, who was smiling at her. "Don't look so happy. We could be going into a serious melee."

"Like you said, Lily, let's get this over with. I'm ready to rock. This is what we do."

Once in the air, stewardesses served hot meals and even offered to serve drinks. The entrée was filet mignon.

Lily advised the group. "If you want a drink, take one only, guys. We don't want anybody drunk going into this mission. Any questions?"

Lily shared a bottle of White Zinfandel with Patty, Donna, and Grace. It mellowed everyone for the flight. Joe and Andy went with beer and tried to romance the stewardesses, without success. The ladies smiled politely but ignored the clumsy advances from the macho men.

Donna joked with her comrades. "I see you haven't lost your touches. You sent the stewardesses scurrying for cover."

"Shut up, Donna. It's their loss," Joe replied.

"Some loss." Donna snickered and the other ladies chuckled.

Lily dozed off after eating the food to awake later as the plane touched down.

"Where are we?"

"We're in Cairo," Hassan answered. "This is my territory, so you're all under arrest."

They laughed heartily. Hassan didn't normally make jokes. Ari, however, laughed the least of all of them. He eyed the security forces assembling to greet the plane.

"You're in no danger, my friend." Hassan smiled reassuringly. "They're here for our protection."

"I'll take your word for that." Ari still looked uncomfortable.

Coming off the plane, they were whisked past customs and the normal intake processes to a special room in the airport. Waiting in the room were two men. They arose and went straight to Lily.

"Hello," she said.

"I'm Mohamed Sheik, and this is Abdul Hamma. We're sent from ISI to join your group."

"Welcome, gentlemen. I can introduce—"

"We know who you are. We got dossiers to study and have been fully briefed about the mission."

"Oh, well, that's good."

"I will say, we accept you as our leader for the mission."

"Thank you. I realize that's a big thing for you having a woman in charge. I'll try to be worthy of the honor."

Both men smiled at her. However, she didn't feel warmth in the gesture. Rather, it was more like Cheshire cat smiles, like she was about to step into a bear trap.

"Everybody, please take a seat. Patty, can you join me?"

Lily and Patty went to the rostrum. Lily started.

"Let me tell you two, our newest additions, we still haven't received orders for a final destination, so we're speculating at this point. Obviously with the attacks in Kabul, that is a strong possibility. It's not viable to just leave the British ambassador in limbo. The enemy side is broadcasting daily using her continuing captivity to the fullest extent to poke us in the eye. On your end, being much closer to the scene, have you gotten any inkling of where they took her?"

"No," Abdul replied flatly. He did not elaborate.

"My understanding is we're supposed to add a couple of Afghan intelligence officers. If they were going to fly you guys to Egypt, I'm not sure why they didn't also fly them in too."

The ISI men simply sat eyeing her. Neither said anything.

Patty piped in. "I anticipate a fast turnaround here in Cairo, so everyone should stay close. That's all for now."

The ISI agents stood up and walked away to leave the room. Lily noticed them eyeing Hassan as they walked by. It didn't look to be friendly glances. Hassan stared at them coldly.

Lily went to Hassan. "What was that? I'm picking up a bad vibe from these guys."

"I'm concerned also."

"Do you know them?"

"I don't personally. I can make a quick call to my people."

Lily walked out of the room with him. The ISI agents were down the hall talking on their phones. They turned their backs when they saw her looking.

"My bad feeling is growing, Hassan," she muttered.

"I'll make my call."

She walked to the restroom followed by the other women. As they passed Mohamed and Abdul, they hung up from their calls and gave the women smiles. Those smiles seemed phony.

Lily nodded to their nods.

Once in the restroom, Donna spoke. "Team building with that pair is going to be a problem. I don't trust them as far I can throw them."

"Everybody, be cautious about handling this," said Patty. "They've been vetted."

"Why doesn't that reassure me?" Grace asked. "Who did the vetting?"

"Patty, can I suggest we be guarded with what we share with them?" Lily asked.

"I see no problem with that. I think we all have serious concerns about them."

"Thank you. I think this mission will be worrisome enough without adding more self-imposed troubles."

"I do wonder where this idea to include ISI came from?" asked Donna. "Going back to bin Laden living down the street from their training academy in Pakistan and their favoring terrorist forces living within their borders, how could that not jump out at the analysts?"

"I have no answer," Lily replied. "Caution is our buzz word. If they can plaster on fake smiles, so can we."

CHAPTER 3

Patty was right about the fast turnaround time. When they boarded the plane again, this time Lily sat between Ari and Hassan.

"Do you mind if I join you?" She smiled, acting nonchalant.

"Of course you can join us," Hassan replied. He smiled warmly at her. Speaking low, he filled her in. "I talked to my headquarters. They're suspicious. The two names we were initially given to join our team and the ones we had vetted are not these men. We've long believed there are severe divisions in ISI favoring opposite sides of the conflict. I think the side we want is not the side these men are from. What happened back in Pakistan we have no way of knowing, but your instinct seems to be right. We should deal with these men very carefully as they may not have our best interests at heart."

"I try to be ready for anything, but I didn't see this coming. It seems like the curveballs are starting to mount up."

"In this part of the world, you can't depend on anything. Currents and tides shift in unanticipated directions very quickly. What's true one day can be the opposite the next day."

The aircraft departed, soaring into the sky and banking to go eastward initially.

"I think we're headed for Afghanistan," Ari reiterated. "I'm surprised we're still on this luxury jet though."

"I see our ISI friends aren't shy about dabbling in the high life. They're both drinking liberally and trying to chat up the stewardesses," Hassan muttered.

Lily smirked. "I'm sure you noticed the stewardesses aren't even bothering to act civil. It took them about a minute to figure it out. They serve the drinks, leave immediately, and don't even speak to them."

"Good," said Ari. "This isn't a time for political correctness."

Lily's phone beeped.

Reading the text, she got a thoughtful expression.

"More good news?" asked Ari.

"Washington is advising us that the team idea needs to change. They just got word that our ISI recruits were replaced, so too late they tell us ISI is off the table and we're not to let them in."

"We can toss them out the plane door," Ari joked.

Lily had a rueful smile. "They sat in our meeting where we said basically nothing. I'd bet they called home afterwards, but what could they report?"

"They could verify our identities."

"That's true. We're not going to sneak up on anybody in the Middle East."

Ari commented, "Actually, you were never going to sneak up on anybody anyway. With the bizarre politics in the USA these days, the new normal is disturbing on so many levels. Nobody outside of your borders can get a handle on American policies. You seem to be governed by senseless whim and whichever way the wind blows on a given day. Competence seems to have disappeared in favor of political expediency or worse. Pandering to administration hacks is a strong possibility. If this situation is an actual strategy, that would be even more disturbing."

"I'm not sure what to say, Ari. I'm subject to bosses and the chain of command. All that we can do at our level is to find a way to cope. I have my own political views, but when it comes to my job, I must do what I'm paid to do. I worry like everybody else about the division and hatred being fostered out in the world."

"There should be competency tests for leadership in every country," Hassan added.

"I agree with that," Lily replied.

She stayed seated with Ari and Hassan for the balance of the flight. The plane landed in the dark.

"This is Bagram AFB," the pilot relayed over the intercom.

The plane door opened quickly.

"Everybody off!" a huge sergeant shouted. "Move, move, move."

As they hurried off the plane, they noted the base was stirred up with troops and vehicles moving all around them. Base floodlights were blazing. A flight of choppers was launching, and some trucks transporting combat troops were rolling toward the gates.

Hustled into a hangar, they waited for instructions.

Eventually, the base commander appeared with his staff members.

"We've gotten a tip about a possible location for the British ambassador. We're supporting Royal forces that are spearheading this operation."

"How much faith do you have in the intel?" Lily asked.

"It's iffy, like anything here in this country, but it's the best lead we've gotten so far."

"Are we joining this operation?" Patty asked.

"No, we've got all the firepower we need if we have the right place to find her. I'm not the one giving your orders, but I gather you're here for something else."

Lily happened to glance at Abdul and Mohamed. They were whispering and looking around at the ongoing military staging operations. Hassan looked also but at them. Again, his facial expression was not friendly.

He whispered, "We need to stay nearby. If they try to call their handlers to sabotage this operation, we can't allow it. Forewarnings to the enemy could cause the death of the Ambassador before rescuers can get there."

As the two ISI agents started to sidle away from the group, Lily walked over to them along with Hassan and then the SEALs.

"Stay with us, guys," Lily advised. "Whatever we're supposed to do will probably happen quickly, so we need to be ready to move quickly. See what I mean, they're loading our supplies onto trucks."

Mohamed and Abdul looked at each other. "Of course," said Mohamed.

"No phone calls, by the way. It's mission silent from now on," Lily added.

The SEALs eyed them grimly.

They looked angry for a moment before returning to placid expressions.

Abdul muttered softly to Mohamed in Arabic, not realizing Lily heard him say "patience" as she understood their language.

She led the whole group back to the center of the hangar. Patty saw her stern facial expression and moved over to her SEALs for a short chat, while Lily chatted with her CIA comrades.

"Something stinks with our ISI friends," she whispered. "I'm debating whether to cut them loose rather than take a chance later in a difficult situation."

"So if they want to play us, maybe we play them first?" Ron suggested.

"Playing games, I don't know if we can contain the threat if we're backed in a corner."

"I'd rather have them in front of me," Steve added. "If they try something, they're toast. Besides that, we don't even know anything about our assignment, so how could they set any traps."

"That's true. I'll see what Patty thinks. Maybe I'm being too cautious."

Before she could talk to Patty, the team was escorted to the waiting armored trucks.

Boarding quickly, Lily sat down beside Patty. "I can't believe they're sending you on a combat mission."

"I'm not helpless. I can pull my weight. This isn't my first rodeo."

"I didn't say you weren't competent. I was referring to your rank."

Abdul and Mohamed were sitting side by side staring at Lily with smirks on their faces. They were flanked by the four SEALs. Ari, Hassan, the three CIA agents, Wesley, and two Afghan soldiers were riding in the other vehicle. It struck Lily that some members of her new team would be wielding AK-47s. It was a first time having the Russian army weapon in her presence in her unit if there was combat.

Pulling out fast, the trucks sped out of the gate and headed for points east.

"Where do you live?" Lily asked. "Are you near the border with Afghanistan?"

"I live in a village in the mountains, in the territories. So does Mohamed."

"Interesting."

"What is interesting?" asked Mohamed.

"Politics there can span a whole range of ideologies."

"Is that different than your country? Your current leaders pose plenty of their own challenges. I've never seen an America like you are now."

"I can't disagree with you there."

"How do you reconcile differing political views from doing your duty? If your commander-in-chief orders you to do something against your conscience, what do you do?"

"That's a complex question. It's the same elsewhere. For example, Americans don't have anything against average Russians. Moms, dads, and children are the same everywhere, just trying to have good lives and raise the kids. Their leaders can cast them in unfavorable lights, no doubt about it. Do you have wives and children?"

"No, we don't."

Something in their expressions set off danger signals in her mind.

She continued, trying to gloss over her ill feeling. "That's too bad, guys. Marriage with the right person is the greatest thing in the world. That's how it is for me anyway."

"I'm sure you're a very fine wife." Abdul grinned, as did Mohamed.

"Do you find that funny?"

"No, what strikes us is that circumstances can change radically in moments. Where you're set in one mode, confident of yourself and your place, the opposite can occur where instead of being the greater, suddenly you're the lesser. Was that not true for all of those foreign embassies? Some people taken with self-importance met with a new reality where the oppressed rose up to strike them down."

Patty was watching her SEALs. They were like bombs with lit fuses ready to explode. She made a subtle gesture for them to remain passive.

"Well, bad things can happen to good people. If you're speaking about the late American ambassador, I didn't know him, but to attach a label after he's gone doesn't seem a fair—"

"No, we didn't mean your deceased representative. I was speaking in general. Muslims don't speak ill of the dead, even deceased non-Muslims."

"Good to know."

The trucks drove for an hour before the roads became bumpy, and they started to climb. It was impossible to rest as they were jostled about. Pulling into a mountain village later, they piled out of the vehicles for relief and to stretch their legs. Opening some food packs, they ate and drank water. The villagers eyed them fearfully. They would only talk to the Muslims in the group.

The sun was already much of the way across the sky.

Lily muttered to their driver. "I assume we won't be driving in the dark in this area."

"That's true, ma'am. We may not be stopping in a village for the night. We don't need somebody calling ahead to arrange an ambush."

"Are there cell phone signals here? I'm not receiving any updates since we've been driving on the ground."

"It's getting remote, so I'd say probably not. I'm no tech though."

The trucks resumed the journey. The road got bumpier and the incline steeper. Driving for several more hours, the trucks pulled off the road to park behind some stone outcroppings out of sight of the road. Lily glanced around, but the light was too dim to see very far.

"I'm just going to lay out a sleeping bag. No time for a tent."

Joe and Andy walked up. "You, Patty, Grace, and Donna need to sleep in the vehicles. We'll stand guard out here. That includes watching those ISI snakes."

"Okay, but just for this first night," said Patty. "You need to rest too."

"We'll be fine spelling each other."

As Lily climbed in a truck with Donna, she noticed both ISI men watching her closely. Patty and Grace getting in the other truck didn't draw their attention.

When they put down the bedrolls, Donna spoke.

"Those guys are paying a lot of attention to you for some reason, so it seems more than just you being a pretty woman. It feels to me like there is a game in play."

"It's creepy, and yes, I noticed. With dossiers on all of us, I wonder if it's more than just us going up a dusty mountain trail."

"Give me some time alone with them. I'll beat the crap out of them and loosen their tongues for you."

Lily laughed. "You're kind of a one-track girl."

"It's worked for me so far."

"I'll keep your idea in mind."

"You do that, babe."

In the morning they arose early. Keeping a cold camp, they ate rations and drank water before returning to the road.

Both ISI agents came to sit by Lily. Their expressions looked even more smug than the prior day.

"Did you sleep well?" asked Abdul.

"I did, thank you for asking."

"It wasn't too cramped in there?" Mohamed asked.

"It was snug, but we made do. Why all of this interest in me?"

"You're our leader on this mission. What is our mission, by the way?"

"At this point, we haven't been told."

"I assumed we were going after the ambassador."

"That's yet to be determined. Did you have somewhere else you need to be?"

Both men laughed. Abdul replied, "You're a rare treasure, if you don't mind my saying so."

"Thank you, but it's not necessary to compliment me. I have a husband for that job."

"Get a clue, dude," Donna interjected.

They grinned nonetheless.

"Yes, you do have a family," Mohamed muttered thoughtfully. Again, Lily's warning signals went off.

The climb up the road became more difficult. The bumping was worse, and the weather got difficult with a rainstorm, which turned into snow the higher they went.

It was difficult to keep their seats without slipping onto the floor.

"I could have used some coffee this morning," Donna muttered.

"We all could have," Lily answered. She turned her face to the ISI agents. "Do you have any idea how close we are to the Pakistani border?"

"It's hard to say," Abdul replied. "It's a dangerous region. Lawless, I think you say in the West."

"I don't know that we're going into your country. I was just curious. Does your army maintain a presence hereabouts?"

"They don't try to rule over the territories, if that's what you're asking. The people here are less civilized than the residents of the rest of the country. Why do you ask?"

"I was just wondering if there are assets nearby in case they're needed."

"Do you suspect we'll need backup?"

"We try to be ready for anything."

The ISI men eyed her thoughtfully.

At noon they stopped, having reached the peak of the mountain they were climbing. Getting out and stretching their legs. At this altitude, Lily's phone finally beeped.

"Hey, I've got a signal."

Reading the text, she pondered telling the group fully with the suspect ISI agents standing there.

"Did you get instructions for us?" asked Abdul.

Rather than answer him, she took Patty aside.

"We got a target, but I don't really want to tell our friends. Our orders are we're taking the risk by crossing the border. Apparently in a village in the territories there is a Taliban leader who is more than just an opponent for our forces in Afghanistan. He's instrumental in this worldwide conspiracy. I think they may have made some progress back home in decoding that dark web chatter. We're supposed to capture the guy and put him on a plane to Langley. This could be a serious encounter. The villagers could hate him, but because of their rules about guests, they would defend him to the death."

"I understand. I think we should keep it to ourselves for the time being, Lily. I hate to think about a firefight with innocent villagers though. They don't deserve to be mowed down, not to mention they could do some damage to us."

Returning to the vehicles, Lily spoke. "Everybody, mount up."

They drove the balance of the day, slept, and then drove another entire day to cross the border. They slept that night in Pakistan.

"Welcome home." Donna smiled grimly at the ISI agents. "You're back on your home turf."

Abdul and Mohamed looked almost giddy. They spoke in low tones in their own language of Urdu. However, they weren't close enough for Lily to be able to hear them.

Finally, the time had come. Lily called all the team together.

"We're going into a village tonight. Our mission is to capture an insurgent leader staying there. He's an Afghan Taliban boss, but apparently there are also connections with this global threat too. We've got to use the element of surprise to strike before the villagers can mount a defense. Obviously, we'd like to minimize casualties. There will be Taliban troops with him, but most of the villagers are innocent. Keep that in mind. We get in and get out in a hurry. Any questions?"

No one spoke.

"Abdul, Mohamed, any observations or suggestions?"

Neither replied. They merely shook their heads.

Abdul then said, "I can contact our army to dispatch units to support our operation."

"Thank you, but there is no time to wait for them to arrive. It falls on our shoulders. Everybody, gear up. We leave in an hour to take up positions at the village."

Wesley walked beside Lily. "Don't bother telling me to go elsewhere. I'm going to cover your back during this operation."

Lily smiled. "Thanks, Wesley. I'll cover your back too." Wesley snickered.

It was a long walk trudging to their goal before it got dark. They were heavily armed, including Ron Gray carrying a minigun. The ISI agents were side by side now, carrying American weapons, AR-15s rather than their Russian AK-47s. Lily had made that decision. They hadn't objected.

As they knelt down near the village, Lily spoke. "We're going in from three sides. Patty will lead an attack from the west, I'll hit from the northeast, and Hassan will come in from the southeast. Quick, clean, grab the dude, and we get out of here fast. This will stir up a hornet's nest, so we don't hang around. I don't know how far the villagers will go in chasing after us if there is a firefight."

Lily made a point of splitting up Abdul and Mohamed. She took Mohamed in her group and Patty took Abdul.

It was a timed operation. At the appointed moment, three teams raced silently into the village. They were spotted immediately. It took very little time for villagers to grab their weapons. However, various Arabic-speaking unit members were there to confront them before they could engage in a battle. Lily arrived at the suspect dwelling at the same time Patty got there. Bursting inside, they were surprised to find a villager family and no one else.

Looking at the ISI agents, she asked, "What happened?"

"It seems he was tipped off."

"How is that possible? We just found out the mission."

"Perhaps your intelligence was bad. He may not have been here at all. You may have an issue in your intelligence services."

"There are only villagers here from what I can see. No Taliban soldiers. Hassan, can you talk to the village elder?"

"Sure, Lily."

They went with him for the conference. The village leader looked very angry.

"Hassan, please apologize for us for the misunderstanding. You can tell him what we thought, that an Afghan Taliban leader was here."

After some conversation, he calmed down.

"Lily, he says they know of this man we seek, but he was never here. They think he went back to Afghanistan."

Patty looked at the ISI agents. They looked amused.

"Why are you smiling?"

"I believe we tried to offer the assistance of ISI with intelligence, but your people chose to ignore our help. It's fortunate you didn't kill any Pakistani citizens in Pakistan as that would have had major ramifications," Abdul answered.

Mohamed piped in. "You must admit, we haven't been treated as a part of this team. We were met with suspicion and outright distrust from the start, and that hasn't changed."

"When you were plugged in replacing men we expected and had vetted, that was off-putting. It's no secret some in your agency do not share our views. We don't know you."

"A fair point, but you never gave us a chance to work past that. How are we supposed to gain your trust?"

Taking him aside, Lily spoke Urdu to the villager leader. "Again, I want to beg your pardon for our intrusion. We're not your enemies. Can we leave you with some supplies to make a gesture of good will?"

His wife leaned over to whisper to him.

"My wife trusts you, so we accept your apology. I know our ways are different than in your country. You may go in peace. As a gesture from our side, I can offer our best tracker to accompany you back across the border to be sure you face no trouble."

"Thank you, and we accept."

The villager volunteer was surprisingly young. He rode in the front seat of the lead truck. Lily sat between him and the driver to translate anything he had to say.

In Urdu, she chatted to get to know him. "Thank you for helping us. I hope we're not taking you away from important duties."

"There are others who can step in for me in the village. I'm happy to fulfill our offer to aid you. I speak English, by the way."

In a way, he acted shy, as young men do, but at the same time, he was confident and competent about his job. When he looked at Lily, he smiled warmly.

"What's your name?"

"Gamal."

"I'm happy there were no shots fired or casualties."

"That was very fortunate. There are men in the village quick to take insult. It happened so fast they didn't get a chance to take any bad actions. Believe me, they would have. We don't fear conflict with invaders, no matter how advanced their weapons."

"That's fortunate indeed."

"I want to say, I desire to prove my worth to you."

"What do you mean?"

"I can do much more than merely sit in your truck. I've been to Afghanistan many times. I can help you, and as I see those ISI agents in your party, I must say you need me."

"Do you know them?"

"I'm surprised you include them. ISI has many faces, and some openly aid your enemies."

"So are you saying they're part of our enemies?"

He looked at her without replying.

"I'll admit, we've had a bad feeling since they first showed. They're not the men we were promised."

"That should doubly worry you. If you depend on them, I believe there will come a time it will cost you dearly. Perhaps I'm wrong."

"Thank you for the information, Gamal. We'll continue to use great caution."

The trucks moved forward on roads made dangerous by the weather. The drivers had to decrease speed to avoid mishaps.

They barely made it back across the border before they had to stop for the night.

With the winter storm, all the team members stayed inside the trucks, trying to sleep as best they could. Lily took Gamal into her truck partially to help her keep an eye on ISI. It made for cramped quarters. Gamal acted slightly embarrassed.

"What is it?" Lily whispered.

"I'm an unmarried young man who wouldn't normally be lying against a woman. I'll be fine though. I need to accept in my mind that I'm not in the village with elders around to chastise me. Your world is different than mine."

Lily grinned. "That it is, Gamal. Just look at it as us sharing the warmth in a winter storm."

He grinned also. "I like you."

"I like you too."

They left early the next morning. Again, it was a slow go on the treacherous road.

They still had far to go down the mountain when the attack started. A mortar round exploded in front of the lead truck. It was at a bad place as they were exposed and vulnerable there.

Swerving, the drivers tried to continue downward to at least get to a defensible position.

"Friends of yours?" asked Donna in a hiss.

"I think perhaps you've found your Taliban leader," Abdul replied.

The mortar rounds continued. Fortunately, though some rounds landed close, they missed while the swerving trucks tried to escape the noose.

"There's a place ahead we can stop and make a stand," said the driver.

"No, keep going. The enemy has set a trap. If you stop and get out of your trucks, they are there to shoot you dead."

"Keep going," Lily ordered. "Thank you, Gamal."

As they raced through that point, Taliban gunmen opened fire, but their rifle fire couldn't penetrate the armor shielding of the vehicles.

As they raced ahead, Jeeps and trucks pulled out full of enemy soldiers to give chase.

Patty and Lily both tried to connect with headquarters, but reception was spotty. The enemy wasn't willing to give up their prey and followed the two allied trucks racing down the mountain. By chance, two American helicopters happened to pass overhead and saw the pursuit and the battle in progress. Swinging around, they strafed the Taliban vehicles, allowing Lily's unit to break away.

"That was close," said Patty. "I'd forgotten what it was like to be in harm's way. My heart is still thumping."

"Thank you again, Gamal," said Lily. "You spared us from a really bad situation."

She looked at her ISI agents. "How do you suppose we got bad intel sending us to that village, and then how would they know to set a trap here?"

"As I said, perhaps you have a problem with your own security services. Any side can have leaks. Weak people will sell anything for bribes or other inducements." Abdul smiled.

Both of them looked at Donna, who was glaring. Before she erupted, Lily spoke again to head off trouble.

"That's true. It's a hazard for any organization. Thankfully, Gamal was here to give us his valuable guidance."

Gamal joined Donna in glaring at them. They were undaunted under the harsh scrutiny.

"Indeed," said Mohamed.

The trucks sped along as the helicopters headed back to base to refuel and reload.

Abdul added, "I think you've made an enemy. Sheik Rahman will not be happy you avoided his trap. For his purposes, you would have been a great trophy to taunt your people, the darling American superspy caught, helpless in his hands. I think you haven't seen the last of the sheik."

"Why don't you call your pal," said Donna. "Tell him to bring it on. We'll be waiting."

"Again, this distrust…why? What have we done? We're giving you advice just as Gamal gave you his opinion." Mohamed shrugged. "Your suspicions are misplaced."

"Right." Donna balled up her fists. Both Mohamed and Abdul got deadly looks.

"Stop!" Lily shouted. "Enough of this posturing, it serves no purpose. Stand down, Donna."

Donna backed off but continued to glare.

"This isn't over." She turned her head to talk to Andy sitting beside her. He was similarly provoked.

"Navy SEALs," said Mohamed.

"Yes, brother," Abdul answered. "We are truly blessed to be among them."

Lily noticed for the first time, both of them now wore large knives sheathed in their belts.

"Gifts from our fathers," Abdul explained. "It's traditional, like when boys in your country get guns from their fathers."

When the trucks finally left the mountain road arriving back to flatlands, Lily's phone beeped.

"I guess we're back in touch with the world."

Gamal looked at her screen as Lily pulled up the text message.

"Do you read English, Gamal?"

"I can speak it, but I've never been taught. Can I know what it says?"

"It's updating me about events. They're warning us the sheik could be in the area. Take all precautions."

Everybody in the truck laughed, even the ISI guys. Strangely, it eased the tensions in the truck, at least for the moment.

Lily typed out a reply, an update of her own.

She smiled at Gamal. "Now they will know the sheik is in the area. I'm sure they'll dispatch forces."

"Surely they must know it's too late. He wouldn't sit around for them to come after him."

"Do you have any idea where he goes? Where his base camp is located?"

"No, I wish I could help you with that. He's hated in my village. If he was gone forever, we would have a celebration. His forces have taken girls from my village and other villages as child brides for his men."

"That's evil," said Donna. She looked at the ISI men. "Where is that in your holy book where it's okay to steal underage girls?"

"Why do you try to put this on us? We don't condone such actions. It is despicable. We agree on that."

"Where to now, Lily?" Her driver glanced over.

"We go back to Bagram for the time being."

"I'm ready for a hot shower," Patty opined.

"Amen," the rest of the crew agreed.

"Are you okay with this, staying at an American base, Gamal?"

"Yes, it will be a new experience."

"Does your village expect you back soon?"

"I'm of an age to make my own decisions and to choose the things I do. I will give you my help for us long as you wish. I would defend you with my life."

She looked at his face. His pronouncement, the determination and devotion, struck her deeply. It was a surprise from an unexpected source.

"I appreciate that. I'm honored."

"The honor is mine."

Arriving back later at the air base, Donna and Lily went to their shared room.

"Lily, you've got an admirer."

"He's a young guy. I think it's sweet."

"I'm just saying, for him to make that statement in front of everybody, he was serious about devoting himself to you personally. In this part of the world, it's no idle pledge. You know part of his interest is infatuation. He'd love to impress you."

"I realize that. What do you want for me to say?"

"There's nothing for you to say, but keep it in mind for the future. He might make some magnanimous act to prove his devotion that costs him his life. Remember, they don't see women like in the West. His need to 'protect' you could come into play at the wrong time."

Lily pondered the issue and what to do about it.

"I've got an idea, Donna. Let's invite Gamal to the gym. Maybe when he sees us fight, he may see us in a new light."

"Sure. I can beat the crap out of him for you."

"Donna, I'm not going to humble him. We owe him thanks about that ambush averted."

"Okay, but if you change your mind, let me know. I'm always ready to rumble."

Picking up Gamal as they went, he changed into gym clothes they provided.

There were a large number of men and women working out as they walked in. Gamal was agog for a number of reasons. Women in shorts was scandalous where he came from, but quickly his attention focused on the sparring battles as women fought men on equal terms.

"Why don't you watch for a while? Donna and I will show you a few things, and then we can ease you in to get some training."

He nodded his head.

Donna and Lily started an aggressive fight landing solid blows often. Gamal heard them grunt from the heavier impacts.

The male SEAL members walked up to Gamal to watch the women in action.

Wesley joined them. "Gamal, our women are trained for battle. They can take care of themselves."

"Yes," he muttered, but he struggled to contain himself from jumping in to end the heavy blows.

Finally, he looked at Wesley.

"Relax, they have it under control. I've known Lily since college. She was driven back then, and nothing is going to change. It's who she is. Do you understand?"

"Yes." His response was tepid.

CHAPTER 4

Lily ended her fights with Donna and called Gamal onto the mat.

"Just relax. We're not going to fight. I want to take you through the fundamentals. Learning hand-to-hand combat is a step-by-step process. Is that okay with you?"

"Of course, I'm eager to learn. If it makes me a better warrior, that is a good thing. Perhaps I can learn other things while I'm here?" He grinned.

Lily chuckled. "Okay, I'm not sure what you have in mind, but I'm game."

Lily stood in front of him. "Okay, when you face an opponent, this is deadly stuff, him or you. It takes absolute concentration. You can't be thinking about anything else. Don't face them straight on to make yourself a bigger target. Turn so you're sideways and flex at your knees to be nimble. Have your attack plan in your mind already so you just react to opportunities and strike quickly."

She almost chuckled as when he turned, he tried to show a fierce facial expression.

Lily took him through various moves and countermoves, leg sweeps, fundamental punches, and how to maximize impacts in how you swung. "Remember, in a fight to the death, there are no rules of good conduct. Expect your opponent to fight dirty, because he will. Turn the tables, if need be. Another thing, your emotions can be a problem. You should never engage in a serious fight unless there is no other way. Sometimes you can be in a situation that the only choice is to escape from harm's way. You may be fighting multiple opponents. Do you understand?"

"I didn't think about retreat. We think of your army as always charging ahead."

"Often we do, but you need to use your head, live to fight another day."

She smiled at his reaction, like she was revealing the secrets of the universe only to him.

"Also, when you must fight, you've got to play to win. That means you might need to do some difficult things, gouge eyes, chop their throats so they can't breathe, go for vulnerable parts of the body. It isn't some noble contest of honor, it's simple survival. Defending yourself can also involve fighting women attackers. They can kill you too, so you can't be vulnerable."

"I understand," he replied soberly. "It goes against our nature, but one must survive."

"Most fights will involve weapons, not personal battles."

She continued instructing for hours before they broke off for a meal. The mess hall was another first for Gamal. Looking around at the pandemonium, he frowned. The scent of food, loud talking, and laughter, it assailed his senses. Looking at the food pans, he wasn't sure what he was about to eat, which didn't help.

Standing behind Lily in line, selecting what she took, he looked at the full plate uncertainly.

"It's filling, Gamal."

Donna was behind him. "Gamal, these meals are gut bombs. Don't let her fool you."

"Shut up, Donna." Lily laughed.

"What is gut bomb?" He looked confused and concerned.

"Don't pay attention to her. She's trying to be funny, and not successfully so."

They were joined at their table by others of the team. Notably, Ari and Hassan seemed to have become fast friends as the edginess of their differing politics was accommodated successfully. It was a vital step for the team dynamic to flourish.

When Abdul and Mohamed sat down, it chilled the conversations at the table.

"Greetings, Lily." Abdul smiled, but Lily wasn't warmed by the gesture.

"Hello," she responded in a neutral tone.

"May we join you?" Mohamed asked.

"Of course. You don't need to ask. You're a part of this team, remember."

He sat down beside Gamal, while Abdul sat across from them.

Both spoke in Urdu with each other, but mostly they talked at Gamal. He said nothing, but his facial expression hardened, causing both ISI men to grin. Again, they didn't realize Lily could listen and understand their words. However, when her expression subtly changed also, Abdul noticed. He nodded at Mohamed, who changed the subject and switched to English.

"It is a fine day today. Lily, I must say the allied forces are impressive. The technology and equipment here are daunting. It's a wonder your enemy hasn't been conquered with such might all of these years later."

"It's been a tough battle." She eyed them coolly. "We don't take opposing forces for granted."

"Is there a problem? You seemed perplexed? Is that the right word?"

"When I face problems, or tasks, I tend to carefully ponder options and solutions. Perhaps you're misreading me. We're a team working together. You seem to me to have trouble remembering that."

"Perhaps you're right that I'm not interpreting you correctly. Both Abdul and I wish to contribute to the team, but it is a difficult task overcoming—"

"We don't judge people on words, we watch their actions."

"Have we not done our part thus far?"

"I'm talking about serious confrontations like a firefight. We can't afford misunderstandings then, where lives are at stake."

"That goes both ways. Our security services offered to aid in your quest, but you remain resistant."

"Hey, you can leave anytime," Donna piped in.

"Donna, cool it," Lily said it to head off any argument. "This is a tough assignment for everybody. We all need to try harder."

Abdul and Mohamed glowered at Donna, who smirked at them. "Anytime," she muttered.

"Donna, stop that." Lily was angered.

After the meal, Gamal stayed close to Lily as they walked back to their barracks.

"You heard what they said?"

"I did. I think it finally dawned on them I know their language."

"I'm sorry for…what they said. It's an insult. I hope you don't take offense."

"Gamal, you've done nothing wrong. Why they're needling you, I'm not sure, but we have our eyes on them."

"They imply I'm a collaborator along with, you know…the other thing."

"Ignore them. The mission is what's paramount. I think they're worried you can pick up on little cues between them that we might miss."

"I have. I think they're not fully honest with you. There is more going on, and I want to say you must be careful. They're danger-ous. With them against this daunting team, it's too easy to dismiss that they are a force to be reckoned with. They're not afraid of Navy SEALs. I think Donna should not continue to taunt them. They're highly trained also."

"I understand."

"Can you forgive me?" His head went down with embarrassment.

"For what?"

"They accuse me of wanting to…eh…"

"That's their way of getting to you. Your presence helped save our lives. I suspect the sheik's ambush was a planned operation. They weren't randomly in the area. It's possible those two are plotting against us. I lean toward it's probable they're enemies."

"That's what I'm trying to say. I should have known you'd understand this. You're very perceptive."

"Thank you, Gamal. I'm heading back to take a shower after the workout."

"I will do this too. We don't have showers in my little village. It's new to me."

Lily returned to her room. Donna was already there.

"Donna, you've got to stop poking the bear with our ISI friends."

"If I knock them off their game and they slip up, I see that as a good thing. They try to be smooth, but nobody is perfect. They can stumble too."

"I agree, but on the outside chance they're not working for the other side, use your head."

"Yes, ma'am."

"I'm going to get cleaned up."

"Go ahead, I already did."

Afterward, while she was drying her hair, they received a knock at the door.

"Ma'am, you're requested in ops right away."

Quickly dressing, she hurried to the command center.

"Lily, we just received this message from Langley. They intercepted chatter, but it doesn't seem to make sense. It looks like random letters and numbers. There is no sentence structure we can discern. The pattern isn't systematic. The analysts are stumped. Take a look and see if you see something they missed."

Sitting down, it took her only a moment to glance at the message.

"I agree, I see nothing helpful here. I assume they checked for codes."

"The supercomputer analyzed it in moments and concluded it was gibberish."

"Can I take this with me to study it? I feel like we can't afford to dismiss this. It means something to somebody out there."

"Certainly."

She started to walk away and then turned back.

"I thought we could trace anything back to the source. Some computer or device generated this thing."

"I can't explain it. If it was a government agency somewhere in the world, we'd know about them. If there is an individual who is such a computer genius that he can completely mask his location, device, and message, that is unique and chilling."

Lily continued back to her room. After viewing the strange message from all angles, she gave up.

Donna tried her luck, but that attempt had a very short duration.

"Sorry, Lily. Computer stuff isn't my strong suit. Maybe it is nothing more than gibberish."

"Gibberish accomplishes nothing. There is a reason that we need to figure out. I worry that there is a time limit running out if we don't crack this. The people this is being sent to know what it says."

Donna got a serious look on her face. "I really do wish I could help you."

"I do also. I just can't let this slide. I really think there is something important."

"Do we show this to our ISI pals? We watch how they react to see if they get it?"

"You're banking on them dropping their guard and screwing up? Even if they understand, I don't think they'd give us an inadvertent clue. I wouldn't if the role was reversed."

"You're one of a kind though. You know you're perfect."

"Will you shut up with that stupidity please?" Lily laughed, shaking her head.

"It's worth a try if we've got nothing else."

"I'll think about it."

"Well, think fast. I agree with you time is ticking away."

Lily glanced back.

Donna smiled. "Let's…"

"No."

"You don't know what I was going to suggest."

"It doesn't matter. The answer is still no."

Donna laughed heartily. Lily ignored her and stared at the mystery message again. It remained an impossible puzzle at that point, which frustrated her a great deal.

"Come on, Lily, let's go. Staring at that thing will just give you a headache. Try it later and maybe something will click."

Lily sighed a moment before she got up. "Okay, maybe you're right."

Folding the paper, she put it in her pocket. Going out of their room, they wandered out of the building, ambling toward the nearest aircraft hangar.

"Hello."

Turning to look back at the voice, they saw Gamal approaching. "May I walk with you? I didn't want to sit in the room."

"Is everything okay? Who are you rooming with?"

"No one at this point, I just wanted to get out."

Lily pulled out the paper from her pocket. "Does this mean anything to you?"

Gamal stared at it. His expression changed to anger, but he said nothing.

"Gamal, what is it?"

"I…I'm sorry. This is difficult for me. It is vile, like a call to evil."

"It was put out around the world over the dark web. What does it mean?"

"In my religion, there are those people who have warped it to their demented purposes. They have tried to act as if they represent all Muslims. They do not, but what they do draws attention, so the bulk of us that hate what they do are ignored. Do you understand?"

"I understand completely. When you say that this thing calls forth evil, help me to understand."

"To your eyes, you see nothing, gibberish as you call it. We see within the message characters that reveal the intent. What it means, I can only say that not only here, but everywhere, like-minded people will see it as a call to arms. It looks to me like a call for action."

"Amazing. As you said, I would never have discerned that, nor would I discern anything."

"See this." Gamal pointed out particular characters within the string.

At that moment, Lily's phone rang. "Hello."

"Is this Lily Carson?"

"It is."

"This is Kevin Simmons, I'm a CIA analyst. I got a message you wanted to talk to us."

"I do. I'm trying to get a handle on this weird message. I was hoping you can give me some background?"

"If you liken back to an example of Ross Ulbricht, a.k.a. Dread Pirate Roberts, the inventor of the Silk Road back in 2011, we looked at this challenge as something analogous. Back then he basically invented the deep web to facilitate criminal enterprises and activities, including illegal drug sales, human trafficking, weapons sales, and so forth. They used Bitcoin for the financial transactions and netted $13 million in three years. The FBI was able to take them down then, but we have our hands full this time around. This event seems to encompass a far wider scope and operates on a vast scale. I personally have never seen anything like it. I'm sorry we couldn't distill an answer out of the muddle, but regardless, I felt it important to get the message to the field even with us stuck in the interim steps. At least you have a prior warning of something big roiling all around. You guys being wary like never before goes without saying. Does this help?"

"It helps me understand to an extent. Obviously seeing the whole picture would help, but we'll take whatever we can get at this point. I appreciate what you found, and I agree this thing has us all worried. In the meantime, we need some direction about how to approach this. Pass that on to the powers that be, we need step-by-step instructions."

"I will. Goodbye, Lily. Stay safe."

"Goodbye, Kevin. You be careful also."

Lily stared away, wrestling with an uneasy feeling.

"I gather it wasn't good," said Donna.

"It's kind of what we expected. Whatever is going on seems to be unprecedented. When the CIA analysts are stumped, I get worried."

"Uh-oh. Did they have any idea what we should do next?"

"Not really, or maybe I should say, not yet. Kevin is passing on our concerns and the need for an action plan."

"So we twiddle our thumbs in the meantime? The enemy isn't standing still."

"I'm sure they know that."

"I hate giving the bad guys a head start."

"You're not alone in that feeling."

"By the way, have you noticed the sharp increase in sorties departing the airfields?"

"I have. Locally, things are definitely percolating."

"Maybe that sheik is planning to come a callin'."

"That would be a bold move, a mistake in my opinion, but you never know what these true believers will do."

"They can't wait to get those seventy virgins, I guess."

"Donna, you're demented." Lily chuckled.

"I call it like I see it."

They heard a rap on their door.

Lily opened the door to see Wesley.

"Hi, what's up?"

"They've called a meeting."

"When?"

"Right now."

"Okay. We're coming."

The three walked to the headquarters to a meeting room. All the unit members were assembled there.

The base commander stepped to the podium.

"I'm sure you've noticed our escalating threat level. Our available resources are being stretched past the limits. Originally, an aircraft carrier was going to sail close enough to the coast to add naval aircraft assets supporting our missions. That has since been compromised as other challenges are arising elsewhere, drawing them away. Developing a comprehensive plan to address every incident everywhere is not a rapid process. We're being forced to play whack-a-mole, picking and choosing which site is the point of greatest need, the very thing we worried about. I think Langley is overwhelmed. I've already instituted an order no one is allowed to leave the base for anything other than an actual combat mission. As far as you folks, you're in a support mode for our operations until such time as we get orders dispatching you elsewhere. If we get somebody pinned down here, you could be called in as reinforcements. That means stay frosty. You're our only quick reaction reserves here. Any questions?"

Lily raised her hand.

"Yes, Lily."

"When you say picking and choosing, are you talking about only in-country, or does that include cross-border operations?"

"Both."

The team members muttered and glanced at each other.

The commander added, "Listen, folks, I know this is pretty nebulous, but the situation is what it is. We need to be flexible because we don't know what's coming down the pipe or when."

"We know that, sir. It's just that normally we're dispatched for a specific purpose, so this is new ground for us."

"Lily, it's new ground for all of us. Our bathtub is full to overflowing, so nobody knows how to deal with this glut of danger everywhere all at once."

Lily glanced around the room to see numerous glassy-eyed expressions.

"I don't suppose we can call our families, sir?" Andy asked.

"I'm sorry, but that's not possible at the moment. This situation requires secrecy on all of our parts. We'll see how things shake out. Possibly you can have civilian contact later."

Looking around also, he continued. "Any more questions, folks?"

Nobody spoke, but numerous faces were riled up.

"You're dismissed."

They filed out of the room relatively quietly, although there was some muttering.

Andy and Joe were directly behind Donna and Lily. Once down the hall out of earshot of the commander, Lily heard from them.

Joe spoke. "This is BS, Lily. I don't get it."

"Nobody likes it. My opinion, they're taking no chances. I think these are unprecedented times."

"What the…"

Lily stopped and turned to the men. "Why do you suppose it's a violation for anybody to disclose our current position? That's true for the location of any Navy SEALs on an operation. I guess the other side could be monitoring our calls home, but I get the strange feeling we're being singled out. I don't know why that would be."

The men scowled but didn't reply.

"Do you think they know all of the SEALs and the details on our families?" Donna asked.

"Why not? Hackers break into anything these days. With our American egos, we think we're above the skills of our opponents. I don't think that's true. A lot of overseas kids go to the USA for college. They're taught the same things as our kids. I don't make assumptions about the security of my family or our country for that matter."

"I never thought of it that way," Donna replied. Her face mirrored deep concern. "It's a chilling idea. I'm not married, but I've got family too, parents and siblings."

"It's why I feel stressed so often. What lies ahead for us could be a problem unlike anything we've ever faced before. I really believe that."

"I don't disagree."

Joe spoke. "It makes me want to smack somebody. I need a beer."

"I'll drink a beer," Andy added. "How 'bout you, Lily?"

"I'm more of a fine wine girl, but thanks. I'm going to study this message a little more. Maybe something will pop into my head."

"Okay, but it's your loss. You have a chance to hang with genuine certified Navy SEALs in their natural habitat. Nothing could be better than that."

"I'm sure you're right. I'll just absorb the hit as best I can."

Donna spoke, smirking. "You two are a couple of knuckleheads."

They laughed and walked away to claim their adult beverages.

"You aren't joining them, Donna?"

"I don't need a headache at this time of day. Those two don't drink just one beer."

"Well, I guess everyone has their own way of maintaining combat readiness."

Lily's phone rang. "Hello."

"Lily, this is Todd."

"Hey, Todd, what's up back at the agency?"

"I'm calling…as your friend."

"Okay, what does that mean?"

"I…eh…well, things are getting a little weird here."

"That doesn't sound good. Weird in what way?"

"I'm sharing this because I believe we're kindred spirits of a sort. This isn't a place for politics, but nonetheless, there seems to be a new element seeping in the door."

"Explain."

"We've talked about some worrisome aspects of the current domestic regime. Lately, some of the secrecy and mystifying meetings that seemed inappropriate are bearing fruit and not in a good way. Remember we joked about the USA adding May Day as a new national holiday based on governmental contacts outside our borders? We just had a large Russian team arrive to join us at Langley. Can you believe it?"

"What? What possible reason could there be?"

"One other thing, they think the British ambassador has been taken out of your area, though there's no evidence to support the theory. I can't even tell what our strategy is. If you were initially dispatched to try a rescue, it would seem you'd be moved. However, with no good intel, we don't know where she might have been taken, assuming she's not still there somewhere in tribal lands. Do you get what I'm saying? I get the feeling we have a rat, or maybe I should say rats in this building."

"That is an incredible accusation, Todd. It seems impossible."

"I've never seen us so clueless. If there is a power struggle at the top trying to pull us in opposite directions, that is unprecedented. I'm not the only one who's noticed. You definitely need to watch your backs out there."

"If you're right and there is some background agenda in play, how do I respond to any subsequent orders? It has seemed strange to me here we're sort of in limbo reacting to things instead of going toward a goal."

"That limbo may continue. I don't see progress here, and it's getting worse. We get orders and directives that get countermanded the next day. It's paralyzing. We look around and wonder who we can trust. Listen, I've got to go. There are other serious worries I wish I had time to explain. Goodbye, Lily."

"Goodbye, Todd."

"What was that?" Donna asked.

"I'm not sure. Todd kind of warned us to be wary."

"We always are. What did he mean?"

"He thinks something is amok in the agency."

"This isn't him joking?"

"Not at all, he was dead serious. There are Russians at Langley now."

"Huh…what's happening? So…what do we do now?"

"I'm going to make a call to a knowledgeable friend. I asked Todd how we judge future orders. He didn't give an answer, but he alluded to possible infiltrators. He said bad politics could be bleeding into the agency."

"That makes me mad. As if our jobs aren't tough enough out here already. Being set up is—"

"I know that." Lily looked concerned. "It's a possibility I didn't see coming."

"I'm not out here to get burned. Make your call to your friend. Having this kind of situation is unacceptable."

"Let's go back to the room. I don't want to have that conversation out here."

"May I come with you?" Gamal asked, frowning.

"Sure."

Returning to the room and closing the door to the outside world, Lily dialed the number.

"Lily."

"Yes, Bret, I—"

"I know why you're calling. I've talked with Todd. He said he was going to warn you."

"What he said, it boggles my mind."

"Have you told anybody else?"

"Donna was with me, so she knows. We have a young local guy with us too."

"Keep this under your hat. Even in your unit, you shouldn't share this with anybody."

"Explain."

"Briefly, there seems to be a contrary element in our government that goes all the way to the top. That element is orchestrating actions that run opposite of the path we've taken forever. Whatever is their end game, it has the establishment worried. That's in addition to serious threats popping up within our borders as well as everywhere else on the globe. If we have a fifth column deep within every agency that protects national security, that could mean danger on a scale we could never have imagined before. I know I'm saying that phrase a lot lately."

"Are you saying part of my team could be threats too?"

"You need to operate under that premise."

"We've had questions about our Pakistani friends, but does it go deeper than that?"

"It is possible. Whatever loyalties service members might have back home, it's hard to say."

"What does that mean? What other loyalties can there be?"

"You know the background groups that have risen to the surface in recent years. It's possible some troops may sympathize with their goals."

"Wow, that's kind of open-ended. Once you open that wound, the poison can spread and infect other people."

"You see what I'm saying. If your associates have hidden feelings and agendas, who knows what might set them off. Having a meltdown in a combat situation would be catastrophic."

"I asked Todd how I should judge new orders coming in from Langley."

"I'd just say, remember that an unlawful order is not a legitimate order. In some circumstances, we have choices."

"That is a slippery slope. I don't really have a good answer to that problem."

"There probably isn't a good answer. Countermanding or ignoring orders from above is obviously a dangerous move, but at the same time, polarization at the top with competing agendas is an equal threat, if not worse."

"How could we get into such a nightmare?"

"What can we do about it? Who do we trust? That's our problem here at Langley. That makes it true for you in the field also. Listen, I've got to go. Stay frosty out there and keep to trusted friends only as much as possible."

"I'll try."

"I hope to get back to you later. Things are in serious flux, so I can't say when or if."

Lily hung up and stared at the wall. Donna commented. "Now I think we need a beer."

"I understand the feeling, but I need to keep a clear head. I suspect there is something big coming for us real soon, and we need to be ready at an instant. You can go join the guys at the bar if you feel the need."

"It's a thought, but I guess I'll pass. Hanging around you is making me a better citizen."

"Yeah, right."

"Plus, we've got Gamal here. Showing him good examples is probably the better choice. So what now, Lily?"

"I wish I had a good answer. I think I'll get in a little weapons practice. Gamal, you're going to train with US weapons with us."

"Yes, thank you. I'll join you. Should I get my AK-47 from my room?"

"No. American weapons only. If these jarheads hear the sound of an AK, who knows what they'll do."

Donna laughed.

Going outside into a very hot sun, they walked slowly as they silently pondered the situation. When they arrived at the range, it was jammed. So many weapons were in action it sounded like a battle in progress.

"I guess we aren't alone with our ideas," Donna muttered.

"We aren't the only people hearing from friends. The story is consistent from everybody everywhere."

"With the backup, do you want to stand around and wait?"

"I guess not."

In the distance they heard explosions. These were not occasional booms but sustained blasts.

"Is that ours or theirs?"

"It sounds like a serious event. I'd say theirs. It would take a little time to get our assets to the site after we're hit."

"That's pretty bold for them. Noon attacks out in the open aren't their usual MO."

The thumps from the battle continued. Overhead, choppers flew in waves, and above them fighter wings raced toward the fight.

"That is a major response. The battle must be a lot bigger than normal."

The sounds of the thumps of explosions changed as aircraft ordinance erupted in the battle, shaking the ground even at this far distance away. The firing at the range ceased as the troops were called to man their defense stations. Soldiers sprinted past, racing away to assigned points along the perimeter.

Lily glanced at Donna. She had a feral expression as her battle frenzy ignited. They hurried to the room to don battle gear. At the sound of an explosion nearby, the women raced outside, weapons in hand. Perimeter guard stations opened up firing with heavy weapons.

"They're attacking this base?" Donna sounded astonished.

"We need to gather the unit members."

"I see Joe and Andy sprinting this way."

When they arrived, Lily asked, "Have you seen the others?"

They glanced around before shaking their heads.

"I don't know where they are," said Andy.

A mortar round flew over the wall, landing in an open area near enough to knock them off their feet.

Rising back up, Lily looked around.

"What do we do?" asked Donna.

"Let's jump into the perimeter defense until I hear otherwise."

Racing to the wall, the four of them aimed at the muzzle flashes as the enemy was not charging the wall. In the distance in the nearby mountains, a serious battle continued to grow. Even with bombing from aircraft above and considerable strafing from attack choppers, the enemy was returning significant fire. It was the largest firefight Lily had ever been in.

In this engagement, Lily noticed there were far fewer wild shots coming at them. Instead, the marksmanship of the enemy fighters seemed unusually competent. It added to the normal fear reflexes. Clearly they heard the distinctive sound of Russian AK-47s.

Donna flinched at a round kicking up debris into her face.

"Are you hurt?" Lily cried out over the din.

"I was startled more than injured. I'm okay."

"Take a minute to collect yourself."

Lily resumed firing. Donna joined her in moments.

A wave of helicopters roared overhead to attack the enemy positions. That dampened the attack significantly. Enemy troops could be seen scurrying for cover as the minigun firepower of the copters was too much for them.

"My heart is still thumping," said Donna.

"Mine too. Donna, you're bleeding on your arm."

"It's just a scratch. I've had worse. I'm fine. It's probably a little shrapnel."

"Get it looked at, just in case."

CHAPTER 5

After the lengthy battle, Lily led her nearby SEAL team friends to locate the other members of the team while Donna went to the medical clinic for treatment.

They found unit members dispersed to different places along the perimeter. She was mildly surprised to see Mohamed and Abdul, the ISI members, had participated in repelling the enemy assault.

They looked up as she approached. "Are you guys okay? That battle was a surprise in a lot of ways, out of character for what we usually see. Those enemy troops were really good shooters."

Abdul replied, "Westerners give too little credit to the people they face. Why do you suppose that is? Does your cultural bias color your opinions so deeply? You do so at your own great peril. Your enemy has skills too."

"I hope that's not a correct critique of our army. Personally, I don't dismiss any threat."

Both of them smiled at Lily but again more like Cheshire cats sizing up prey.

"That is wise, Lily," Mohamed added after a moment. "Our culture is different than yours. We are all tenacious to the end…in everything we do. We strive for many kinds of goals and don't stop short of any of them."

She eyed them thoughtfully. "I get the feeling there's more in your implication than just this mission."

They grinned broadly. "Now you understand us." Now it was Abdul answering.

She eyed them in curiosity. "Should I take this as threatening me?"

"We're just giving you an overview, some added perspective. You make decisions that include us too. Do you see? We need good decisions."

"I see. That's fair."

"The point is, stop thinking here with your Western mind and try to see things through Arab eyes. It's not so easy to do for you, I think."

"Thanks, an excellent suggestion. In the future I'll depend on you to help me with that."

Mohamed spoke. "We're well aware that you and your team don't trust us, and that's fine. You should be cautious, but that should apply with everybody in your country too. We respect you personally a great deal. I hope you will realize that someday. We're your allies too."

"Thank you, guys. I will say again I judge people on their actions rather than their words. Watching you fight with us in this battle caught my attention in a good way."

"That's what allies do. We will defend you like you're our family."

"And I'll do the same for you."

Lily's phone rang. "Hello."

She stood for a time listening and then hung up.

She spoke louder to all her people. "Follow me, unit members. This battle was recorded and just posted online. We need to see it."

Gathering around a computer operator in the command building, she pulled it up for viewing. It was shot first aimed toward the mountains and the first battle and then turning and aiming toward the camp when the attack started there. A narrator spoke infrequently in Arabic.

Once the post ended, they looked at Gamal as well as the ISI agents to translate.

Mohamed spoke first. "It was intended as propaganda but wasn't a polished product. The speaker glorified the attacks, but…"

Abdul added, "It stopped before the battle ended. Had they won, I'm sure the recording would have continued. They didn't film when the allied aircraft bombs exploded and the fight turned badly for them. I don't know what their ultimate expectation was. It was a significant fight, but one doomed to failure."

Gamal suddenly spoke up. "It was a call to arms to any and all Muslim peoples."

Donna joined them. "So it was an opening salvo."

"Yes," Gamal replied tersely, grim faced. Everybody stared at him. "My friends, you must understand our teachings point to the ultimate end of the world you call Armageddon. Our teachings say we win that final battle. There are many who strive to hasten that outcome by starting the final war."

"I've heard that," Lily commented. "Other than fanatics, I didn't think most Muslims believed that. We see such theories as the ravings of lunatics."

"It is far more widespread than you think. I'm sorry, but you need to know these background things when you're planning your strategies."

Donna asked, "You don't believe that, Gamal? It's your religious tenet."

"I can honestly say I'm not sure. Also, I can't say this attack is the start of the final war. I'm too young to be a scholar."

Everybody chuckled, even Abdul and Mohamed.

Gamal smiled sheepishly and shrugged his shoulders. "I probably shouldn't talk."

They all laughed heartily.

Patty Baymill hurried over to the group from the command building. "Everybody inside for a meeting, we've got new orders."

Once inside the room, Patty took to the podium accompanied by the base commander.

"They've got a lead on the captured British ambassador. We'd assumed she was taken across the Pakistani border into the territories, but this lead has them going across a different border possibly into Uzbekistan or one of those countries ending in 'stan.' They haven't told us for sure the exact location, so it could be another country there altogether. At any rate, we're wheels up in an hour to investigate. It will be full gear, so ready your minds for a possible serious firefight. They just released another tape on the internet. This one is really disgusting. The Brits are ready to go to war after seeing it. Those enemies are soulless animals. We're going first because we're closer than any of their Special Forces units. They won't be far behind us."

Hurrying to their rooms, it took them little time to gear up as they lived out of their duffels. It was afternoon, which coincided perfectly with the plan. Arriving in the dark at the destination was the first best option.

When Lily went to the helicopter, Gamal edged up to her along with the other unit members.

"Gamal, you're not required to go into this battle. It's going to be dicey, and there could be casualties. We're soldiers, so it's our job to take risks."

"I know. I'm not afraid. If it's the will of Allah that it's my time, so be it. These jihadists don't speak for all Muslims. We must make an answer to their vile ways."

Donna spoke. "Good man." She bumped fists with him. Gamal smiled broadly at the unexpected gesture of acceptance and comradeship.

Climbing onto the large transport chopper, Capt. Patty Baymill took the SEALs—Donna, Joe, and Andy—near her. Ari and Hassan went on next; then Wesley; the three CIA agents, Ron, Steve, and Grace; and lastly, Lily boarded. Gamal gestured to her; he'd saved a seat beside him. Lily glanced at Donna, who smirked sitting on the other side of Gamal.

"Okay, Gamal."

He started to chatter happily at her immediately when she sat down. She merely smiled and closed her eyes, leaning back against the bulkhead.

The aircraft departed quickly. With Lily ignoring him, Gamal turned his head to talk with Donna. She chuckled but joined his conversation.

It was a bumpy flight as a storm roiled ominously ahead directly in their flight path. Lily's attempts at a nap ended as they were battered by high winds buffeting the helicopter all about. Gamal bumped against her after a particularly savage jolt.

"I'm sorry," he sputtered apologetically.

"It's not a problem. We're all being knocked around."

It took nearly an hour flying higher to navigate the bad weather. Once they cleared the storm, the choppers veered back on course to head toward the landing zone, which was still some distance away. The lost time meant a later arrival deeper into darkness. Any margin for error was rapidly shrinking.

Lily glanced over past Gamal at Donna. Somehow, she'd managed to doze off in spite of the bumpy ride.

"I don't know how you do it," Lily muttered.

"What?" Gamal asked.

"I was envying how Donna can sleep in this storm."

"She is very good at many things."

"You're right about that."

"I learn so much from being around you." He grinned broadly.

Lily gave him a shrug. Glancing at him, his cow eyes spoke volumes. "Oh my," she muttered.

The sky darkened as they continued the flight. It became dim inside the aircraft. Lily closed her eyes and thought about home, smiling as she imagined her family sitting down to a peaceful dinner. It caused her a pang that she couldn't be there with them or even call.

She heard one of the male SEALs start to snore. Whether it was Andy or Joe, she couldn't tell in the dark. Lily smirked.

Lily dozed off, finally, then waking up later in the dark. Dim lights were just actuating. With a chirp, the pilot alerted them.

"We're approaching the LZ."

"Gear up, everybody," Lily announced.

The copters banked and headed for an elevated position of grasslands for a quick landing.

"No enemy response. The immediate area is clear," the pilot added.

Hurrying off the choppers, the team gathered around Lily and Patty.

Patty spoke first. "Our intelligence indicates a small village a mile from here. We approach on foot after surrounding the perimeter."

"Approach what? Do we have a specific target house?" asked Joe.

"Not exactly. Watch for guards on duty. That will clue us to the probable place they have her."

"That's kind of sketchy," Joe added.

"We work with what we've got."

Lily spoke. "Remember that village of Gamal's. If this is a bad lead, we don't want to start trouble. If there are no outward signs, we may be in the wrong place. Keep that in mind. I'll be in the lead along with Gamal. He may spot something helpful. We'll go to our approach points and move in half an hour. Donna, you're with me."

Lily felt anxious, as she always did before an engagement. Donna outwardly looked calm and composed. Gamal looked intense. She pondered what they were thinking, but just for a moment.

"It's time," said Donna.

Creeping forward in the dark, they approached the closest house. It was dark, relatively small, and seemingly unlikely as their target.

Inching past, they moved toward a collection of houses. It was cloudy, so there was no moon to add light.

Donna touched Lily's shoulder, holding up her fist. Gamal was stopped, down on a knee staring at one of the houses.

Lily waited along with Donna. Gamal continued to be motionless. Lily squinted in the dark but couldn't make out what Gamal saw.

At last, she saw movement in the dimness. Gamal started creeping forward. The two women followed him. Moving deliberately and slowly, Lily could now see what could be two persons. Before they could edge closer, suddenly two shapes struck, taking out the guards.

Gamal hurried them forward. Andy and Joe nodded.

"This must be the place," Lily whispered. They waited until the other unit members emerged from the surrounding approaches.

"Breach all the doors and move fast. If she's here, don't give them a chance to harm her."

Breaking open the doors nearly simultaneously, Lily entered the back door, while Patty came in the front door. The startled militants were too slow to jump out of bed and were caught flat-footed. They were disarmed without shots fired.

Grace Bailey found her in the basement on a bed, shamefully chained to the wall.

The ambassador wept as they released her from bondage. Gamal was livid at what he saw. Taking her upstairs, they went to a bedroom to find clothes for her. Gamal went to the man and his wife enraged, lecturing them on proper Islam. Even Mohamed and Abdul were visibly upset. Surprisingly, it was the wife who was verbally defiant, shouting at Gamal. They slapped her into silence.

Others of the team gathered materials from the basement, including copies of the recordings.

Lily radioed the base. "Hostage acquired. Call off the Brit operations. They can pick her up from us later back at the base. We're racing out of here right now to the extraction point."

Even with their goal accomplished, it was nerve-racking trying to slip out of the village to escape, especially when a dog started to bark.

The ambassador wasn't in shape for a long run, so Andy and Joe took turns carrying her at the sprint.

At one point, Andy jogged up to Lily. She glanced at the ambassador. She was holding onto Andy for dear life.

"Thank you for coming for me," she whispered.

"I'm glad we found you, ma'am."

"It was awful. I'm so ashamed."

"Don't say those things. All of that stuff reflects on them, not you. A lot of people didn't survive the militant attacks."

"You're right. I need to collect myself. I should be happy for my life. I don't know what to say to my family."

"Don't worry about that now. Let's get you home first. It will work itself out later. You survived an incredible ordeal. That's what's important."

"Thank you. You're giving me the right perspective. As bad as things were, it could have been much worse. You're right."

Moving at best speed, it took nearly an hour to arrive at the proper location. They got there none too soon as they could hear the helicopters approaching, including gunships.

When everybody was loaded on board and they took to the sky, the ambassador moved to sit beside Lily. Donna moved so she could sit between them.

"Now, I feel like I can relax. I didn't think I'd leave that basement alive."

"You're safe," Lily replied. "It's a long flight back to Bagram, but it should be uneventful. If you want to sleep or talk, just let us know. Are you hungry?"

"Now that you mention it, I could eat."

"Here's a bottle of water, and we've got energy bars to tide you over."

"Do you have any chocolate? I haven't had any since I was taken."

"I've got a candy bar," said Donna.

"Thank you so much. This probably seems silly."

"Hardly. With what you've been through, you deserve anything you want. Even though your captivity was the most aired and publicized in history, don't let it define you. Those people were pigs. I'm glad we got to you before they could do even worse things."

"I never imagined such horrors could happen to me. My career is over, but I'm okay with that. I just want to go home now to live in safety. Don't pretend the stigma of what they did to me will just melt away. I'm going to close my door, no interviews, no appearances, nothing like that. I may have my meals shipped in."

Lily spoke. "I think it will get better with time. Staying within your support group is a good choice in the beginning, I agree. I'm not saying I'm some expert about traumatic issues. I think the body heals itself."

"I guess I'll see. Right now, it feels good to sit here safe between you two warriors. I might hire bodyguards."

"I suspect the British government will provide ample protection details."

"I'll take it."

"Do you need another energy bar?"

"No, I'm good for the moment, but maybe I'll try to sleep if I can borrow your shoulder to lie against?"

"Sure, let's get a blanket to cover you."

The ambassador was asleep very quickly. During the long flight, nearly everybody else dozed off also. Lily thought about home again and then pondered what it would have been like to face what the ambassador had endured. Imagining being helpless in their hands broadcast all over the world, she vicariously felt shame. How Lily's family would have coped with it, how she would explain it to her husband what was done provoked Lily to great anger. She mused, *I will never let them take me alive.*

At long last, they landed. British forces were waiting anxiously for their ambassador. She turned to Lily and Donna with tear-filled eyes.

"I can't thank you enough. You've given me the courage to face this. I'll suck it up and endure this gauntlet ahead of me."

"You can call me if you want to chat to a friendly ear," Lily offered.

"I just might take you up on that."

"This way, ma'am," said a large fierce-looking Royal Marine.

She was whisked away in moments to start her journey back to England.

"That operation went surprisingly well," Gamal commented. "They were stupid in thinking you could never catch up to them."

"It was lucky," Donna replied.

Gamal eyed her. "It wasn't so much luck but more like incompetence with them. I was so angry I could have shot that man and woman myself. What that wife said, it will haunt me forever."

"You weren't alone in feeling that, but in our army, we control those feelings for revenge. We must."

"As I tell you, I'm learning a great deal from you about many things. I know I say the same things. I apologize."

"You're welcome, Gamal. There's nothing to apologize about."
He chuckled. "Also, I think I understand your humor better."
"Good for you, dude." They all chuckled.

Lily glanced over as a messenger approached. "Your team is requested for a meeting right away." He spoke tersely.

"Okay, we'll be there shortly."

Half an hour later, they sat down. The base commander spoke. "Consider this something of a debrief about the recovery operation. We've got a live visual link back to Langley to include them in the discussion at their request." When the screen activated to the CIA where it was nighttime, Lily recognized a number of faces, including Todd and Kevin. She noted the grim looks on their faces. Sitting in silence, their stone-faced expressions triggered her concern.

This collection of agency personnel had a new person in charge, and shockingly, Russian agents were sitting in attendance, staring into the monitor at them.

"Greetings, folks, I'm Director Paul Mayne. We want to talk about your successful recovery of the ambassador. By the way, the Brits are very grateful we got her without her being injured or killed. With that being said, I'd like to hear your interpretation of the op. Specifically in the aftermath, do you have any observations we should know about? Do we have a list of all the resources you used? This needs to be read into the official record."

Lily's feelings of danger signals erupted. Looking at Todd and Kevin, they were glassy-eyed, grim faced, staring straight ahead, and unmoving. Neither said a word.

Lily cautiously answered the question. "Sir, to my knowledge, you have all of that information. On our end, we merely reacted to data sent to us and followed your orders accordingly. The sources of information, including any tips, were never made known to us. Is there a problem?"

"I'm new to you, so I'd like to explain there has been some changes made here. I believe in running a tight ship. Everything goes through me with no exceptions. I make all strategic calls, and only I give authorizations. Are you clear on that?"

"Crystal clear, sir."

He stared at her grimly, like she was disrespecting him.

"Yes, there is a new sheriff in town. I want everybody on board because I don't tolerate failure."

"Yes, sir."

"Now going back to my original question to you, what did you observe that we should know about?"

"It struck us that this operation seemed far too easy. Where the tip came from that you received would be helpful in understanding. Once we landed, we approached a lightly guarded house, secured that home, and recovered the ambassador with minimal opposition. For an asset of this magnitude, it struck me as something was askew. The enemy mounted a coordinated operation in Kabul inflicting considerable damage and death to numerous foreign embassies only to have this lame ending? It doesn't make sense."

Director Mayne looked at Todd. "What do you say?"

Todd replied, "It seems like they kept the ambassador briefly with the usual threats, anti-Western pronouncements and with inflammatory online footage until some point where they inexplicably dumped her in the laps of those backward peasants for their subsequent disrespectful handling. It was like they wanted her found but as damaged goods, soiled, if you were."

Finally, the director looked thoughtful. "Interesting perspective, I tend to agree with you."

At that point, he turned to the Russian agents, speaking in fluent Russian. If he was aware Lily spoke Russian, he didn't seem deterred.

"Do you agree with this theory? I'm also surprised that opponent would have an accidental episode of incompetence. It does seem intentional."

"It does, comrade. We're working on the same conclusion."

"Keep me advised."

"We will. Have you cleared us to all of the CIA areas we want to visit?"

"That's a difficult task. We're replacing problematic people with our folks, but it takes time. There is still a great deal that can go wrong in these early stages."

"*Da.*"

Turning back to the screen, he spoke. "May I call you Lily?"

"Yes."

"We're sending you on a different operation shortly. I'll be back in touch to explain. In the meantime, any calls you make to Langley are placed to me alone. If there is a need for consultations with others, I'll decide and make the arrangements. Do you agree?"

"Of course, sir."

"Any violations of this policy will have serious consequences."

"Lily out."

She abruptly severed the feed.

"Oooooo," said the team in unison. Some members chuckled, and others gave martial shouts.

"He won't like that," Donna muttered. "What do you say, Patty?"

"I'm as conflicted as the rest of you. Seeing Russian agents in our house at the CIA, it's scary at the least and ominous at worst. Openly speaking fluent Russian was like a shot across the bow to the field forces."

"When they called him comrade, it put severe doubt in my mind about what's going on. Also, apparently their trying to gain access to every secret we have. Did you see the looks on the faces of Todd and Kevin? How would those comrades like it if we walked freely around the GRU offices?"

"What should we do? What can we do?" asked Andy.

"Support and defend the Constitution of the United States of America against all enemies, foreign and domestic," Lily replied.

"This is turning my stomach," said Donna. "It reminds me of that old movie about Russian children back in the USSR days bred and groomed for long-term insertion into American society that someday rise up against us. That was farfetched as a movie, but now it makes you wonder. That was eye-opening, enemies in our midst."

Patty remarked. "Now we really do have a problem judging the orders we receive."

Lily replied, "We'll get our first chance to deal with it soon. We're supposedly being sent somewhere else."

They looked at Gamal.

"I'm going with you, no matter where it is."

"That may not be possible. Here you're invaluable, you blend in, know the language, local customs, and can read between the lines. If we leave this region, none of that is true. Also, you're not authorized. You're untrained in tactics and have no papers for traveling."

Gamal looked stricken. "Lily, there must be something you can do. I've made a life pledge to defend you. That is a sacred oath for my people. I can't simply wander back home. I'll be treated as a failure, rejected."

Lily felt a pang. Patty spoke. "Gamal, I can't tell you how much you've meant to the team, but—"

"Can I say I think you still need me? If ISI is traveling with you, I need to be your eyes and ears about them."

Patty looked at Lily. "Listen, we'll inquire from our bosses if they'll approve you as a new part of the team. We can make no promises. The probability of success about that is slim."

"Can I speak to them?"

"No, they wouldn't talk to you, and it wouldn't help your cause. We appreciate your offer. They would not understand it."

"This is terrible for me but also for you. Can't they see I'm valuable?"

"We see it, and they're aware of what you've done. Still, I wouldn't hold out a great deal of hope."

When they left the meeting to return to their rooms, Gamal followed Donna and Lily.

"Do you mind if I sit with you?"

"No problem," Donna answered.

"Do I not see everything about this? Are there things in your culture I'm not getting?"

"Culture has nothing to do with it," Lily explained. "Our ISI friends are of your culture, but they're trained in the craft."

"I think I can do whatever they can do."

"That may be true, but there isn't some test we can give to validate you. What you gave to the unit, the question is whether you could do the same in different countries. Do you understand?"

"I can adapt, I can learn quickly."

"I have no doubts, but this isn't a situation to learn on the fly."

Gamal scowled. "Do you not want me to go? Have you lost faith in my value?"

"It's not our decision."

"But…you are my advocates. Without your voices, none stand for me."

Lily was at a loss. Secretly she agreed with Gamal. They felt close to him, like he was a relative, a nephew perhaps.

"I'll tell you what. On the outside chance you get approved to join us, you can't be carrying around a Russian army assault rifle. Let's go to the range to get in some qualifying rounds on US weapons starting with an AR-15."

He smiled, like his problem was solved. "Yes, I agree."

As they walked, he added. "I think I like US basketball."

The women laughed.

Donna replied, "Nice try, Gamal, but that won't get you in the door. Have you ever seen US basketball?"

"No, but I believe it must be good. I hear your soldiers talk about it."

"Duh." Donna smirked.

"What does that mean?"

Lily answered, "Don't listen, Gamal. Sometimes Donna's brain slips out of gear." Donna laughed.

"That is a joke?" He had a puzzled look.

"Sort of, don't waste your time on it."

Their session at the range lasted for hours. Gamal was a good shot and got better as he practiced with rifles and pistols.

At the end, he remarked, "I think I am pretty good."

"You did fine."

He smiled warmly at Lily. "I can get better."

"I'm sure you can."

"I will get better."

"Okay, Gamal, we've got it," Donna said. "It's time for dinner."

They made their way to the mess hall. The scent of roast beef wafted through the air.

"That actually smells pretty good," Donna commented. "I'm shocked."

"Hopefully it tastes good too," Lily replied.

They were joined at their table by several team members and then others of the group. For Gamal, these were now his family. He felt accepted and talked freely joining in with some of the banter.

The American basketball topic arose, and Gamal became the instant target of some harmless needling. Moving on to football, they explained the difference between football, a.k.a. soccer, and "real" football.

Gamal smiled and nodded his head, but everybody realized he had no clue what they were talking about. He was an emotional fixture with them too. Getting to the point of seeing him as other than a stereotype was a big step for some in the group.

After the meal, Lily and Donna decided to make their attempt. Contacting Langley, they asked to speak with the director.

Lily was surprised he would talk to them without a prior appointment time.

"Hello, Lily, Donna, what can I do for you? Thank you for following my protocol to run everything through me."

"I know you're busy, but we wanted to add some perspective so you see things as we do on the ground. As you're aware, we developed an incredibly valuable asset locally from a village we entered. We were going on bad intel about a militant sheik supposedly being there. It was really fortunate we avoided a disastrous firefight with friendlies. Their head man gave us this guy to help us back to safety. Gamal is a young man we found to be highly skilled with weapons, but unusually perceptive and shrewd ferreting out enemy schemes. He spared us some traps and guided us in the rescue of the British ambassador. I realize this will seem a weird request, but we'd like him added as a unit member, even if we travel out of the region. We've trained him on US weapons, and he's already more than competent. His skills would be useful in any situation. We can get him dressed in appropriate clothing for any country we go to. He will be a great help for us. He already has been."

"You're right, it does seem a strange request. However, I'll give it serious consideration. Your success frankly is unrivaled, so I'm willing to give you some leeway. Whether the top brass agrees, I'll let you know. You're right about leaving that theatre. We've got hot spots all over the globe at this point. Stay sharp out there."

"Thank you, sir. Do svidaniya."

"Do svidaniya." He answered like a reflex, thinking after he said it. "Wait. You speak Russian?"

"I also speak German, French, Spanish, Chinese, Japanese, and a number of Middle Eastern languages."

He got a calculating look with a sly smile.

"That's very interesting. Good to know. I think we're going to do an in-depth conversation in the near future. Call me at any time. I will always take your calls. Stay safe, Lily."

"Out."

"Wow," said Donna. "Did you just trap him?"

"Just a little test, for my understanding. I want to know what we're dealing with. Russian came to his mind really easily."

"But now you've tipped him off you understand what he says to his Russian pals."

"He would have discovered it sooner or later. He has my file. I showed him I'm not hiding anything."

"We're hiding our suspicions."

"That's true, but letting him know I speak and understand Russian doesn't necessarily tell him we don't trust him."

"I hope it doesn't start a new level of danger for the team."

"I think maybe he'll sign off on Gamal joining us."

"I hope it doesn't lead to bad things for Gamal."

CHAPTER 6

The call came back in a day.

"Hello, Lily. Gamal is in. I hope that makes you happy."

"Thank you, Director Mayne. I think it was the right call."

"It isn't necessary for you to be formal with me. Call me Paul."

"I hope this is a good move for Gamal. He's determined to work for us, but the dangers we face in this line of work can be fatal. I don't think he fully understands the risk he's taking on."

"Are you having second thoughts?"

"No, I just want you to know how I think and what I feel. Gamal is very brave."

"Okay, good to know. Moving on, you're wheels up in two hours for your next assignment. As with before, you'll get mission details after you're in the air. Can you be ready that quickly? All of your equipment goes with you."

"I assume that means the team as currently configured. I'm sure you're aware we've had concerns about our ISI twosome."

"Have they done anything troublesome?"

"They're very good at what they do. I do have a question about the intel sending us to the wrong village and then immediately being attacked on the ride back by the sheik. I can't pin that on them, but we remain cautious."

"That makes sense. It's exactly what I'd expect from a top-tier operator like you. That is why you were selected to lead this team."

"Thank you, sir."

"Paul, please."

"Sorry, it's habit honoring the chain of command."

"Of course it is." He chuckled. "I'll let you go. You've got a lot to do in a short amount of time."

"Lily, out."

"Your new pal Paul, eh?" Donna smirked.

"I trust him as far as I can throw him."

"Do you think we can throw him all the way back to Moscow?"

Lily laughed. "That would be a heck of a toss, even with two of us. Well, let's get cracking. We've got a flight to catch. I'll go tell Gamal the news."

"He might kiss you right on the spot." Donna laughed heartily.

"Will you shut up with that?" Lily rolled her eyes and shook her head.

Donna laughed all the harder.

Gamal was ecstatic upon hearing the news. He eyed Lily agog. She worried momentarily Donna was right about a kiss. "I knew you could save me."

"I'd hardly call it saving you. I suspect we have difficult troubles ahead of us."

"Do you know where we're going?"

"No. They keep it secret until we're in the air. We don't need any leaks. Pack up your stuff. We're flying out in a couple of hours."

"I'll be ready. I'm very happy."

She couldn't help but smile at his youthful exuberance, however misplaced it was.

Later the team assembled at the aircraft. All their equipment was already packed on board. Gamal looked strange out of his tribal garb. Wearing Western-style clothing was a first for him. He eyed his teammates for their reactions.

"You look like one of us now," said Patty.

"I was worried I wouldn't be accepted."

"Gamal, you're not judged on your clothes."

Walking onto the plane, they took seats. This time Lily made a point to sit beside Patty.

"If I get a call, I want you to hear it with me."

"Sure, Lily."

The plane soared into the clear sky and banked to travel westward initially.

"I suspected we would leave this country. That's partly why I wanted Gamal in different clothes."

"I agree. Although I have no idea where we're going, our purpose here ended up being the ambassador's rescue. That's over, so now we travel. What I'm curious about is the first orders we get from the new regime and what we're told to do."

"That has me worried also, Patty. Letting the new director know I'm fluent in Russian was a gamble. I hope I didn't make a mistake. When you say a new regime, that's how I feel too. There's something weird going on."

As the flight continued westward, eventually they turned to fly southwesterly. Afterward there was a chirp as the pilot came on.

"We've just gotten orders to head to the eastern shores of the African continent. Settle back and enjoy the flight."

Immediately afterward, Lily got the call.

"This is Lily Carson."

"Director Mayne here. We're landing you at a safe airport, but then you'll travel south across the border into Somalia. There is an individual that's proven to be troublesome we need to deal with. I anticipate a rapid resolution and then a speedy exit for your team."

"By 'deal with,' what do you mean? Who is this person?"

"His name is…eh…hold on a moment while I get it. Jaffar Abdul Salmond. We'll transmit mission details shortly."

"What is it we're supposed to do?"

"You need to take him out. He's our enemy."

Lily looked at Patty with concern.

"Yes, sir."

"I knew I could count on you, Lily. Good hunting. Out."

Donna piped in. "So we're in the assassination business now?"

Lily looked at her. "I'm going to Google him."

Lily was appalled with what she found. Jaffar wasn't an enemy of the USA. Instead, he was the opposite, one of the leaders who was a moderate and trying to work past Somalia's checkered past toward a better future. He was an enemy to the warlords.

Patty commented, "I think this guy is Russia's enemy, not ours. This is worse than I thought. It might be a litmus test for this team to see what we'll do."

"What should we do, Patty? If we make a stand, it's crossing a line. There's no coming back from it. We'd be culpable if we do this nasty thing, and any future orders could be worse."

"Whatever we do, I'm not going to kill one of the good guys. I'm thinking we find a way to pretend staging an attack, but only after getting word to this guy so he can escape. We go through the motions and blow up a few things and then fail the mission."

"That will not make the director happy. We're not a unit that ever fails missions."

"Regardless, we can't sell our souls."

"Okay. Do you have any sort of back channel to your friends back home?"

"I think they're under surveillance. I might be able to call a friend that can talk to them after-hours to get the word out. We need help and in a hurry. Do you agree we don't start assassinating people?"

"I do."

Lily looked around at the unit members. They were staring at her intently.

"There's no way to sugarcoat this, folks. We've been ordered to make a political killing. Thwarting that order, which I see as illegal, will place us all in jeopardy. I don't want to speak for you, so each person please say your piece."

Andy spoke. "Lily, you know we're with you, all of us."

"Do you all agree?"

"Yes," they said in unison.

"Okay, Patty and I are going to make a Plan B."

She called home. "Bob, I'm sorry to get you out of bed. I'm still overseas, and time is of the essence. I need a favor, a very big one. Can you drive over to talk to Kevin Simmons? Here is the situation which you can repeat to nobody except him. The clock is ticking."

Lily explained the mission and their counterplan. She also explained what she needed for Kevin to do.

"I owe you big time, Bob. I will find a significant way to pay you back."

"Lily, that's not necessary. You know whatever you need from me, I will always be there for you."

"One other thing as I think about it. We're worried about repercussions. Can you call Jack to warn him to take precautions? If I call, they'll know. I want my family safe."

"Of course I will, ma'am."

"Thank you. I'll let you go because we've got very little time to get a new plan in place."

"Stay safe, Lily."

"Do I know him?" Grace asked.

"No, I knew him at school. He doesn't work at the agency, but he knows some agency folk from school."

"Oh...good to know. Ron, Steve, and I share your concerns about this strange twist. This sudden integration of Russian spies is alarming. We can't think of any innocent explanation for it. This new director, is it possible he's a Russian operative?"

"I'm not ruling out anything at this point."

Later after landing, they were met by a small army of thuggish-looking armed men.

Their leader leered at the women as he greeted them.

"Who are you?" Lily asked.

"We're soldiers of General Mobutu. I am Bulogo. We'll accompany you and assist in the operation against that criminal Jaffar Salmond."

"I didn't realize we would have your help."

He smiled and laughed, but it didn't strike her as genuine mirth. Speaking to his men in his language, they laughed also. The women looked grimly at the frank perusal from him and his men.

"Come," he said. "We have trucks ready to drive to Somalia."

The unit armed themselves, leaving the storage cases on the plane. Following the militiamen to their many trucks, they tried to separate the unit, putting small numbers together, but Lily would have no part of it.

"I've looked forward to knowing you," said the leader. "We hear about you often."

"This isn't a vacation excursion. My unit stays together."

"Ah, yes, of course. I must say, I've never met Navy SEALs before. I'm honored."

Nobody replied. Their grim stares spoke volumes. The best they could do was splitting in half as there were no large trucks to accommodate them all together.

Patty took a contingent onto one truck and Lily the other half onto another. She didn't succeed in excluding Bulogo from sitting beside her.

Gamal stayed close to Lily openly glaring at Bulogo, who smirked at him.

Lily spoke in Urdu. "Gamal, ignore him. This is going to be a dicey operation, so don't draw his attention."

"He treats you with disrespect."

"I'll handle it, now relax. Stop glaring at him."

It was a bumpy ride in the old pickup trucks. All the trucks had heavy machine guns mounted in the bed of the trucks. The flags flapping on the trucks were not Old Glory. It irked the unit members, but there was nothing they could do at that point. The implication they were siding with warlords was aggravating.

Their periodic stops were to eat and to relieve and never in populated areas. The women went together away from prying eyes. Once apart, they could talk.

Donna spoke, "These militia slugs look like we're the main course for their dinner. It takes all of me to keep from decking them."

Patty answered, "Stay sharp because if they're taking us into an ambush, we've got to stop them in a hurry." Grace nodded in agreement.

Lily added, "I wondered about that same thing, but my thought is their plan is they go through with the mission to kill their opponent and then try to kill us in the process. Who knows how many of them are waiting wherever we're going? There's no way Langley would have set up an operation like this and certainly would never have arranged transportation with these guys. Let them think they duped us and we're at their mercy. Don't let the seamy smiles provoke you to act prematurely. We'll have an answer for them at the right time."

As they prepared to return, they spotted a leering soldier watching them.

She walked straight to Bulogo. "What's with the peeping Tom act from that dude?"

He laughed. "No, no, I placed him there to guard you."

"That is not necessary. We guard ourselves. Keep your people away from us and we'll be just fine."

"As you wish, Lily. We are your friends."

For once, Lily couldn't mask her ire. She eyed him balefully.

It added to his glee.

"Let's get going," she said tersely.

Continuing the travel, they approached the Somalia border. Lily was surprised they were merely waived through without checking identifications by the guard station.

Donna was sitting beside her now. She muttered, "Somebody paid off these border guards."

"So true. From this point forward, stay frosty. We're assuming they'll take us to their target, but they may hit us earlier."

"I'm ready for a fight, especially with these ——."

Instead of driving toward the city, the caravan took a detour to one of their camps.

"We can eat good food at the camp," Bulogo explained. "You will like it."

The camp was a large one. Of the troops she could see, Lily estimated there could be over a thousand stationed here. More leering faces populated the road into the camp. Some of the troops were women but equally mean looking. The women leered as much as the men of the camp.

"We're sitting ducks," Donna muttered.

"This definitely is not a sanctioned op."

Piling out of the trucks, the unit informally assumed a defensive array to cover every direction.

Sitting down, they stayed very vigilant, weapons at the ready.

The "good food" consisted of a meal of a stew of an unknown meat and vegetables. The women serving the meal were timid and cowed by the soldiers.

"I wish we could set them free," Grace whispered. "They're not here by choice."

"I hope this stuff doesn't give us the runs," Donna added.

"They're eating it too," Lily replied.

After the stew, the hosts offered beer.

"No, thanks, we don't drink on the job."

"It's your loss. This is very good beer." Bulogo grinned.

"I do have a quick question. After this operation, how do we exit the area?"

"We will drive you back across the border to your plane at the airport."

"I see."

"Is that a problem?"

"No, I was just curious. Normally we have full knowledge of an operation, start to finish."

"Ah, yes. We got late notice also from your Langley."

Lily stared straight ahead so he wouldn't realize his error or that she noticed.

"We will take good care of you."

"Thanks."

Traveling farther, they spent the night at a different camp, a smaller one. The unit stayed in a single hut in cramped conditions. Lily posted guards all night.

In the morning, Bulogo approached her. "You posted guards here in my camp?" He sounded offended.

"We maintain vigilance during any operation until it's over."

"I see. Do you not trust me?"

"No. No offense, but we don't know you, and your side has been against us in the past. Is that a surprise? I find it hard to believe if you can't understand my position."

He grinned. "You're right, Lily. You're exactly as we expected and exactly how you should be. Under different circumstances..." He had a distant look.

"We'd be friends. I don't think so. You can't do atrocities to the innocent and think there are no consequences."

For a moment, his face hardened, but then he got a calculating look. "I appreciate your honesty. Not everything we do is by our choice. You think I'm a barbarian, but you don't know me. You haven't walked in my shoes."

"Granted, but people respond in different ways to hardship and, in some cases, in opposite ways."

"Perhaps in your world there can be happy endings, but not so much in mine."

"I have no need or desire to judge you or your decisions, but decisions have consequences. That's a good thing to keep in mind as we go forward."

He smiled. "I will keep it in mind."

"How soon will we arrive at the target?"

"About half a day."

Lily pondered carefully before continuing. "Bulogo, you can't be so naive as to think we can't see through your plans."

"What do you mean?"

"I suspect at one time you may have been a decent man. Who you are now and what you do, we won't tolerate it in dealing with us. I'm giving you fair warning up front so there are no misunderstandings at the wrong time."

He got a sad look. Glancing away thoughtfully for a moment, he looked back and replied, "I had a wife and daughters, but one day when I was gone away, they were taken from me. I lashed out seeking revenge, finding and killing those men. It didn't soothe my soul, and I became worse than them with no good purpose left in my life."

"That's terrible, but how many innocents have suffered since your tragedy?"

"Too many."

"When you look at us women, you and your men, we know what you want to have happen. Do you think we're here for that? I

94

looked up the target on the internet and found he's a good guy, one of the voices trying to have a better Somalia, not this lawless criminal den you've got now. We're not going to attack him, and as far as our own CIA setting us up here for an ambush, that will not go well if you try it."

"I did not like this job. How is this possible what they asked of us? What did you do to earn their wrath?"

"It's possible we've been infiltrated. People are being replaced in the agency, and there are Russian agents present right in the CIA."

"What do you plan to do?"

"Here, we're going to make a little noise, maybe blow something up, but we'll defend the target. Afterwards we'll scamper out of there and escape."

"Don't go back to your plane. Your people called it away right after you left. You're not supposed to survive. We were given leeway to keep you captive, like the British ambassador, for public humiliation that can be put on the internet."

"I guess we'll commandeer ground transportation and go inland. They won't expect that. We'll maintain radio silence while on the move during the escape."

"It is a serious matter. Your agency is very powerful."

"I'd like to propose, you could change your ways. Join the man who is your target and do some good for your country. You need to atone for your sins."

"I don't know if that is possible. My boss does not forgive."

"You must have some men that are trustworthy and loyal to you."

"Perhaps, but some of them here are vile. They set goals to have Western women at their mercy for the first time and won't want to be turned away. You know what I'm talking about."

"I can't help you with that. We're tier-one operators, so it's best to stay out of our way and let us do what we must. If they try anything, they're dead men walking."

"I understand. I'm sorry for this."

"I doubt it, but at any rate, what's your decision?"

"I won't attack you. We will try your ploy of a false attack."

"Good answer. Maybe you give us two trucks afterwards?"

"I can give you my best man as a guide. He's someone who does have some good character. He hasn't been with us long and should never have joined General Mobutu. His name is Hussain Bedoin."

"Okay, let me meet him and I'll decide."

"He lost his entire family, so he has no ties here any longer."

"Are you sure you want to lose him? He sounds like someone you need going forward."

"He will be missed, but later if you're safe in western Africa, he can return if he chooses, or he can go with you to save America."

Lily smiled. "Save America, what a concept. I wish that was possible."

"I will tell the men before we reach Jaffar's compound."

An hour later, the caravan halted for refreshment and a brief break. Lily spoke to her team.

Bulogo talked to his forces. They were shocked at the turn-around. Some of them eyed the women balefully. Benevolence wasn't something in their normal playbook.

"Let's check our weapons, make it obvious, especially with the miniguns," Lily advised the team.

It was a sufficient move as intimidation as the full range of team weaponry was revealed. Donna decided to parade around a minigun. It cast her in a completely different light to her "admirers."

Thereafter, the hostile glances were replaced by mere occasional mutters.

When they finally approached the fortified compound, Lily walked to the gate along with Patty and Bulogo. She yelled up to the guards.

"Did you receive our message?"

Their captain stepped to the gate. "We were surprised, but yes, we did. Come in."

Jaffar himself was there, just inside the fencing.

"Greetings, my friends."

"Hello, sir, it's an honor to meet you. I'm Lily Carson, this is Patty Baymill, and you may know Bulogo."

Bulogo chuckled as he received universal frosty stares. "I come in peace."

Lily spoke, "I'm not sure what you were told, but we have real problems back home. This attack they planned against you would seem to originate in Moscow. You need to be very wary because our failure here and now, it won't protect you from future attacks. I've talked with Bulogo about taking a new course in his life, bringing any loyal forces of his to join you. Your country needs more good men, not less. Do you understand we need to stage a mock fight to perpetrate the ruse you fought off this attack? We will slip away afterwards, but I'm sure this is just the start of difficult things for you."

Jaffar looked at Bulogo. "We welcome all help, but to trust you after all the harm you've done, it's a difficult proposition. How many men do you have?"

"Of my force here, there is around a hundred men I would trust. I think that half of them are worth your trust too, maybe more."

"And about the rest of them?"

"They would return to the general. I would be marked for death as a traitor."

"You accept that?"

"I do. Lily pointed out I need to atone for my mountain of sins. Whatever is left of my life, that will be my task."

"I will meet with the men you feel are worthy. Lily, I'm grateful to you for my life. I will contact the other moderate voices to form a joint defense against this kind of outside aggression. Someday we may be able to stand up among the other nations without the shame of our past."

"We need to stage a realistic-seeming battle, so that means explosions, a lot of rounds expended, and some damage."

"I understand. I don't want to say we need injuries, but having wounded fighters adds to the illusion. If anybody is willing to endure flesh wounds, on both sides, for the sake of the cause, let them step forward. Also, my team is supposedly here to take you out on behalf of our Russian friends, so we need to open up with some high-powered weaponry. It will be dangerous even with trying to avoid casualties."

"It's better than the actual attack they want. I will be one of the volunteers to take a flesh wound. It will be far more convincing."

"You're a brave man, sir."

"No, I'm frightened too. I haven't been shot before."

It took several hours for Bulogo to comb through his forces to pick the converts to send them to meet Jaffar. The other men, the rejects, were sent away immediately to return to the general.

Afterward the "battle" took place. It was well staged with plenty of sound, plenty of superficial damage to the compound, and with the requisite injuries. Jaffar took his wound stoically but smiled afterward at his "red badge of courage."

Even Bulogo decided to endure a wound. When it was all over, Lily and Patty talked with Hussain Bedoin. He was polite acting.

"Hussain, are you on board with this? You realize there will be negative ramifications for you in leaving your general, but more than that, by coming with us, you're exposed to the considerable dangers we will face. Defying the CIA even for corrupt orders can be a fatal choice. They will never stop looking for us. If they find us, they find you."

"I know, and I accept the risk. I will share your fate."

"Okay, I'll introduce you to the team."

He followed them to where the team waited.

"This is Navy Captain Patty Baymill, she's in charge of the Navy SEALs, Donna Smith, Andy Reiger, and Joe Gilson. This is Ari Goldstein from Mossad, Hassan Aboud of Egyptian intelligence, Ron Gray, Steve Sawyer, and Grace Bailey from CIA, Mohamed Sheik and Abdul Hamma from Pakistani ISI, and this is Gamal. He volunteered to aid us back in Pakistan, and he has traveled with us ever since."

"You're like me," said Hussain, smiling.

"They are good people," Gamal responded. "I've pledged my life to them and to Lily, who is my inspiration."

"Please, Gamal," Lily answered with a chuckle. "I hardly deserve anything like that."

Hussain took a long admiring look at Lily. "I understand, Gamal. I will make the same pledge."

Donna laughed. "Your posse is growing, princess."

"One of these days, Donna." She smiled ruefully.

Donna laughed all the louder and was joined by the other team members, even the ISI twosome.

"Let's get going. Hanging around here is not a good idea."

They loaded supplies into the trucks and climbed aboard. Hussain sat with the driver of the lead truck, Ron Gray. Lily sat between them to be able to make decisions on the fly.

The two-truck caravan pulled out heading west toward the far Somali border. Once they were out into the countryside, the danger level decreased although they stayed vigilant.

"Do you have any ideas, Lily?" Ron asked.

"About the agency?"

"Well, that too, but I meant our current destination."

"I think Nigeria. I believe there is a secret CIA site there. We can formulate a plan from safety."

"Are we safe going to any agency location?"

"We're still a force capable of defending ourselves in the short term. If we arrive safely, we call Langley with a concocted story. I'll be curious how our new director handles our still being alive."

"This is really bad."

"It is really bad. By the way, Hussain, don't be shy. If there is anything we need to know, say so before we drive into trouble."

"I will, but what has happened to America? What you're saying, it's what happens in places like Somalia."

"I wish I had an answer. At this point, we just roll with the punches."

"Can I ask you something?"

"Sure."

"We hear about your prejudice in America. Is it as bad as they say?"

"I guess it depends on your perspective. If you're rich and white, life is ideal, but for people of color, not so much. They must fight for acceptance, validation, and security, all the while biting their tongues on their jobs as they're passed over for promotion and marginalized."

"That would make me angry."

"America is not a perfect society."

Suddenly on the road ahead, armed men stepped out to block the way.

"Are these General Mobuto's men?"

"I don't think so yet. This is probably just their territory we've stumbled into. Be careful though."

The trucks stopped short of approaching the men. One of them yelled out.

Hussain translated. "He wants you to slowly drive over where they can see you."

Lily noted he spoke into a walkie-talkie.

"Safeties off," she said to her troops.

Idling forward, the man moved to get a better look at the truck. Her people hunched down to mask their numbers.

"Don't shoot unless they fire first."

"Don't go all the way to them," Lily muttered.

They stopped and Lily got out.

When the man saw her, he grinned and spoke to his guards. They laughed. Lily had no trouble grasping their words and intent.

The man gestured for her to approach. She took a couple of steps but stopped short again.

The guards edged toward her but watched the trucks too. Their leader was talking steadily on his radio. Finally, he spoke in broken English. "You will surrender to us now."

Lily merely stood watching him.

His expression changed at her passive resistance. Reaching for his sidearm, his soldiers aimed their rifles.

Lily remained passive, but the unit leaped out of the truck beds with weapons at the ready.

The leader realized what he faced, and the colossal mismatch. Putting his hands in the air, the guards lowered their weapons.

Lily walked up him accompanied by Hussain.

"You never saw us pass by. Do you understand?"

Hussain spoke for her.

"Yes," he replied.

"Remember, we always have drones overhead. There is no hiding from us. Don't get any bad ideas, or it will be your last."

She climbed back into the truck, and the unit drove past them. They were looking up into the sky for those drones.

"Do you think they'll contact your general?"

"They may not be in his militia. I didn't recognize them. They are aware of American power and your threat. That is a good thing for us."

"Good, we need to make tracks as fast as we can. Somali warlords aren't our only hazard."

As they rode farther, Lily got a phone call.

"Hello?"

"Lily, this is Bob. I wanted to be sure you made it past that trap."

"We're still in one piece. It was fortunate I could reason with the militia leader. Half of his force defected, the target was spared, and we got out without casualties."

"You live a charmed life, ma'am."

"So my boys at the agency, were you able to talk to them?"

"What you worried about, it could be even worse than you thought. It isn't just the agency where career folk are being replaced. There are movements all throughout the government and I'm hearing it's transmitting down into state governments too. What are your plans?"

"Right now, we're trying for Nigeria. I'll call the agency from there and see what happens."

"That's risky, but what isn't nowadays. Give me a call at any time. By the way, I talked to Jack, and he has rearmed. He'll make defensive plans for him and the kids."

"Thank you, Bob. I'll talk to you when I can."

"Bye, Lily."

Ron commented, "I wonder about my family. All of us are worried. We know the risks when we sign on to this job, but our families didn't sign up for any dangers."

"We're all in the same boat, Ron."

"Damn them."

"Amen, brother."

"Hussain, what do you think we'll face at the border?"

"I think you have less danger. The border guards are from the central government. They are not your enemies."

"Good, we need some good luck. Just so you know, we don't really have papers for crossing the other countries in our path to Nigeria. There could be difficulties."

CHAPTER 7

Riding in pickup trucks bouncing across the African continent got old in a hurry. In spite of their desire for speed, it wasn't always possible, although once across the border, they felt freer to use main roads. In a surprise entering the next country, the guards in the border station recognized them as dangerous American operators and let them pass without demanding papers.

Donna elbowed Lily. "Your reputation precedes you."

"We were lucky. It saved us a needless complication. I want to avoid gunfights as much as possible."

"We've been lucky a lot on this trip. I wonder if there is a limit to that luck?"

"If so, we'll deal with it."

Hussain and Gamal had quickly become friends, being young and of similar ages. They were chatting in English.

"I would like to go to America," Hussain said. "The land of the free and the home of the brave, eh?"

"I would like to see America too," Gamal replied. "However, I miss my village. I think I would go home eventually."

"You probably have family there. I'm an orphan. There's nothing drawing me back to Somalia. Life means nothing there. The strong take what they want and exploit the weak and then usually kill them."

"Don't the strong take what they want everywhere?"

The boys chuckled.

Lily piped in, "Yes, the strong are a problem everywhere. However, we learn how to cope. It's what must be done. I fear humanity is deeply flawed, no matter what country they're in. People can get weird ideas and then take contrary actions that hurt people who disagree with their slant. The internet gives an outlet for radicals to spread lies unfettered. If they repeat them long enough and loud enough, some people start to believe. Truth takes a hit."

Donna added, "We cope by being stronger than the strong."

"I like this idea of yours. Evil needs to be answered," Hussain replied. "Will you teach us?"

"Sure, if you survive long enough."

"Donna," Lily said reproachfully.

Gamal and Hussain laughed heartily.

Hussain continued, "I do like this. Navy SEALs are much better to be with than Somali pirates. Are there any Somali SEALs in your Navy?"

"Not that I'm aware of," Donna answered with a wry smile.

"Then I will be the first to become one."

"Good luck with that, dude. For your sake, I hope you can swim."

Andy and Joe sat nearby, smirking at the exchange. They chuckled and bumped fists with Donna.

That evening at their stop, not only the women, but the male SEALs tried to explain to the young men what they were pondering.

"I don't want to burst your bubble," Patty explained, "but the chances of either of you gaining residency in the USA, gaining green cards, getting into the Navy, and then qualifying to even try out to be SEALs is…well, virtually impossible. Do you understand?"

"No," Hussain replied. "I'm very determined in whatever I do. I strive to be the best. Is that not what you seek for your best unit?"

"It is, but determination is only part of the story. I'm not saying it can't be done, but there are so many hoops for you to jump through and over a long period of time, that's what I'm saying. Overcoming those challenges is…difficult."

"Then I repeat, I will do this impossible thing. We will prove you wrong, Gamal and me. We will become Navy SEALs."

Patty, Donna, Andy, and Joe smiled at each other. Joe commented, "Hussain, you're kind of a blockhead."

"Yes," he replied, laughing along with Gamal.

In the distance, they heard the roars of wild animals. Everybody tensed and went quiet.

Finally, Andy asked softly, "What's more dangerous right now? Being surprised in the dark by predators or militants chasing us down from behind?"

Donna looked at Lily. Lily frowned before answering. "Well, I guess they're equally a hazard. We're fleeing potential enemy pursuit without prior planning. Inevitably in this circumstance, there are going to be challenges."

Hussain spoke. "Your biggest danger is those following us. Animals don't usually approach groups of men. The enemy will be angry at being thwarted, and with you escaping their trap, they will come at you with deadly intent. We cannot allow them to capture any of us. It would be better to shoot yourself in the head. What they do to prisoners is…horrible."

Joe replied grimly, "If they want to tangle with us, God help them. We will drop the hammer."

"Boo-ya," the others added.

Lily smiled at his confidence, as well as the group's answer. "Macho," she muttered contemplatively.

Wesley and the others riding in the other truck looked over at the sound.

"Relax, Wesley, no danger here. Gamal and Hussain are getting a little education, SEAL style."

Wesley chuckled. "With those SEALs as teachers, I suspect they're getting very little education."

"I can't disagree."

Late in the night as most of them slept, Andy was on watch along with Steve Sawyer. The night sounds suddenly went silent. Both guards perked up staring around into the darkness. They carefully crept backward to their sleeping comrades. Andy put a hand onto Lily's mouth. She awoke with a start. Collecting herself quickly, she crawled along, waking others, and soon everybody was alert and armed. Quickly they deployed into defensive positions to cover every field of fire.

The tiniest of sounds, a metallic cling, warned them danger had come.

Enemy fighters arose and started to creep forward, weapons at the ready. Suddenly one of them squeezed off a round before their leader signaled an attack. The allies responded with withering fire, catching the enemy attackers by surprise. However, in spite of quick early casualties, the enemy rallied to mount a determined assault. They had come in force.

The fight was not over quickly. Grace jumped onto the truck bed to fire the .50 cal and was nicked in the arm. Wesley Bromwell took shrapnel wounds from a grenade explosion. Patty was nicked by a flying round. Joe Gilson, Ari Goldstein, and Hassan Aboud all suffered flesh wounds too. It was a dangerous situation out in the open.

The enemy tried a charge that was doomed to failure with two .50 cals and miniguns lacing them with overwhelming firepower. They did get close enough for Lily to see them.

Once the survivors withdrew in defeat, the allies cautiously examined the large number of dead and dying. Gamal was shocked. "These are Sheik Rahman's men."

"Chasing us in Africa? How would they know where we went, and how would they get here?" Lily asked.

"It's said the sheik now has outside help."

Patty spoke. "I'd say this verifies that theory. Let's get everybody patched up and ready to go. We've tried to go fast, but now we go faster."

"In this country, I didn't think we'd be attacked. I expected something in places where there are local rebel forces, like Boca Haram."

"We may still get a chance to battle them, Lily," Joe muttered.

"Are you okay with that wound?"

"I've had worse nicks shaving."

The entire group chuckled.

Mohamed and Abdul had remained in the background, although they did join in the fight against the militant forces. Lily walked over to them. "Are you guys hurt?"

"We are fine, Lily," Mohamed answered.

"Thank you for fighting with us. I know some of those militants may be people you know."

Abdul spoke. "Have we not proven ourselves yet? We have tried to show you loyalty, yet there is this doubt all the time. It's annoying. We did not know those men."

"I'm sorry you feel that way."

Gamal came over to stand beside Lily. He looked at the ISI men darkly. They glared back at him.

The unit members climbed back into the trucks before sunrise and resumed the journey. Breakfast was ration packs eaten on the move. Patty mixed up the seating on this next leg. Mohamed came into Lily's truck along with Wesley and Grace. Andy went to the other truck along with Gamal and Hussain.

Trying to drive faster was only partially successful. Some roads were paved, but there was considerable slow traffic, and other parts of the roads were not paved, which restricted their speed.

Lily was in the trailing truck where they kept a watch behind them for signs of pursuit.

Donna looked at her. "That sheik following us here, it doesn't make sense, any more than that British ambassador rescue. I'm worried how they could track us. I think we've got other players involved here."

"I've been thinking about that very thing. With what we've heard about the confusion at Langley, I agree. We need to keep our heads on a swivel."

"Who would have a motive?"

"I don't know."

"Taking out this unit, that's a bold move for the enemy. When you consider who would have the ability to accomplish that, the resources needed, the technologies...it narrows the pool of possible candidates down to some very concerning groups. Not the least of those groups is our own government."

"I know that. With us basically going dark after Somalia, who could find us here? You're right, we need to guard against threats from any source, including back home."

"I also notice you're not getting any calls on your phone. Your phone rang up constantly before. That's pretty telling to me. I wonder what might be waiting up ahead of us? This isn't good."

Wesley piped in, "Whatever happens, I'll protect you, ladies."

They all chuckled. Donna replied, "I feel safer already."

"You're welcome to apply for refugee status in the UK. I'll vouch for you."

"Does that include us?" asked Grace.

"Sure, the more the merrier. As I think about it, instead of seeking out that agency secret location in Nigeria, we may want to detour to British bases. Calling home to America from London seems like a stronger position than sitting vulnerable out in the field somewhere."

"What did you have in mind, Wesley?"

"Instead of this mindless trek across the heart of Africa, why don't we detour north? If we're being set up by people at Langley, leaving the path they expect will buy us time for one thing. I trust my mates at home, so from my perspective, we can't go wrong. We might actually survive this mission from hell."

Lily pondered the matter.

"Listen, we've had pursuit on our tails since the start, even going back to that ambush by the sheik in the Middle East. I can't say the trouble is with the CIA entirely, but I suspect there are corrupt elements there. As unlikely as it would seem, we must face the facts of what's happening here. If enemies have successfully infiltrated your spy agency, it's not impossible they've made inroads in other agencies too. However, I trust my contacts in England. I truly believe we're better off going there."

"We'll talk about it tonight when we stop."

"I understand your hesitation, but if we're going to follow my suggestion, the turn north is not far ahead. We'll reach it before we would stop for the night."

"Okay, Wesley."

He moved to sit beside Lily.

"One other thing I'd suggest. If you get a call on your cell, let Gamal or Hussain answer it in their own language. If we have traitors at Langley that are trying to pinpoint you and your location, it will throw them off thinking your cell phone is in enemy hands. They may think you got killed. We need time out of the gun sights to collect our thoughts and make a good plan."

"I like that idea, Wesley. I hope your agency hasn't been corrupted. With all that's happened, I'm feeling paranoid these days."

"We have no choice. Whatever is going on may be the most dangerous threat any of us, or our countries, have ever faced."

As Wesley predicted, reaching the road northward occurred within fifteen minutes. The trucks stopped while Lily pondered the difficult decision. She got out of the truck to pull Patty aside. Donna and Wesley joined them.

"Wesley told me we should change our route and go to a British secret site. There are too many questions about Langley for my liking."

Patty eyed Wesley. "How safe are your people? If our agency has been infiltrated, how do we assume yours hasn't?"

"I don't trust my agency any more than yours. I trust certain friends. Harold Smith, in particular, is stationed where I propose we go. Lily, you remember him from university, but think about it. We have people in the intelligence agencies that try to anticipate moves. Our best plan is being unpredictable. Do what they wouldn't anticipate."

"I...eh..."

"Actually, he may be foggy in your mind. You met him at a party we went to. We'd both had a bit too much to drink."

"Okay, I'll take your word for it. Wesley's plan is probably as good as the choice I made heading west. What we would have found there may have been worse than going to this British base. What do you say, Patty?"

"I have no preference either way. If Wesley feels this is a better choice, I'm for it."

Donna was staring at Wesley and also at Lily.

"I guess we do it. Let's go north," Lily said.

Walking back to the trucks, Donna edged close to Lily. "You have history with him, don't you?"

"This isn't the time or place to explain. Another time, okay?"

"Sure, but I want all the details. I think you must have broken his heart."

"We've got more important things to worry about, like staying alive. How can you think about something like that at a time like this?"

"I notice you didn't deny it."

"Donna, we dated in college in England. I thought I already told you that. It was before I met my husband."

"I get the feeling he didn't like you getting away from him."

"It was a long time ago, and it's over. That's all I'm going to say about it."

Boarding the trucks, they resumed the journey. As they made the turn northward, the road went through increasingly open arid stretches. It made for uncomfortable conditions with no clouds overhead to block the searing sunshine. Combined with gusting hot winds kicking up dust clouds and eddies, they all covered their mouths and faces to avoid breathing in the grit. Their clothing stuck to their perspiring bodies like bandages.

"This is fun," Donna muttered sourly. She'd covered her weapon with a blanket to keep the grit from clogging up its functioning. Everybody else followed suit similarly protecting their main protective pieces.

Additionally, this was a dirt road, so they hit considerable bumps. The jarring effects of the jolts added to the misery of the long ride.

"I hope we don't break an axle on these roads. Walking would be a real pain and may not be doable under these harsh conditions." Lily looked at Donna, who'd closed her eyes.

"I'm not asleep," Donna replied. "Just resting my eyes."

Lily snickered. She glanced up, noticing Wesley staring at her. "How much farther to your facility?"

"It's hard to say. My guess is maybe a day or two at the most. I could be way off. We can't make great progress on these roads. I've only been there once."

The long trip continued into the evening. As darkness approached, they decided to stop at a village for the night.

"Is there danger for us here, Wesley?" Lily asked. "Are they allies of our enemies?"

"Not here, quite the opposite. Their enemies are their own government, which is Muslim. We're saviors to these people."

"Good. I need a good night of sleep."

Driving into the village, the team drew a crowd. Strangers weren't normally trustworthy in this part of the country.

Wesley spoke to the chieftain, and soon they were welcomed for the night.

"We invite you share our meal," the chieftain offered.

As they looked around, it was obvious these were poor people barely able to feed their families much less to feed strangers.

"Wesley, tell them we'd like to feed them from our supplies in return for their hospitality."

The chieftain grinned. The villagers cheered, and the occasion took on a festive air.

With the exception of Gamal, Hussain, Abdul, Mohamed, and Hassan, all the Arab folk at whom they cast leery glances at, the others were treated as celebrities. The women in particular—Lily, Donna, Grace, and Patty—drew crowds of village children. It didn't take long to decide the Arab team members were benign and no threat. Soon the villagers included them into their acceptance and let them join the festivities.

Having full bellies was a rare treat in an area accustomed to poverty and want. Laughter was an unusual sound here, where they needed constant vigilance.

It was a surprisingly relaxing and pleasant time given the circumstances. The children waited patiently to receive their portions of the evening meal sitting in concentric circles around the allied women. After filling their bellies, the littlest children became sleepy. The mothers came to claim their babies and take them to their beds.

Wesley spoke with the men at length about local matters and what to expect ahead.

Lily and Patty went to listen in.

He turned to them. "From what I've been told, government patrols are increasing the last few days. If they're looking for us, he has no way to know. He advises caution but also taking alternate roads."

"Roads worse than this one?" Patty asked.

"Probably. However, the route he suggested would cut off some distance to our base and would avoid a couple of larger towns jammed with government troops. We'd be going northwest."

"It sounds like a no-brainer of a choice," Lily replied.

"They invited us to stay as long as we like. As a matter of fact, they'd like us to stay for the rest of our lives. They feel safe with us here."

Patty and Lily smiled.

Wesley continued. "They said we can sleep inside huts with village families, which is better than truck beds."

"Okay," Patty answered.

"With our Arab folk, I'd say we split them up joining with us so no family gets spooked."

Lily took Gamal along with Donna into a hut. The family smiled warmly, even at Gamal.

"Thank you for inviting us," Lily said.

The father responded in his language. They both laughed at not being able to communicate. The mother directed their guests to a place near them to place their sleeping bags. The children were on the other side of the parents. It was dusk outside, moving toward darkness.

The three allies lay down whispering quietly for a time until they dozed off to sleep. When they awoke in the morning, well rested, it felt good to feel revived. The sun was high in the sky.

Walking out of the hut, they were the last of the allied troop to arise. Wesley sauntered over. "I thought we might lose a day with you guys sleeping straight through."

"Not funny, Wes," said Lily. "Have you eaten yet?"

"There was no formal breakfast meal. Everybody just snacked out of the supplies, somewhat."

"Okay, let's load up. The three of us can munch on something as we travel. We need to get to our destination."

The villagers were sad to see them go, crying out and waving their hands in genuine regret. For the allies, there was business at hand, so they could afford no lingering distractions.

Driving as rapidly as they could on terrible roads gained them too little progress forward for Lily's liking. During this leg of the trek, Wesley paid closer attention to the surroundings.

"Are you expecting trouble?" Donna asked.

"Not really. I'm trying to spot signs of where to go to find the secret camp."

"Like an exit ramp?"

"Real funny, Donna, but no. There are no posted signs along the way to a secret base."

"Hopefully, your British friends haven't abandoned that base in the meantime."

"That is a chilling thought."

"You don't have a Plan B?"

"No place nearby."

"Leave him alone, Donna. We're all struggling here," Lily advised.

The trucks drove for several hours before Wesley signaled a turn to the left onto a dirt track. It was little more than two ruts worn into the dirt. Ahead they saw a ramshackle wood building.

"That's the camp?" Donna asked in disbelief. "I've got a cabin in the woods back home bigger than that."

Wesley merely smirked.

Stopping near the door, Wesley led Lily, Donna, and Patty inside the shack. Going to what looked to be a closet, he opened the door, stepped inside, and held a card against a scanner.

Immediately they heard a beep, and a small panel slid open to reveal a phone. Wesley dialed and spoke to the on-duty officer.

"We've experienced some trouble..."

After explaining their misadventure, another panel slid open to reveal an elevator. Donna retrieved the other unit members, and everybody rode down to a large underground facility. The British staff members were more than surprised at unexpected visitors, especially non-Brits.

Wesley made his way to the facility head, Nigel Smythe. Nigel did not look happy.

The Americans, Lily and Patty, waited discreetly out of earshot as Wesley had a spirited "conversation" with Nigel. Finally, the two men walked over to greet the "guests."

"I'm sorry if I seem rude, but this isn't an operation designed to entertain foreign visitors."

"That's understandable," said Lily. "I'd like to apologize for showing up unannounced, but dire circumstances drove us here. I'm sure Wesley has explained developments back at Langley have been worrisome. We're in a position we don't know who we can trust at home. That coupled with Sheik Rahman being in close pursuit all the way from Pakistan and seemingly knowing when and where to find us…well, the possible explanations are not good. The newly appointed CIA head speaks fluent Russian, and he has a Russian team right there with him right in the agency."

"I'm not unaware. The security services of the other Western countries have adjusted how we deal with the Americans."

"I'm glad to hear that. Safe havens for us are few and far between. We won't impose on you any longer than is necessary, but we need to get a plan in place for our next moves. Is that acceptable to you?"

"Yes, of course. I just needed to be sure what we were dealing with before I let down my guard."

"I've got friends in Langley, but apparently they're being watched closely, so they can't really open up or maintain any dialogue with us."

"What a state of affairs. In my wildest imaginations I could never have seen this coming."

"Likewise. As you can see, we have nearly no options. Whatever has infected us back home, is it also infecting European agencies too? Are you guys in the same jeopardy?"

"Excellent points. Along those lines, I assume you have a reason for bringing Arabic and African gents with you."

"We trust them. They fought with us and proven themselves to me."

"Okay, I'll accept your assessment. However, bringing ISI agents here is a debatable choice. Regardless, they're here now. Feel free to relax and get some food in you. We have showers to wash off the grit. I'm going to make discreet inquiries to ascertain both of our situations. Lily, I do remember you from school. You still look good."

"Thank you, sir. Your help is much appreciated. You look good too."

"Lynn, will you take the ladies back and get them set up for a good scrub."

The girls laughed.

Lynn stood up from her terminal, smiled, and led them away. She was fairly young, pleasant, and in good physical shape. Her long brown hair was braided down her back.

"Are you trained for the field?" Donna asked.

"Yes. You can't be stationed here if you're not. I would say some of you are US Navy SEALs."

"Yes, ma'am, you would be correct," Donna replied with a chuckle.

"Correct me if I'm wrong, but women SEALs are rare in your military. I don't know that I'm at your level, but I suspect I could give you a pretty good tussle."

They all laughed at that.

Donna replied, "I'm sure you could. I don't need to refight the Revolutionary War."

"Good answer," Lynn replied. "We wouldn't lose a second time."

Again, the ladies laughed.

"I like you, Lynn," Donna added. "You're my kind of gal."

"Are the guys going to separate showers?" Patty asked.

"No, they wait for these showers after the women are done. You'll find towels, soap, shampoos, and there are hair dryers in the bathroom. If you'll excuse me, I need to get back to my terminal."

"Thank you again, Lynn. We owe you."

"Don't say such things. I just might take you up on it. You never know what I might think up."

"Whatever you ask, we'd pay gladly. This is life or death for us at this point."

After washing away the grit, the ladies returned to the office area so the men could take their turns.

Nigel approached Patty and Lily.

"I wanted to say, that issue we've all been watching, the background strange encrypted messaging nobody can figure out, there's been a spike in internet traffic. I'm talking about a big surge in messaging. I can only assume that some sorts of instructions are being transmitted. Who's listening out there, it could be anybody. I don't like it when I don't know who my enemy is."

"I tend to agree, this can't be good," Lily opined. "I suspect this also plays into what's happening at Langley. I wonder what else can be happening in the background."

"I think your desire for a quick departure may need to be put on hold, at least in the short term. There are going to be major storms sweeping through this area this week, the kind where you don't want to be sitting in the back of a pickup truck. You break down around here you've got huge trouble, and there is nobody able to come to the rescue."

"That was going to be true anyways. We have no place to go yet. I'm sorry to impose."

"Don't worry about it. We'll conserve our supplies and apportion them to make do."

"Don't short yourself on our account."

"We can probably arrange to get some supplies locally. We'll be fine."

"May I borrow a sat phone? I need to make a secure call back home."

"If you want to call your family, I'd advise against it. Your home phone is surely tapped. You can't alert them you and your team are still alive out here. They may think you're out here, but verifying it for them isn't a wise choice. Keep them in the dark while we all get our ducks in a row. If they have confederates in European agencies too, we're all under threat."

"You're right, Nigel, but there is somebody else I want to call."

Nigel glanced at Patty, who remained quiet.

He walked away to retrieve the satellite phone and came back to give it to her.

"I'm sorry there aren't really any private places to make your call in this small area."

"That's not a problem. I'm not spilling any classified secrets. I just need an outsider to help me figure out the lay of the land."

Lily dialed a number and waited. It took a little time before someone answered.

"Hello, who is this?"

"Rick, it's Lily. I'm sorry to disturb you in your retirement."

"Lily, I wish I could say I'm surprised to hear from you, but I had a feeling you'd reach out. I think I know why. My retiree friends and I have been monitoring this weird situation, and it gets markedly weirder by the day. What can I do for you?"

"Have you tried to talk to anybody in the agency?"

"I haven't called. Our information came from outside of their knowledge and control."

"Good. Let me explain my predicament. My last call with Langley talking to the newly appointed director was eye-opening. He actually has Russian intelligence officers in the CIA building going everywhere unrestricted. Incidentally, he speaks fluent Russian. At any rate, he sent my team on a mission to the Afghan Pakistan border region into an ambush by Sheik Rahman. The sheik has apparently marked us because he's followed us into Africa and seems to have inside information on our whereabouts. We've had a number of running battles with his forces. I think the only reason we're alive now is I decided to take us off the grid. Nigel Smythe has been kind enough to let us hunker down here until we can come up with a plan."

"That makes me angry to hear, Lily. I want to help you, but we can't really phone home to the agency."

"I don't want that. The last thing we need is putting you guys in the crosshairs. What I want is if you can get all your friends into the fray to get me good intel and some way to try to survive and still do something useful. Also, if you can keep an eye on my house and family for me, I'm worried about enemies using them to get to me."

"Sure, I can do that. We've been busy being subtle anyway. Expanding the envelope won't be much of a stretch."

"I owe you. I will find a way to—"

"Stop, Lily, you owe me nothing. Let me know when you have a secure phone number I can call. Stay safe out there. It's a scary world. We'll get busy back here."

"Was that Rick Reick?" asked Nigel.

"The same."

"So you're pulling him out of retirement?"

"People like Rick always have their fingers in the cookie jar. I need his connections to make sense of things. Can I see any codes you've seen? I'm trying to piece it together in my mind."

"Sure. I'll take you back to Lynn. She's working on it."

Lynn was studying her computer screen when they walked up.

"Can you go over the latest on the messages with Lily and Patty, please?"

Lynn looked up. For a moment she had a sharp glint in her eyes before she relaxed.

"Sorry, I can get fixated on my tasks, and being interrupted is annoying."

"I understand. We've been studying it back home, so hopefully we can work off each other."

"Okay, you're on. This is the latest transmissions, and honestly it's just as much gibberish as the rest of the messages."

Lily eyed the encrypted message. Though she couldn't understand it, there was a familiar feel. Whoever was the mastermind, this was his, or her, work.

"I've used every tool in my kit to break this down, but I can make no progress of any kind, Lily."

"Trying to break the encryption is probably not the answer. I banged my head against the wall too with no success. We need to figure out a different way to solve this puzzle."

"What did you have in mind?"

"At this point, nothing, but maybe we brainstorm any thought that strikes us. Perhaps some nugget will drop out we can act on."

"Okay, I'm game. Nothing else has worked."

"Patty, are you in?"

"Sure, I'm not a computer guru like you two, but I'll try."

Lily smiled. "I know the situation seems tough, but we've got to try. If we don't, who else is there to take up the slack? So let's get to work."

They displayed the latest messages to contrast with the prior messages. The similarities were obvious to trained eyes.

"If we had the key, it would be helpful," Lily muttered.

Patty and Lynn snickered. Lynn spoke, "If we had the message itself, we'd know what it says."

"You know what I meant. I was just thinking out loud."

CHAPTER 8

Lily pondered a moment before continuing. "It seems familiar, but at the same time, I suspect it's meant to lull us into our usual conclusions and approaches. This guy or girl is a master at this stuff."

Lynn frowned. "I agree with you. If we tried our normal approaches, it might be like a Mobius strip, an eternal loop with no conclusion possible."

"Therefore…any new ideas?"

"Rather than struggle with the coding itself, maybe we can trace back to the originating source? If we can't solve that riddle, taking out the author works just as well for me."

Patty and Lily chuckled.

"You've got a hard edge, Lynn," Patty muttered.

"When it comes to the mayhem and madness they're causing, it's no-holds-barred for me. I've got family at risk too."

"That's a sore point for me also. I don't dare call my husband and children because it will tip off our enemies we're still out here. Right now, my hope is whoever they are, is they're uncertain if we were killed off and, if not, about where to locate us. I have no delusions that we're now suddenly safe and the threat is over. Dusting off those thugs chasing us will set off alarms somewhere."

Lynn stared away for a moment, digesting Lily's words. "Well, back to work. I'll start the search to pin down the source. I can see things are being bounced all over the world. This won't be easy."

Wesley wandered over. "Any luck, ladies?"

"We're just getting started," Lynn replied.

Wesley glanced at Lily and nodded to Patty.

"We're thinking we pin down a location for the author of these messages. Langley is supposedly trying to translate the message, but cracking this encryption may not work."

"You also mean Langley may be a player in whatever is going wrong."

"That would be true. I'm planning for all possibilities."

"That's the only choice at this point, I agree."

Patty spoke, "Have you heard back from your retired friends yet?"

"No, I didn't expect anything promptly. They must be ultracautious with anything they do for their own protection and that of their families. It will take time on their end."

"In the meantime, here we sit. Our safety in this hole has a time limit and probably shorter than we'd like."

"I know, Patty. Lynn, I'm sorry we've brought our danger onto you guys."

"If it's meant to be the end for us here, it's my fate. I don't blame you. What else could you do in that killing field your enemies set up for you? Lesser units wouldn't have survived. I'll keep working on finding the origin of these messages to end them once and for all."

"That's a brave outlook, Lynn. You humble me."

"Hardly, Lily, you humble me. Your legend is built on a career of actual deeds in the field."

"Don't downplay your importance in the big scheme of things. Without people like you, people like me go nowhere. Then the bad guys win."

Lynn smiled.

"By the way, what legend are you talking about?"

"Are you fishing for a compliment? You know you're as well-known amongst your enemies as much as your friends. That sheik has probably got your swimsuit picture hanging in his bedroom."

The ladies chuckled.

"What a sickening thought." Lily shook her head. "At any rate, I'll let you get back to work. Thanks again for your help, Lynn."

"What are your thoughts about exiting here, Wesley? Making our way to Britain, is that doable and is it wise under the circumstances?"

"I suspect there is great jeopardy no matter where we go. If the CIA has been compromised, I can't guarantee England isn't also vulnerable. It's a slippery slope. I wish I could be more helpful. I wish I could be more hopeful."

"I understand, and down deep I feel the same way."

Lynn added, "By the way, along that same line, we haven't advised anybody about your arrival."

"We appreciate your looking out for us."

"Like Wesley said, there could be spies and corruption in our agency too. I still can't believe what's happened to the Americans."

"I think I need to gather all of my people together for a talk. We must develop a plan immediately for a lot of reasons."

Wesley patted Lynn's shoulder as he walked past her. She concentrated on her computer search.

Moments later the entire team huddled together for their brainstorming session.

Lily took a moment to look at each and every face before opening the meeting.

"You're all proven commodities, so I'm not going to pull any punches. We're in a pickle and need to develop a viable strategy. If it's nothing more than dodging the bullet to get out of the gunsights, at least it's a start. Without agency help, it's a daunting challenge. I've asked for help from some retired friends back home, but there is probably a limit to what they can do. That being the case, I'd like to have you guys speak. No matter how wild your ideas, please tell us. Once we leave this facility, it's back into the fire figuratively and literally. Depending on pure luck to save us is a poor situation." Lily frowned and paused a moment.

"Well, I don't need to explain it, you can figure it out. I'm not saying we shouldn't or couldn't take risks, but we need to find a way to prevail. A unit of this size cannot save the world, but hopefully we can save ourselves. Does that make sense to you?"

There were various forms of response between nods, muttering, shrugs, and yeses.

"Anybody want to start?"

Grace Bailey spoke. "Lily, have you totally ruled out the agency?"

"As far as normal channels and protocols, I'd say yes. I prefer to keep any enemies in the dark. My feeling is we're only alive now because they're not clear on what happened in Somalia and our current status."

"The reason I asked is there are friends back at Langley I trust with my life."

"That's true for all of us. My fear is all of their communications are compromised, and not just the agency. There is no secure line for us to call them without somebody else recording it. Remember that apparently there are foreign assets infecting every unit and department back home. That means there are people in high places allowing it."

"That would be a breach of our government of biblical proportions. I'm feeling pretty small right about now."

"I know that feeling. I'm going to give a call to my retired friends. I hope I haven't put them in the gunsights too. We'll talk again later, but think about plans of action."

Lily called Rick Reick. The phone rang a number of times.

"Hello."

"Eh...I was calling for Rick?"

"This is his wife, Mariann. He's not home right now. Who is this?"

"I'm Lily Carson. We worked together before he retired."

"Oh, hold on a second. I'll get him. He's being very cautious these days."

"Hello, Lily. I'm sorry for the subterfuge, but the situation here is deteriorating. Once I and my associates started looking into things, it seems to have put us on some radar screens."

"I'm sorry, Rick. I should never have drawn you into this."

"Don't be sorry. It's our country too. Somebody needed to do something."

"We're at a loss here. I can't imagine a strategy or plan to get out of trouble. Have you been able to learn anything?"

"There are fifth column elements everywhere. They're becoming more blatant in their activities and worrying less about any consequences. It's inconceivable. We tried to get people out to watch over your families, but plans about them were already in motion."

"What…what does that mean?"

"Your husband suddenly pulled your kids out of school and took them away secretly. At least that's our assumption. I can't be sure if they were actually taken by—"

"My God, I needed to be there."

"Don't say that. If it was some enemy after you, your being there might have meant your capture or worse."

"I've got to do something. This is intolerable."

"If you could find a way to get home, you going to your house would be the last thing you want to do. Your family isn't there. If the mysterious *they* don't know you're still alive, that's part of your advantages, one of the few."

"What do you think about a boat trip across the ocean?"

"As I said, coming home is a bad idea, but getting some private boat is probably the best way out of your current predicament. I'd head north to the Mediterranean shore."

"Where else could we go? Sitting mired in another continent is a bad situation."

"If you decide to do that, call me back, and I'll try to facilitate your arrival. We'll arrange vehicles, food and water, and replenishment of your ammo."

"That sounds great, Rick. Thank you so much. If you hear about my family, call me immediately."

"Will do, stay safe, Lily."

Lily went back to speak to Lynn, who was working diligently on the coding issue. "For lack of a better idea, I think we'll go north to try for a private boat to sail home. Do you have any connections up there?"

"I think we can help you with that. I'll make some calls and let you know. What kind of time frame did you have in mind?"

"The sooner the better. My family is gone from our home. I need to get back to the USA to find out what's going on with them."

"I understand. I'll get right on it."

Lily gathered the squad again to discuss the latest. Mentioning her family-in-jeopardy situation caused similar concerns with everybody else for their own loved ones.

"We're going to start loading up the trucks for a quick exit. Lynn is trying to make arrangements to get a boat on the coast."

"Are you taking all of us to America?" Gamal asked.

"Yes. We'll sort out those details later. We're a team. Listen, everybody, assuming we can manage to get home, you can go to your homes to check on family, but use great care. If you call, the lines could be tapped, so don't call. If you go in daylight, there could be surveillance. You go in the night and sneak in without tipping off the enemy. Make whatever arrangements are appropriate, and then we gather again later, whether a week or a month."

No one objected.

"What about us?" Hussain asked.

"We'll divide up the non-Americans and each take somebody. Gamal and Hussain, you can come with me, for example."

Gamal grinned broadly. "Thank you, ma'am."

Lily noticed the ISI agents eyeing her. "Did you gentlemen have a question?"

"It's very generous of you to take Muslims into your homes."

"It's not a problem. I think you're judging America based on news reports. Those incidents are hardly the norm. Muslim folk get along in the USA better than most other countries in the world. The 'Death to America' crowds you've seen in your area on Middle Eastern television are fomenting a skewed and inaccurate narrative meant to further their warped agendas. Generally speaking, life in America is pretty good for everybody."

"Good to know," Abdul replied.

Donna edged over. "Nice speech. If you're taking Gamal and Hussain, are you taking me too? I live alone and have no family to check on."

"Sure, that will work. If we run into a dicey situation, having you along will be a good thing."

"I guess we can get to it and get the trucks loaded. We leave after supper so we can drive in the night and not draw undue attention."

They walked over to Lynn's desk.

"I've got you set up. Here's where you go. There's a captain with a large enough fishing boat that can sail directly to the US coast. We'll give you some of our cash to grease the skids for smooth sailing. You will definitely want to load your supplies and weaponry on board at night there. We're depending on both stealth on your part and the fact there is too much area for the enemy to cover so you can evade detection."

"Thank you, Lynn. You're a life saver."

"Initially, you'll drive west going the last direction that your enemy would expect you to go before you turn north. You'll be straddling the border of two countries so be careful. No karaoke from the back of the truck."

They all chuckled.

"Understood," Lily answered. She patted Lynn on the shoulder. "I owe you, ma'am."

Lynn turned her head to smile. "You absolutely do."

After their evening meal, the trucks loaded, Lily led her team into the dim light of dusk to resume their trek to survive. It was overcast but still hot outside. Again, gusts of wind kicked up sand, causing them to cover their faces.

Wesley had seated himself beside Lily. She spoke.

"I'm surprised you opted to continue with us. You were relatively safe amongst your people there."

"Lily, either we're a team or we're a collection of individuals and individual goals. I choose to do my part for all of our dodging this bullet. Our Arab friends are out of their element and going to America where they'll definitely stand out in the wrong way. That takes courage, so how could I expect less from me."

"Thank you, I appreciate that."

After departing, it wasn't long before they completed their initial westerly drive before turning northward. The generally northerly route veered often, and with the poor quality of the road, it was slow going. The cover of darkness had a limited duration. The trucks were unable to get to their destination before sunrise. They did manage to get close enough to smell the salty air of the Mediterranean.

"What do you want to do, Lily?" Ron Gray asked. He was driving one of the trucks.

"We'll just have to lay low for the day. Watch for a secluded spot where we can hole up until dark. Tomorrow will have to be soon enough to get there and find the boat."

He drove for a short distance before pulling behind a hill into a small grove of trees. It was sparse cover but out of sight from the road. Feeling restless made for a long hot day stuck in place. They recessed under the trees, but it was very little relief. The sounds of the nearby town kept them alert. Being discovered wasn't something they could allow.

Patty came over to Lily. "I have an idea. Let's send our Somali friend Hussain into the town to find our boat captain. He won't stand out amongst the populace, and we can get directions about how and where to go. Wandering around in the dark isn't a good idea."

"That is an excellent idea. We can give him some US money and a letter from us so the captain trusts him. I agree, it certainly beats stumbling around in the dark."

Hussain was sitting nearby listening.

"What do you say, Hussain?"

"I can do it. Thank you for trusting me. I will go now."

"Okay, I'll write a brief note."

Soon, Hussain was walking away from the camp back to the road to walk into the nearby settlement.

"This can't go wrong, can it, Patty?"

"We're good. Hussain has no reason to double-cross us. He's out of his country with no support other than us. Plus, the fact the chance to go to the USA is a huge lure for non-Americans."

Sooner than they expected, they heard a vehicle on the road, an old jeep. Hussain was riding with a stranger. They pulled behind the hill.

"I have returned. The captain sent one of his men to escort us to the boat."

127

The man nodded, eyeing the attack group appreciatively. He had the look of a former soldier.

"So we leave at dark?" Lily asked.

"We go at dusk," he replied.

They ate supper before piling into the vehicles to head for the coast. Lily rode in the jeep with the soldier.

"Do you expect any trouble?"

"Not here."

"You understand, we can't be spotted and identified. We have serious enemies chasing us. They have technology available if they get a hint that we're still alive."

"Yes, our captain told us that. You're in good hands. The boat crew has extensive prior military experience in various armies."

"Good. Thank you for your help. We need it. How long will it take to get to your boat?"

"About half an hour, I'd say, but we will wait into the dark to unload your weapons and supplies."

"How soon before we can set sail?"

"Basically, as soon as you're loaded on board. We've already loaded extra fuel and supplies for the long trip."

Driving along the dusty road, they veered around the town onto an even worse road. Here they bounced and rattled their way in a bone-jarring final leg of the dangerous journey on the African continent. By the time they approached the shoreline site of the piers and the boats moored there, it was dark enough to attempt the transfer of personnel and materials.

Lily and Patty walked on board to meet the ship captain.

"Hello, ladies, welcome to the *Kraken*."

Both women chuckled. Patty replied, "Interesting name."

"Not my doing. I got this boat used. I guess the original owner liked sea monster movies. As I look at your team, I see tier one operators mixed in with…I'm not sure what."

"We're a conglomerate," Lily answered. "We do work well together, as unlikely as that might seem from a casual glance."

"I'll take your word for it. By the way, this isn't my first rodeo. I do these transport tasks fairly frequently."

"Traveling to the US coast won't be a problem?"

"No, not for you. For me, I do owe some money a few places though, so taking a long voyage is good for me. I really need to avoid gambling."

"Your man said you were fully apprised of our situation."

"Yes, we'll keep you below decks. I've noticed drones in the area. That doesn't happen here. This backwater has little to no importance. It seems they're not assuming you were killed in your Somalia firefight."

"It was weird. The warlord's men assigned to attack us in Somalia, we actually turned them, and they joined the other side, our side."

"That's amazing. Well, Lily, it looks like all of your equipment is on board, so I'll let you join your people below decks while we get underway."

"Thank you, Captain. Did they take the mounted fifty cals and ammo from the pickups?"

"Yes."

"I have a feeling they might come in handy."

The boat was not huge, but the team had ample room to move and sit in relative comfort. The ship's crew took to their guests readily. All the crew had military history in common, although in different armies. However, soldiers understand each other.

The boat churned out of the small harbor, gradually turning westward. Being a windy day, the swells rocked the boat to the point many of the team struggled to hold down their latest meal. The Arab contingent especially suffered through getting their sea legs. None of them had been on boats on the ocean before.

The boat captain, Charles Whalen, came down to speak with the ailing passengers.

"Tear off pieces from this loaf of bread to swallow. Your sick feeling is fluid in your stomach sloshing around. The bread soaks it up. You'll be fine after that."

All the team shared in the bread and were startled to find the captain's cure worked well.

"I feel better," said Gamal. "There is much I don't know."

Hussain mentioned, "I knew of this. I once was on boats of Somali pirates raiding ships off our coast."

"Why?" asked Donna. "Why would you do that?"

"My country is not rich like your country. My family needed food, and it paid well to do their work."

"Were any of those ships American?"

Hussain paused before answering. "The only American vessel I faced was a private yacht. They were fools to sail into our territory. The owner was on board at the time. He was a pale fat man, disgusting to see, but he brought many pretty young girls. They were very afraid of us and should have been. The yacht captain and crew were competent, but we were heavily armed. They were forced into our harbor. I was young, so other than hold a weapon on them, I didn't do anything. Others of us, older guys, were not respectful and…did things."

"You don't need to say it. We understand what they do," Donna said grimly.

"It was why I left that job. I wasn't like the others who reveled in doing such evil. The memory of those actions, the anguished cries of the girls, it haunts me to this day. I feel shame, and I didn't even touch any of them."

"Bastards," Donna muttered angrily.

"All of them went home when the ransom was paid, but I think they're emotionally scarred for life."

"It isn't something a woman forgets. You're probably right they needed therapy after the traumas. If you ever see those guys again, let me know. They're overdue for some retribution, Navy SEAL style."

Captain Whalen poked his head in the doorway from up top.

"Lily, did everybody eat? Is the sea sickness under control now?"

"Yes, sir. How long before we exit the Mediterranean?"

"We need to act like a fishing boat, so we'll have periodic stops to mimic fishing. If we cruise steadily to the US coast, it will draw the kind of notice you don't want. These days there are drones everywhere watching everything. It isn't just America anymore. It seems like all countries have drone fleets in the air."

"That's good news."

"I'm sorry, it's a new world."

Mohamed spoke. "We've lived with drones for a long time. Now you can see what it was like for us being forever on guard."

Donna eyed him darkly.

When she started to speak, Lily cut her off. "Mohamed, countries do what they feel is in their best interest. Not every decision we make sits well elsewhere. That works both ways."

"That is an understatement, Lily. So many citizens in my part of the world have lost people to drone strikes. That is another thing a person doesn't forget. Your kills don't accomplish what you wish. Taking out a person from above creates new enemies with his sons, brothers, uncles, neighbors, and even women who decide they want revenge also. You never learned your lessons from your Vietnam War."

"I can't disagree."

"Your technology is a double-edged sword."

"I guess we both have things to apologize for on behalf of our countries. Watching helpless people get beheaded should not be out there on the internet."

"That's true. There are vile people in the world on all sides."

The chat continued, but covering fewer incendiary topics as they cruised along. The boat slowed near an area they fished frequently. As the crew prepared their nets and other gear to pretend to fish, one of the crewmen noticed boats racing toward them from the shore. As they got closer, Captain Whalen yelled down the hatch to his guests.

"There are two pirate boats coming. We would normally let them board us rather than get shot."

"Obviously that won't work with us here. My people will crawl above decks and blast them when they get close. I don't know if they've radioed anybody."

"There looks to be five or six each on the boats. They're not acting unusual so far. I don't think they were sent looking for you."

"Regardless, we're not taking any chances."

The fire teams dispersed quickly deploying to offer maximum coverage of the approaching threats.

Keeping their heads down, they waited. They could hear the motors of the approaching enemy craft coming close.

The crew put their hands up as the boats slowed and maneuvered for the boarding attempt.

"Now!" Lily yelled. The troops rose up and opened up with withering and overwhelming point-blank fire, taking out the people but also riddling the boats, which started to sink. It was a ridiculously easy fight.

The allied troops stared silently at the aftermath. Most of the pirates were young.

Lily turned to Mohamed. "There's an example of an action we had to take. I'm sorry it had to go this way."

"As you say, it had to be done for us to survive. I hold no blame on you for this."

They waited long enough to see the boats sink under the waves before resuming their trek.

The crew sat in silence below decks, pondering the fight.

Patty spoke. "Sometimes this job has a lot of issues. Those were barely men we killed. Granted they made some bad life choices about piracy, but they stood no chance against us."

"Hopefully we won't have further firefights," Hassan muttered.

Patty looked at Lily. "I'm uncertain if the bad guys have fully bought our deaths. The drones may be their regular attempts to watch this area, or they may be searching for us."

"We're definitely vulnerable, but we would be no matter if we're here or back in Africa. Somehow, we've risen to the top of their hit list. I'm not sure why that would be. We're not the only tier-one operators in play."

"Maybe we're the only ones left."

"That is a chilling thought. God bless the USA, eh?"

"It may not be safer where we're going, but I'll feel a lot better with my feet on American soil."

Wesley piped in. "It's funny, I can't say I feel that way about getting to British soil. This entire episode has me confused. I'm glad to leave the decisions to you."

The seas became more difficult as the wind picked up intensity. The captain came below decks.

"We're sailing into a storm, so get ready for rough seas. I'm sorry. This won't be pleasant."

"Will that slow down our arrival back home?"

"Probably. We're sailing into the storm. It's going to be a slog fighting through it all."

"We understand. We're just happy to find a way to escape the traps back in Africa."

Sailing across the Atlantic Ocean cramped in a fishing boat was the ordeal the captain predicted. They got no breaks in the weather, and over the long term, the moods on board gradually deteriorated. The captain offered his cabin to any of the women who wanted it. They all declined his offer.

"Captain, you need to be rested and ready, so thank you, but we'll stay out here," Lily replied.

Well on their way to the US coast, they passed US naval vessels traveling toward Europe. The captain sent the team below decks, feinting innocence to the scrutiny of the warships. His crewmen moved about on the deck, pretending fisherman chores. The fact numerous lookouts on the ships studied them at length did not escape his notice. He kept the team below decks for half an hour as a precaution, which worked well as a helicopter flew overtop the boat and shadowed them for a time before returning to the fleet.

At last, the team cautiously came up for air.

"That was weird," Patty said.

"If they used equipment to survey this boat for heat signatures, they may know we're on board," Lily replied.

"If that's the case, somebody really doesn't like the idea we could still be alive."

Donna edged over. "I'm getting tired of this game. If somebody wants to take me out, bring it on, I will not go quietly."

The captain walked over. "We need to use ultimate caution. Don't forget there can still be subs cruising in the area."

As if on cue, behind them one of the crewmen spotted a trail which appeared to be a periscope approaching. The team slunk back below decks.

In a surprise, the sub surfaced as it continued to close the gap. It was a Russian vessel.

"Take us to full speed," the captain ordered. "That's land ahead of us. I think we can make US waters before they can interdict us."

The race was on. Russian sailors appeared on deck and manned their weapons.

Lily and Patty were sitting on the top step of the stairs out of sight of the sub.

"If we lose this race and they decide to fire on us, we will open up with everything we've got. Our two fifty cals can do some damage, as well as the miniguns."

"It's going to be close, but I don't think they can catch us in time."

"Will they honor the boundary or keep chasing us?"

"Normally I would say they'd back off, but these days there are a lot of strange things happening. The US Coast Guard and the US Navy monitor our territorial waters. Russian subs take a chance in testing us. Whether there's something fishy going on, I can't tell. These stories about Russians showing up in all sorts of unexpected places are worrisome."

"I can't disagree. It's a big part of why we're staying dark. I haven't dared trying to contact my family. The last word I got was my husband took my kids away into hiding. That gives me a brief feeling of relief. But sooner or later, he'll need to go back to his job. At that point it won't be hard to put him under surveillance if they're still looking for me."

"This is really messed up," Donna said.

The captain looked through his binoculars back at the approaching sub. "They won't catch us before we cross the line. I'm confident of that now."

"Are they slowing or backing off?"

"No, Lily, they're not."

"I guess we hope shore installations are watching the chase."

It was prophetic as when they crossed the invisible border line, US military helicopters appeared racing toward them from the East Coast. They heard a loudspeaker as the numerous copters circled the sub.

"You're about to enter US territorial waters. If you do not reverse your course, you will be fired upon."

The sub ignored the command for only a moment before ending the pursuit and reversing course.

"Thank God," Patty muttered.

The boat captain maintained full speed nonetheless to get to US soil as soon as possible.

Lily replied, "I'm still worried. The fact they chased a fishing boat leads me to think they believe we're still alive and on board this ship."

Patty spoke. "It makes me wonder what's waiting for us when we get to land."

"I've thought about that very thing."

Lily turned to the captain. "What's your plans about landing?"

He looked at her directly. "If I pull into a port, there could be eyes watching for you. I decided to head for the Maine Coast. We'll put you ashore away from prying eyes in an area of sparse population. You'll need to do some walking through the brush. If I understand correctly, your friends have arranged for vehicles to pick you up. After that, it's in your hands."

"That's fine. We appreciate your taking this risk and bringing us home. We'll deal with whatever comes next."

"Good luck to all of you. Remember that everybody knows you're the good guys, no matter what your opponents say or do."

"They've got the power, so I'm going to be ready for anything. Seeing Russian operatives in the Pentagon speaking Russian with the new director was unsettling, to say the least."

"Be careful out there. We need to have people to stand up for what's right."

CHAPTER 9

The boat slowed later as they neared the Maine Coast. It was just after 3:00 a.m. and still dark. Prior to leaving Africa, the captain had loaded inflatable rafts to assist them in going ashore.

The team loaded the equipment and then themselves into the rafts.

"Thank you again for what you've done. You were lifesavers." Lily hugged the captain before climbing into the raft.

"You're welcome. We have faith in you and your team to make a difference out there."

They took out oars and rowed toward the dark shore. It was an eerie feeling using tactics used for foreign incursion assignments to make a secret landing in their home country.

Immediately ahead was a forested area. Trees here were mostly conifers. Reaching the beach, they quickly moved personnel and equipment into the trees.

Gamal and Hussain looked around curiously. Wide-eyed, they looked at Lily.

"I know it's different, but that's not a bad thing. Don't worry, guys. We'll get to our rendezvous point and get into the vehicles. It will be better then. You won't feel so endangered then."

She smiled to reassure them, although down deep, she didn't feel assured.

"Let's go, folks," said Patty.

The team marched ahead briskly with Joe Gilson and Andy Reiger in the lead, weapons at the ready. The trek took over an hour to arrive at the pickup point. They eased forward cautiously as they emerged from the woods onto a rural dirt road. A parked truck blinked their lights once.

Hustling to get to the vehicles, a dog barked in the distance. A man in the pickup got out to greet them.

"Lily, Patty? I'm Jason Jones. There are five vehicles here for you. There are cars and SUVs. You choose how you split up your crew. I assume you have a plan in place."

"Thank you, Jason. We do have a dispersal plan and a future rendezvous point," Lily replied. He was a balding man who looked to be in his late fifties. However, he was fit and stout with clear sharp eyes, no one to mess with.

"I'm leaving now. I need to be someplace far from here for a number to reasons. In each vehicle there are items for your secure communications. Your friends have preprogrammed phone numbers so you can touch base. Good luck, I've got to go."

He drove away rapidly.

When they went to the vehicles, they also found packets which included charge cards, cash, and other needed documents.

Lily called them together.

"You all know your missions. We head for our assignments and reconnect within a month at the latest. Be very careful when trying to contact your families. If we can remain under the radar, that's our best-case scenario. I'll be looking to meet with our retiree friends to formulate a plan going forward. Be safe and don't do anything stupid. No speeding tickets or bar fights."

The team chuckled. Various members gave her thumbs-up signals.

Lily climbed into an SUV with Donna in the passenger seat. Gamal and Hussain were seated behind them. They were an unlikely-looking foursome riding along US highways, but the plan was to minimize stops and chances to be addressed by the general public during the drive westward. This was especially the case considering the weapons and munitions loaded into the trunk. Also there, neatly packed away, were their military uniforms. That meant Lily, Hassan, and Gamal could dress as if US troops, to join Donna, who already had her Navy uniforms for use at the appropriate times. They were also provided with civilian clothes. Making Gamal and Hussain look like Americans was a challenge.

Being still dark outside, Lily drove in silence without a radio turned on. "I'd suggest everybody take a nap while you can. We don't know what's ahead for us, but being alert will definitely be necessary."

It wasn't long before she heard light snoring from the back seat.

Driving southward down I-95, traffic was light. She tensed for a moment as a Maine State police car approached rapidly and passed her by. The officer never looked over at her or her passengers.

She mused, *At least there doesn't seem to be any alert out on us. That's one less thing to worry about.*

Within a couple of hours, they crossed the state line into New Hampshire. Soon afterward, they crossed the state line into Massachusetts. Continuing the southerly drive, they turned westward onto the Mass. Pike heading across the state. The sun was coming up behind them from the east. She glanced at the street signs, which included images of pilgrim hats. She smiled. This was a part of the country she'd never been in before. Pulling onto an exit, they made their first rest stop visit. Lily and Donna both talked at length with the guys before sending them to the men's restrooms.

Donna spoke pointedly. "Do not talk to anybody. As a matter of fact, don't talk at all. Take care of your business and come right out, after you wash your hands, that is. You meet us, and we'll all go together to get something to eat. Got it?"

The boys grinned. Gamal muttered, "I am hungry."

Ordering the food from a rest stop vendor, Lily picked the food for them. When they sat down a table, they drew numerous glances from other patrons. Both boys' uncovered hair looked wild, making them look wild. The boys stared cautiously at the burgers.

"Eat fast," she muttered.

Walking back to the vehicle, Donna took over driving. She pulled up to the gas pump for a fill-up. Lily sat in the passenger seat and fell asleep before Donna got back into the SUV.

Driving back onto the expressway to continue west traversing the state of Massachusetts, they crossed the state line into New York entering onto the Thruway. Lily slept all that time and didn't awaken until they were an hour into the New York leg of the journey.

"How are you doing, Donna? Are you okay with driving?"

'I'm fine, Lily. I was a little worried when I paid the fee at the Massachusetts toll booth. That woman eyed us a little too long for my liking."

"We get to do it again when we leave the New York Thruway. There are a lot of toll roads going this way toward Michigan. With that last booth, it may have been nothing at all. We feel worried about our circumstances fleeing unknown high-powered forces. With that attendant, it may have been nothing more than two women hauling around two Black boys. There are bigots in the world."

"True. I've kept the speed right at the limit."

"Good girl. Whenever you need me to take over driving, just pull into a rest stop."

"I'll keep going. I like driving."

"I'm going to try placing a secure call to our retired friends to get the lay of the land ahead."

"Go ahead. We've got nothing to lose. Without their help, we're goners anyway."

Lily dialed the number. It rang numerous times before someone answered, a woman.

"Hello."

"Hi, I called to speak with Rick."

"Who's calling?"

"A friend of his."

"What friend?"

"Is he there? Are you a relative?"

Lily heard the woman muttering with her hand over the receiver. Rick came on the line. "Is this Lily?"

"Yes, thank God I got through to you. Is there trouble?"

"That's an understatement. I gather you've made it home."

"Your man Jason had vehicles ready for us to split up and spread out. I'm riding on the New York Thruway right now heading for

Michigan. I've got Donna driving, and we have Gamal and Hussain riding in the back seat. I know enough not to go to my house, but I'm a little unsure of an alternative destination."

"Michigan is a good choice. I've got a cabin up north where I can meet you with some friends. It's old and it's rough, but it will do in a pinch."

"Who answered your phone?"

"It was my wife. I told her to be cautious and not to volunteer information. These guys are tenacious. I'm worried, and I don't get worried. I assume you brought arms?"

"We did. I have one of the fifty calibers in the trunk. If anybody wants to come at us, we can do some damage."

"Good, it's been too long since I heard the sound of a fifty in battle. Listen, we're taking our families with us wherever we go. Local police are cowed, so people can be snatched right off the street. It's a nightmare come to life."

"I can say 'how could this happen,' but at this point, I guess it no longer matters. It's down to what, if anything, are we going to do about it."

"You're right."

"Do you have any idea about my family?"

"Not really. As I said, we can't call the agency. Everybody and everything there are locked down. We'd only tip them off we're trying to make a move out here."

"I understand."

"I realize it isn't what you wanted to hear."

"Listen, Rick, you guys have taken huge risks for us. I'm beyond grateful. We're still in play solely because of you."

"Thank you, but all we can concentrate on now is staying alive at this point. There isn't anything else we can do because we don't know enough. That has got to change in a hurry."

"I couldn't agree more. I wish I had access to agency computers and resources. Clearly that's not going to happen."

"I'm afraid the corruption goes all the way to the top. This country is in big trouble, but too many gullible sheep are content to stick their heads in the sand. They excuse anything and believe any lie he says. It's appalling."

"I'll admit, I would never have thought we could get to such a state. People turn on certain television shows to get their daily instructions about how to act and what to believe. It makes me sick."

"So you're still on the New York Thruway?"

"We'll follow it down around Lake Erie onto the Ohio turnpike. We'll arrive in Dearborn sometime tomorrow."

"You have the address of the house, right?"

"We do."

"I expect it will be late in the day tomorrow when I get there with my group. It will be cramped quarters for a little while, but I can make additional arrangements fairly quickly. The other parts of your team should be arriving starting the next day after I get there. I anticipate moving us north, possibly into the upper peninsula of Michigan. There are cabins and sparse population areas that will suit our needs in the short term."

"Do you see any problem for my two Muslim boys going to a mosque in Dearborn for prayers?"

"It should be fine. They can just say they're visiting because there should be only one day they attend."

"Good, these poor guys have been existing in mostly a non-Muslim environment with us since we left Africa. A touch of their heritage and religion would be good for them at this point in time."

"Sure. The chance of them showing up on somebody's radar are virtually nil. The search for your team wouldn't be looking for Arabs in America."

"That's my guess. I hope I'm not wrong. I think they believe we're still alive. I can't understand what it is about us, or me, that would cause them to show such diligence trying to hunt us down."

"Somehow, you fit into their big picture. I'm focused on avoiding that search for you and for us."

"Thank God you're there for us. We've got nobody else, or at least nobody else we can contact."

"Stay safe and drive carefully. We'll see you soon."

"We're looking forward to it."

Donna and Lily glanced at each other. Donna spoke. "Do you think we have danger between here and getting to Dearborn?"

"Anything is possible. However, spotting us driving through the country would be pure chance. There's nothing to distinguish us out here. I think we're okay for the moment."

"I hope our other teams have smooth sailing too."

"Have some faith in them. They're all highly trained to cope with any contingency."

"Are you sorry you have us in your car instead of the other men?" Gamal asked.

Lily replied, "Why would you ask that?"

"This is not our country. We stand out as dark non-Americans riding with a white woman."

"To everybody else around us, we're just four people riding in a car. They have no idea about our relationships and circumstances. I'll let you know if we need to be worried."

"Okay." She heard the boys chuckle from the back seat.

"Just settle back and take another nap. We'll stop for gas and food in a couple of hours."

"I'm glad we'll be able to get to a mosque in this Dearborn. I haven't practiced my religion enough in my life. I'll let Gamal show me what to do," Hussain added.

Gamal chuckled. "I don't know if American Muslims will accept either of us. We both have heavy accents, and our English isn't so good. Maybe we look scary to them."

Donna replied, "You guys have nothing to worry about. Just say you're visiting relatives briefly. Also, you do look scary to Lily and me."

Everybody laughed.

"Maybe when we stop in Dearborn, we'll see about haircuts to those wild mops on your heads."

The miles passed as they drove steadily along. After several toll booths and state lines, crossing the border into Michigan, Lily mentioned, "We're in the home stretch, boys"

Gamal spoke. "It's much different in America. Everybody has cars."

"That's not completely true, Gamal, but most people do."

Hussain added, "America is a rich country."

Donna glanced at him. "Compared to other parts of the globe, that's true. However, we have poverty here too. Wealth discrepancy is universal. The rich not only have the money, they have the power. It's the more important factor. Also, that income disparity is increasing sharply in recent years."

Lily added, "The effect of that power is infecting our society and our politics and not in a good way. They have all the money they need to buy politicians."

"Dearborn city limits," Donna muttered. "We're almost there, guys."

Gamal replied, "Good, I'm tired of riding. I need some exercise."

They turned onto the street they'd been given and pulled into the driveway at the correct house. There were other vehicles there ahead of them. A gray-haired man came out of the house and directed them to park behind the house. Joe Gilson and Andy Reiger came out of the house following the man.

"Hey, guys," said Donna, jumping out of the car.

"Hey yourself," Andy replied.

"Are you the first ones to arrive?"

"No. Actually, you're the last car to arrive."

Lily got out of the car to a warm greeting from Joe, a firm embrace. Hussain and Gamal smiled but stood back from the others. The gray-haired man stepped up. "I'm Evan Marsh, let's go into the house."

They trooped inside and then down the stairs into the basement. The basement was full of happy faces and warm hugs of reunion. Already, considerable beer had been consumed.

Wesley walked over to Lily. "There were plenty of times in Africa when I thought our numbers were up. I'm amazed we came through that gauntlet unscathed other than bumps and bruises. It feels strange to be safe."

"You mean as safe as we can under the circumstances?"

"Exactly." He laughed heartily.

"I see the beer has taken effect."

"Just what I needed, ma'am. Our hosts have been more than generous with us."

"I assumed if there was any help out in the world, it would be with them. I guessed right."

More cars arrived as the day passed. They were other retired agents and operators. By ten in the evening, the basement was full with nearly two hundred people in the room.

Finally, the informal leader of the retirees, Bob Seine, stood up.

"We need to talk about some things. When I first got word of what was happening, I spread the word for us to get back in the game. After I learned about the traps being set for our teams, I made a point to contact families back here to take precautions. I didn't want your connections at home to lead to trouble for the innocents. I hope you understand. I realize it's been difficult not speaking with family."

Patty spoke. "Bob, we're all grateful for the measures you took. What's been the damages?"

"There have been some teams that took serious hits before word spread about the danger. There are even casualties among some families. It is vile. I would never have thought this possible on US soil."

Lily spoke. "When a Russian sub surfaces to give chase, right after US forces sweep through the area searching for us, I realized something serious is happening. I worried that sub would follow us right into an American port. The new director at the agency had Russians in the Pentagon talking Russian. That was just before we were dispatched to be trapped in the Middle East. After that failed, they tried another trap in Africa."

Andy piped in, "There are a lot fewer of those bastards walking around."

The crowd cheered.

Lily glanced at Gamal and Hussain. They had wry smiles.

She spoke. "Is it feasible to gather our relatives someplace… with us?"

"Probably that would need to happen in Canada. I don't think the Canadians are a part of this, but allowing us to bring our trouble onto their soil may not go over well."

"We got lifesaving help from the Brits to get out of Africa."

"I just didn't want any of us to have false illusions that there is any easy or safe way out of this. We're still in a serious bind."

Lily added, "Another worry I have is resources. I assumed you've been funding this mission out of your pockets. Obviously, none of us are receiving paychecks since we were killed in action."

The people chuckled.

"That's not a pressing issue yet. Eventually, we'll need to address that, but for the time being, we've got outside help coming in. So that we don't draw undue notice, we'll gradually start our migration north in small numbers at a time within a few days. A caravan would stand out. I've had people up in the woods setting up the cabins we'll be using. There will be advanced communication equipment as well as instruments we need to get into this thing."

"Do we have ammo?" Joe asked. "I could see some firefights in our future."

"We're working on that. Yes, there is ammo being gathered, to answer your question. We have some here, but the bulk of it is being gathered up north."

Lily asked, "If we amass large numbers of people there, how concerned are you about drawing notice?"

"We'll have cabins over a somewhat dispersed area, but you're right. There will be no trips into local towns *en masse.* That would be waving a red flag for the locals to notice along with our foes."

"My thought exactly. Our opponents have shown they are tenacious, and they have plenty of resources they can bring to bear. I suspect I can speak for everybody when I say I feel vulnerable about my family. I wish they could be with me, but I don't want them in the middle of a fight. I agree with Joe that trouble is in our future."

"Eventually, we plan to establish a significant presence north of the border in Canada. Our northern friends are well aware of what's happening in the USA, and they're extremely concerned. We've been in negotiations to combine with their security services. Also, there have been secret meetings with other allies around the world to prepare a defense minus American participation. I can't believe it could come to this, but now our country is seen as a pariah at the very least, and an outright ally in the Russian orbit. The American populace has been too slow to recognize and react to what's happening. With the captive media, there has been no reporting of attacks and ambushes of our elite covert forces around the world and populating Russian forces inside our government. We've been trying to gather as many of our current experts and recently removed officials as we can, both to protect them and to build our own team. There will come a time very soon when we're forced to take action on behalf of this country. By the way, we've also made overtures to Mexico, just like we're doing with Canada."

"Thank God you took action."

"I can't guarantee any outcomes, but we can get into a position to take forceful action. Getting the attention of the masses will be the harder job. The tentacles of this conspiracy have sunk deep into American society. I've heard reports the intimidation of the press has crossed a lot of lines to the point of physical violence and job firings. All that are left afterwards are dupes and puppets of the regime."

"That's really disturbing."

"The political attack dogs have fired up the base of a certain party into a frenzy of illogic and cultlike worship. They're so focused on being against they've lost sight of anything else. Don't even pretend they're doing the people's business. There have always been groups with extreme viewpoints, but in the past, they stayed under their rocks and rotten logs. The current administration has emboldened them to come out into the open to spread their brands of lies, hatred, and intolerance. They've become useful idiot soldiers in the attack on mainstream America."

"And at this point, we have no champion to gather around in our own defense."

"Generally speaking, that's true. It's another dire turn in this situation. Admittedly, there is plenty of alarm in many quarters, but taking difficult action against the most serious threat to our democracy in history seems to be too difficult to the few people who might be capable of leading the resistance."

"I assume that means you've looked for opposition leaders?"

"We have, and we are. There are younger politicians who've expressed some interest, but they're not factors on the national stage. Additionally, the current administration and their party have taken steps to gerrymander, suppress voters, cull voter rolls of opponents, and rig elections to guarantee they stay in power forever. It's appalling."

"I had no idea it could get so bad so rapidly."

"It can, and it has. People are already slipping across both the Canadian and Mexican borders. If that is allowed to continue, what's left in this country will be a poison society full of bullies, bigots, and I suspect it will resemble the old Soviet Union's society."

"Well, none of us are okay with that, so we're in, no matter what's required of us."

"Good, Lily. We're counting on the capable people just like you that can make a difference before it's too late."

"Tomorrow, I'm going to take our Muslim friends to a local mosque for their prayers."

"As I said, that shouldn't be a problem. We won't be here that long, so a one-time visit won't draw a response."

"Thanks. Actually, the rest of us might like to attend services with our own churches too."

"Understandable. Getting our spiritual lives in order before everything breaks loose is a logical move. If this ends up being a coup, it will not be bloodless. We could take some hits on our side."

"We were so lucky we haven't lost people already. Those operations in Asia and Africa were dicey. They nearly went south. Turning an enemy into an ally in Somalia was a huge gamble on my part. Honestly, I didn't think it would work. I expected them to shoot first and talk later."

"Thankfully, it did. You having that savvy to know when to roll the dice is part of why you're such a highly renowned operator. You wondered why you were at the top of their hit list. They fear you the most, Lily."

"I'd gladly forgo that renown."

A group had gathered around, listening to the conversation. They all laughed.

Donna gave Lily a playful shove. "You were born for this life. Accept it and let's move on."

After a cramped night of sleep for the group, Lily and Patty drove cars to take the Muslim members to the mosque for prayers. Including some haircuts, they'd done what they could to make them look less foreign; however, that wasn't much.

Driving to a small shopping plaza in the interim, the two women stocked up on some supplies for themselves and the other women in the group. When they picked up the men after prayers, those men were in significantly better moods.

"Thank you for this," said Abdul. "Being with you for this extended time, we're learning much about you. Honestly, at home we tend to see Westerners as opponents, but your genuine decency and compassion moves us all. I can say, we are all your true friends now, and we'll follow you into any battle that is required. I hope you can move past your initial distrust because we're ISI agents."

"We trust you, Abdul, and you also Mohamed." They chuckled.

"Thank you so much," Mohamed replied facetiously.

As per the plan, most of those gathered in Dearborn prepared to drive north into the upper peninsula of Michigan. Traveling separately so as not to draw attention, the migration went to the site of the remote cabins for the next leg of the journey. There were considerable allies assembled there waiting for their arrival. There were also considerable military supplies including heavier weaponry and ammo.

The team toured the cache and smiled, joking with each other.

"Bring it on," Joe boasted. Andy picked up and caressed a .50 cal lovingly, like it was a long-lost child of his. Joe was holding a minigun.

Meanwhile, the leaders sat down in a cabin for a strategy session. Before they started, another tier one operator group arrived. It was a joyful reunion of friends. Lily went out to greet them.

"Lily, you're still alive. There was a rumor that you guys were taken down in Somalia." Susan Schmit was a close friend.

"That story probably helped keep us staying alive. I stayed off the phone there, so when the bad guys called, we had a Somalian ally answer, as if I was dusted off."

"Smart thinking, ma'am. We were actually confronted in country. We were at Fort Riley, Kansas, at the time out on a practice training session for a supposed upcoming mission. There was supposed to be a fake ambush, but suddenly they open up with live ammo. We had to be nimble to avoid that trap. Somebody was really angry we dodged the bullet. They tried to say it was a horrible mistake, but we could read the writing on the wall and instantly 'disappeared' the team. We also sent words of warning to as many other teams as we could reach."

"Unbelievable. I would have never thought in a million years we could come under attack in our own country by our own government forces."

"Amen to that, Lily. So what's next?"

"We were about to start a meeting to talk about that very thing. Why don't you join us?"

"I will. Thank you."

The leadership barely started the meeting before another elite team arrived to join the growing force opposing the national conspiracy. After the usual joyful greetings, new leaders joined the meeting. Dave Johnson spoke to the assembled leadership.

"We suffered our own ambushes during a mission in the Middle East. Unfortunately, we took casualties. I lost five people, friends I knew from basic training. However, we gave those bastards a beating before they ran away. Although we're lucky to have survived at all, it put a fire in our bellies for revenge. Being in the front line of whatever we choose to do as a group is where we want to be. Our comrades deserve that. I'm sure all of you understand that."

It was a sobering statement. None in the room were unaffected by it. Equally, there were none of them who weren't similarly motivated by the story, actually to the point of being provoked to rage. In this communion of the heroic, loss was particularly painful given the egregious circumstances they all faced. For all, putting the families of our bravest into the crosshairs was intolerable.

Subsequently the meeting became little more than tersely discussing details. No grand new plan emerged. This was the type of group who needed to be doing something about it.

What they did decide was some groups would travel west to turn north along Lake Michigan. Others would go the opposite direction to Lake Huron and then turn north, while others would travel northward through the center of the Lower Peninsula.

A small contingent stayed behind to direct any new arrivals to new destinations. Everybody now had sufficient equipment and materials to act as an impromptu army on the move. Not the least of which were the abilities to communicate over secure lines. Solving the need for command and control was critical to their long-term survival chances.

Increasingly, more current Pentagon personnel as well as members of the various security services found their way flooding into the Dearborn gathering spot. They brought invaluable equipment needed to establish separate command centers capable of countering the infected agencies. It was astounding how many and how high ranking were many of the deserters.

Although a hidden network of opposition to the existing government and their lackeys developed initially in the UP, the migration across the Canadian border started immediately. A similar movement happened as forces traveled south into Mexico. In both cases, they crossed along the entire distance of the borders.

Meanwhile federal officials continued their search and pursuit of the escaping skilled people. Increasingly, jobs were no longer being filled only by Russians. Some Turks, Chinese, North Koreans, Iranians, and other nationalities were appearing. Wherever there were autocratic regimes, they were joining the anti-USA cabal.

As anticipated, former American allies had begun severing ties with the USA and forming their own protective unions. It was an explosive situation, and across-border incidents were escalating all over the world. Immigration was nearly nonexistent. America was no longer the shining beacon on the hill and no longer a destination of choice. Actually, the flood of immigrants was leaving the country. It was quickly becoming too dangerous to risk staying behind. Canada and Mexico in particular had formed a defense pact minus the USA.

It was a huge danger that so many of the world's weapons of mass destruction were now controlled by leaders without a conscience.

Strangely, a consequence of the redefining of the world order was Mexico realized they needed massive and radical changes to compete. All the drug cartel leaders were brought in to the capital city and given an ultimatum. All their considerable illicit cash reserves were forfeit to the state, and their foot soldiers were conscripted into the national police and army. Henceforth none of their criminal activities would be tolerated, punishable by immediate death on the spot. Indigents and the poor were rounded up to join the expanding military forces. Particularly with arriving massive US naval and air forces, they exploded onto the scene, cruising into harbors of former allies to add their might and considerable numbers to resistance of the attempt at worldwide takeover.

It happened so rapidly the occupying foreign overlords had no warning or chance to stop it. Virtually overnight, the USA armed forces were gutted, no longer available to what was proving to be the puppet regime in Washington, DC. Not only were vast numbers of weapons and vessels simply gone, the nuclear weapons systems were frozen with complex viral attacks and sabotage. The new overseers had no familiarity to even know where to start in unraveling the attack. Entire naval fleets cruised into the harbors of former allies to add muscle to the effort to deter worldwide takeover. Remote sites were quickly established to operate drones staffed with recent arrivals from the United States. No trained drone pilots opted to stay behind at their former posts. Additionally, nearly all the drones suddenly departed US bases to land out of country. It was a remarkable instantaneous feat of coordination all across the country.

What remained behind, as roads were choked with traffic of civilians driving to borders either north or south, were the avid proponents of the current regime. Those persons with particular points of view and intolerance toward any person who looked different and didn't share their views. Reveling at first with the departures of perceived opponents, short sighted by nature, intellectually limited, they didn't foresee the obvious future. Their "dear leader" assured them all was well and the nation had never been better. It was appalling and insipid all at the same time.

As huge segments of US citizenry left the country, neo-Nazi tiki-torch rallies sprung up, open KKK gatherings, Aryan brotherhoods, skinheads, assorted militias, white supremacists, and many other groups from the underbelly of society, including conspiracy theorist groups. They felt empowered and emboldened to come out into the daylight to perpetuate their extreme credos and practices. The world of their dreams was now at hand, but their total acceptance and ideal society wasn't what happened. Even amongst each other, conflicts happened quickly over the diminishing food supplies and other resources. The economy broke down without workers on the job, farmers abandoning crops, no longer functional transportation systems, missing law enforcement officers to keep order, and banks could neither function nor protect assets as robberies soon were rampant. However, the thieves quickly found there was nowhere to spend the stolen money.

In response, Dear Leader instituted martial law, though it wasn't a tame and humane force that was sent to enforce his wishes. The new authorities patrolling the streets were infused with mostly foreign troops and led exclusively by foreign officers. Their mandate included shoot to kill if they deemed the need. Abuses and outrages against the remaining populace were ignored as "appropriate and necessary" under the circumstances. Speaking ill of the regime had severe consequences.

Enclaves of the poor, minority communities, and basically those unable to flee were forced to hunker down in defensive arrays against the onslaught of dire forces set free to do their worst. Pitch battles were soon to follow.

Lily watched in horror along with her unit members at the speed of the dissolution of America. The Canadian border had to be shut to keep those elements of discord from filtering into the expatriate communities.

CHAPTER 10

Lily was sitting with Gamal, Abdul, Donna, and Patty.

Abdul asked, "I realize this is not my country, but should we not do something?"

Donna replied, "What did you have in mind? What is it you think we could do here at this point?"

"Don't misunderstand me. I'm not talking as an ISI agent with a Middle Eastern slant. I'm appalled as a human being at what's happening before our eyes. The powerful in your society exploiting the weak is nothing new in human history, but this nightmare of yours spreading and happening on a worldwide scale alarms me. I'll grant you ISI had our own interests at the forefront in our planning, but the kind of world I see developing now frightens me. It would be a new world order straight from hell."

None disagreed, and none could think of an answer. He was correct, and they shared his feelings of fear. As if to support that chilling assessment, the march of events outside their camp took over the moment.

Patty walked over. "Everybody, gather around for some announcements."

Momentarily the enhanced collection of retirees, tier-one operators, technical specialists, support personnel, and recent deserters from government and military jobs assembled. The former agency head Janet Smith, she who'd been replaced by the commander in chief by a Russian-speaking toady, stood to speak.

"As I'm sure you all know to a great extent, our country is in trouble. What you don't know is to what extent. As we stand here, US ports on both coasts are receiving huge influxes of foreign troops from Asian and Middle Eastern countries as well as Russia. There is also a start of troops arriving from Cuba and some unfriendly South American countries. With the current administration gutting all of our national defenses, our enemies see a chance to change the world and direct history toward fascism and totalitarian domination. There have been so many citizens flee into Canada and Mexico, American commerce has come to a total standstill.

"Rushing foreign troops into the void, the president intends to impose martial law. I'm sure they intend to line them up along both national borders to keep any remaining people captive here. I'm told the foreign troops have been quick to assume control. Targeting minority enclaves was high on their list of mandates. Also, even amongst those fervent supporters of the White House, the ones at the rallies screaming chants and idiocy, they're discovering their imagined paradise is quite the opposite.

"The uber-rich assumed their obscene money piles isolated them from the fallout. Wrong! Money has become worthless. The president signed a decree nationalizing companies and funneling private accounts for use by the state. Of course, by the state, he means himself by lining his own pockets. Serious skirmishes quickly started in urban centers where the poor reside. They have various small-scale weapons, but nothing that can stand up to what's coming for them. These are foreign army units fully loaded and with no restraints. It won't be a fair fight, and the outcome is predetermined. Basically a form of ethnic cleansing.

"The underbelly of the country, the bigots, racists, and their ilk have seen the handwriting on the wall and tried to organize resistance. They aren't immune from subjugation by foreign armies. However, it's too little and too late for that. Dear Leader has abandoned them in favor of his foreign friends. The president signed a decree outlawing the other political party, stating they were an unconstitutional assemblage, treasonous, and criminal actors. They were among the masses that fled the country. Those remaining congressional members from his party have been rewarded with large cash bonuses, memberships at exclusive resorts, plush estates abandoned by rich citizens, and on and on. Women can no longer bring suit against men for sexual incidents. The president is basically creating his lewd fantasies as the future norm of his insane society. He's decreed that any female coming into the White House must wear 'attractive' dresses or skirts. Also, Dear Leader has established new enforcement tools. What amounts to basically secret police are busy at work patrolling the country, terrorizing any remaining occupants who didn't leave before it was too late. It's appalling." The assembled were stunned. No one made a sound at the chilling turn in US history unfolding before them.

Janet continued. "As you also know, the bulk of American military, air, and naval forces fled virtually in a single night. We left behind only the weak-minded and jaded sycophants, avid supporters of the regime. There are some weapons and assets remaining, but nothing to impede what we plan to do in response to this horror show. Similarly, we mucked up computer systems to the point they probably can never be reclaimed. American defenses are open to these foreign invaders, but they're also open to us. We've created a joint command and control network linking American, Canadian, and Mexican units. They're a formidable force. Our worry is the opposing countries deciding to strike now, possibly with their nuclear weapons."

The assembled muttered with outrage.

"Europe has separately begun mobilizing combined military forces. It is still a serious deterrent to totalitarian countries, even without us. The anomaly is in Britain. Only in England is there a contrary attempt trying to support the current corrupt American regime. However, Wales, Scotland, and the Irelands are favoring NATO. I think the right-wingers in England are losing all support rapidly as this situation develops and deteriorates. They were already in deep trouble because the Brexit move didn't pan out as they had purported. Their idea of them dictating to Europe and the rest of the world in commerce and all other things was never going to happen. The English economy dropped like a rock and left them alone on an island, literally. Starvation and privation don't sit well with the masses. There has also been an amount of societal decay as a cult of personality develops there too, not to the extent of the workings of Dear Leader here, but noisome enough to draw the ire of the citizenry. The issue is whether free and fair elections will be allowed. Right wingers there are following the lead of right wingers here. Now that they have the power, they're digging in to never give it up. Our version of Dear Leader certainly will never gracefully leave office. He feels safe now in declaring a dictatorship for life. Welcome to the banana republic of America."

Andy spoke. "There are some members in Congress that are veterans. I can't believe they would blithely go along with this. Some of the asinine things they say worshipping him are beyond believing."

Janet replied, "I can't disagree. I suspect they've realized the time to escape has passed them by, so protecting their positions is their only option, and that means kneeling down at his altar. It shocks me more that the religious right is still touting him as God's anointed in the world. His secret life of seamy encounters is no longer secret. He blatantly sees pretty young women right in the oval office now, and I think in many cases they aren't there for voluntarily visits. No one is left in Washington to oppose him."

A messenger came into the meeting and whispered to Janet.

"Okay, folks, everybody needs to head back to your cabins to pack up your gear. We need to be on the road in an hour. Enemy forces are heading our way, and even though we could wipe them out, I'm not ready for open war…yet."

Lily turned to see all the unit members gathering around her.

"I've got nothing more for you. Let's get ready to move. We'll take up the battle for America later. I would say stay frosty because I suspect we may see some action as we move. Whatever foreign troops are now the new border guards will be a barrier for us to deal with."

"I'm ready to bring the pain," Donna muttered.

That elicited a martial shout from the entire team, including the Muslim members as fervently as the Americans.

Later when they were loading up the vehicles, Janet walked amongst the troops, surveying the progress of the preparations.

Lily asked, "I think I speak for everybody in asking about our families. Working in the jobs we do, we understand the risks that come with the territory, but our families didn't sign up for it."

"There has been so much human movement. The new host countries need time to catalog them all. I suspect many of your families are safely across borders, but it will be a while before we can know who is where."

She looked over the grim looks in all the specialists eyeing her.

"I know you want to get into the fight and do something about this. Believe me, we're working 24-7 to create a workable action plan. You will be at the forefront of the action, and sooner than later."

Joe spoke. "I've heard aircraft from foreign air forces are landing at American air bases and have started flying across our country. I can't imagine it will be long before they start taking action."

"The USAF is still in play, guys. We already have drones in the air, so we're not defenseless. I'd say our opponents are the most vulnerable in that arena. They're in a new country for them without the use of the American weapon systems and defenses. We've got a big edge there. The Canadian and Mexican air forces beefed up with American aircraft and pilots are beyond formidable. They are rabid to right this wrong."

They heard the sound of many vehicles' doors slamming as the entire crew climbed into the transportation.

"Off we go," said Lily.

Driving out of the area, moving on little-used backwoods roads did little to mask the large convoy. However, it didn't matter as the opposition was already coming for them. The entire command kept their weapons at the ready.

After an hour of northward travel, a helicopter flew over them and pivoted to maintain a position above the convoy.

"They're calling in attack forces," Donna announced.

"No problem," Andy responded. "It's time to get this war started."

Patty spoke. "I think the border is close. There will be opposition troops there. Lock and load, folks, safeties off."

As they approached the border, enemy troops were arrayed to stop them, but it was obvious they'd just arrived and hadn't entrenched themselves.

Greatly outnumbered, the enemy troops opened fire but with small arms. Piling out of the vehicles, the allies deployed and returned considerable fire, including some miniguns.

Lily always felt anxious in the heat of battle, when bullets flew all around her. This fight was no different. When helicopters appeared in support of the enemy, her fears escalated. However, it was a short-lived fright as suddenly drones swept in from Canada, taking out the few helicopters and eliminating that threat from the air. The drones also strafed enemy ground forces, quickly tipping the scales for the allies. The expert marksmen on the allied side dropped enemy troops rapidly until they surrendered rather than be wiped out.

Approaching the kneeling troops, Lily noted this was an assortment of Asian and European troops with a few African contingents. They decided to take the commander, a Russian, to interrogate him later.

He was seated in the same vehicle with Lily. They'd taken one of his aides also. Lily listened closely as they talked, unaware she spoke Russian. The hushed conversation was interesting as they talked.

Lily made a point not to react or seemingly not to even pay any attention. Andy and Joe sat with weapons trained on the two, grim expressions on their faces.

Later, many miles into Canada, they stopped for a break and a quick meal.

Janet came over to Lily.

"What did they say?"

"The aide is very frightened. The officer told him to calm down. He told him they would study our camp, wherever we take them, and then escape to report back to their command center. One center is being set up in the area north of Detroit both to be near the Canadian border and to be close to their ethnic cleansing efforts in the cities. However, the aide remains terrified. Seeing Joe and Andy so dangerous and threatening rattled him badly. Also, watching their forces get mowed down at the border got both of their attention. The officer was stunned we didn't execute their troops that surrendered. Actually, he was contemptuous. Leaving troops alive to face us again was beyond his comprehension."

"From their viewpoint, it makes sense they would feel that way. Anything else of importance I should know about?"

"Not really. There were usual misogynist comments about women in our army. I didn't tell Donna because I know she would have taken quick action. She cuts no slack about that sort of thing."

"Good, we need to keep them in the dark as long as possible. Friendly forces will meet us here to guide us to a camp. We'll blindfold our guests so they have no idea where we go."

A flight of USAF fighters raced overhead heading south. Moments later, they heard explosions as the Air Force wings struck elements and positions of the enemy on US soil near the border.

"It's on," Lily remarked.

"It is indeed, and none too soon. Do you think they'll cross the border to attack us?"

"That would be a poor decision. We have a huge advantage. Even though they're constantly shipping in more foreign troops, we greatly outnumber them. Also, our skilled forces far exceed anything they can mount at this time. By shipping so many from their armies here, they leave their homelands vulnerable if we counterattacked there. This whole plan was risky at best for them and probably foolhardy. I think the ultimate odds are well in our favor."

"Good. I like that. I do wonder what it will be like after this is over."

"We pick up the pieces and start over. This time we can build in safeguards from this ever happening again."

"By the way, I think I heard the administration has started a youth corps for the remaining children back there, kind of like Hitler Youth. It turns my stomach."

"I try to imagine my kids exposed to that travesty, and it angers me to want revenge, even for the children of those toadies that stayed behind. Children don't choose their parents and are totally vulnerable to what adults put on them. I agree, it makes me sick too."

A messenger sought out Lily. "Ma'am, Janet wants leadership to come for a meeting."

"When is the meeting?"

"As soon as everybody can be gathered."

"Okay, I'm coming."

Shortly she joined the assembly, which at this point was a large contingent of military, intelligence, and security personnel.

Janet began, "We're going to start our actions reactively at first. There will be across-border incursions to disrupt enemy troops and camps. As they respond, I think they start to show their hand with what they're planning. We can then devise offensive moves of our own. I realize it hits many of you as wrong that we're not taking the initiative now, but we have our own vulnerabilities, so we've got to use caution and feel our way along. What's important is the outcome. This isn't a situation for mistakes. We bear the heavy burden of the fate of our way of life, and we are the last line of defense. I have total faith in your skills and training. Do your best at all times, work as teams, and protect each other. Any questions?"

There were no questions.

"Good, we're going to break up to meet by specialties. Some of you are going to be dispatched immediately, so get ready mentally for the new missions. We'll be striking within US borders."

Patty waved Lily over, which started the rest of the original unit moving too. Others of the operator units joined them. It was a sizeable group.

"Lily, you're going to be a strike captain for this first action. You'll be flown south all the way into Kansas. There's a central enemy encampment meant to be a regional hub for their operations. I believe that political prisoners are kept there too. Not everybody got out safely, and there are some important people we'd like to rescue and fly them here to safety. This will be a joint operation with southern command in Mexico. They'll also dispatch appropriately skilled assets. We're going to operate in force with this. Enemy aircraft have been landing at US air bases, but they're vulnerable. We'll send choppers to transport our forces supported by drones and fighter wings. Obviously, we're using the element of surprise. I don't think they expect us to strike so soon and so deeply into enemy held territory, especially at a perceived power center. Your mission is one of rescue, and you're authorized to use any level of force you deem necessary. What that means is if any American citizens, supporters of the regime, attack you, they're deemed enemy combatants and subject to a lethal response. Any questions about that? You may find that various special interest groups have organized into militias. In addition to those names you know, like the Klan, skinheads, Aryan brotherhood, neo-Nazis, and so forth, now you'll see the new Confederate army. They're even dressed in gray, the army of God, a radical religious offshoot to punish sins as they define them, which seems to be whatever they can dream up. It's really a mess and getting worse by the minute."

There was utter silence. The pronouncement meant there could be a new civil war in America, though this time foreign aided.

"I'm sorry about this, but from our perspective, we need to strike now before they're further entrenched in our country. Also, for the time being, Canadian and Mexican forces will remain in defense of their own countries. We'll be coordinating closely with both of their armed forces' chains of command. One other thing, the president ramrodded a new statute through his one-party rubber stamp legislature. He's now president for life. We should call it the Duma now since his instructions seem to come straight from Russia. It's also treason, subject to execution, if anybody disagrees with him. Some of his statements have been downright idiotic, off-message topics to the point of nonsensical. It would be farcical if not for the deadly consequences. We've got work to do, folks."

Angry, the troops simultaneously arose and went to gather their gear.

"My god," Patty muttered. "What will we be like coming out the end of this?"

Lily didn't reply.

Shortly, they gathered near the transport plane, the usual cast of characters. She greeted each as they filed past her. Wesley Bromwell was first. A very good-looking man, his stare and warm smile always let her know he'd never forgotten their brief intense college relationship. In truth, it was a pleasant memory for her too. Next came Donna Smith, now among her dearest friends. Her playful look tickled Lily in spite of this serious and dangerous mission. Donna was followed by the other SEALs, the muscular males Joe Gilson and Andy Reiger. Their glances were predictable, perusing her full torso. Macho was baked into their DNA. Their boss followed, Patty Baymill. All business, she nodded, distracted, as she pondered potential hazards ahead. She was followed by the Arab add-ons, ISI agents Mohamed Sheik and Abdul Hamma. They both acted less restrained in eyeing Lily, like their SEALs colleagues. Right behind them were Gamal and Hussain Bedoin. Their adoring smiles were broad, however more agog than seamy. Hassan Aboud from Egyptian intelligence and Ari Goldstein from Mossad were fast friends now. They acted polite toward her. Bringing up the rear were Lily's three CIA, colleagues Ron Gray, Steve Sawyer, and Grace Bailey. They all merely nodded.

When Lily walked onto the plane, Gamal looked at her hopefully, but she sat beside Patty.

"Patty, what are you fixating on?"

"It's just me. I don't like surprises, so I try to work out solutions for all possible contingencies."

"I do some of that myself."

"This action is predicated on catching them unprepared. I don't fully trust that theory. They don't need to be dug-in in order to be competent. We're a small force to go against a potentially large base. We can't be sure our target is there or where they might be."

"I agree. I feel we should strike if possible, but if the target is totally unviable, we use our heads. Rescuing somebody who may already be dead can make us dead too. I know they'd like us to take out a lot of the guards, but our best hope is getting them confused and firing at each other."

"That is what I'm worried about, all of the confusion. There are too many variables for my liking."

There was no wasted time in getting the plane into the air. Joining them once in the air, they were accompanied by a wing of USAF fighter craft. During the flight to middle America, the aircraft wings were not approached by enemy crafts, nor were there radar contacts.

It was after midnight when they were deposited in a farm field not far from the base of enemy operations. Quickly assembling, they set out a trot approaching the camp. It was dark with no guard towers erected yet. Formerly, this had been a series of government buildings, commandeered recently by regime forces, though most of the forces were foreign army troops.

Lily knelt down along with Patty, Donna, and Ari.

Patty whispered, "It's mighty quiet. Having no visible security worries me. Either they're totally incompetent, or they've set a trap."

Ari replied, "I think they've only started their fortification. I don't think they have any fear of locals causing trouble. Us moving against them from across the border isn't something they anticipate."

Lily added, "If this is a trap, let's spring it and get this party started. If they have political prisoners on site, they'll be glad to get out of here."

Patty nodded. "Let's split up and come from all four directions in small groups. Try to stay quiet as long as possible. We'll put one SEAL in each group."

"Agreed."

Lily took Gamal and Hussain. Her SEAL was Donna. They moved around to approach from the east. At the agreed-upon time, all four units cut through the wire. Cautiously slipping inside, they paused for a moment watching for movement. As it was a cloudy night, there was no moonlight to illuminate any dangers.

Lily hand-signaled her people into motion. Creeping to a large building directly in front of them, Donna took the lead to move to the door. It was locked. She'd brought a device to cut through glass. Cutting a circular piece of the glass out, she could reach inside to unlock the door. They crept in following a short hallway to an intersecting long hall. Looking to their right, they saw a light down the hall coming from a room, and they heard some voices.

"What language is that?" asked Hussain.

Lily answered, "It might be Chinese. I can't tell for sure."

Moving cautiously, they slunk down the hall. Their weapons had silencers, but if forced to fire, it might alert others whether in this building or nearby.

As they neared the doorway, they heard a television. The dialogue was in English. Donna was first to spring into the office. The startled guards, two of them, were disarmed quickly and tied up.

"Do you speak English?" Lily asked.

"Yes."

"Are you Chinese?"

"North Korean."

"Where are your prisoners?"

The two looked at each other uncertainly.

Donna spoke. "We can do this the easy way or the hard way." She pulled out a knife.

"Second floor," one of them replied.

"Don't do something stupid or we will hurt you." Donna put her knife to the man's throat. He nodded fearfully.

Leaving the men tied and gagged, the four allies hurried up the stairs to start a room-by-room search. In what had been a conference room, they found seven people trying to sleep on the floor. The two men were in poor shape from beatings, and the five women weren't fully dressed. They hadn't been provided with blankets, so they were huddled together to try to share warmth. They awoke with a start as Donna and Lily shook them awake.

"Be silent, folks. We're US military here to rescue you," Lily explained. "Ladies, where are your clothes?"

A blond-haired woman replied. "I think back at the commander's office. That's not in this building."

"Are there other prisoners?"

"There were more of us brought here, but we're kept apart. I don't know how they are or where they are."

"How long have you been here? Are you from this area?"

"It's hard to keep track of time. My guess is possibly six months? We were brought here in covered military trucks. It took weeks of driving. Most of us are from the East Coast area. The women worked in Washington, DC. Where are you coming from?"

"Canada. My understanding is when we had the big migration, half the people went to Mexico and the rest came to Canada. Were they questioning you about something in particular? Why did they put you here?"

"Initially they asked us some questions, but it was always about how and where to find important people. Because we're seen as opponents of the regime, that is the main reason we're here."

"What's with…"

"Taking our outer clothes. I think to keep us from being able to escape, a humiliation factor as punishment for our views and support and trying to beat down our spirits. Lying on this hard and cold floor takes a toll, believe me."

"I'm sorry. The landing zone isn't far, so we're going to get you out of here. How is it you didn't leave with everybody else?"

"We worked for two senators that stayed to try to reason with the administration. That was a bad choice. We were soon isolated and vulnerable. They took us easily. I worry about my family. I don't know what happened to them."

"Are your senators here somewhere?"

"I don't know. They weren't on our truck, so I don't know where they went or if they're still back in Washington. The administration wanted some scapegoats and sacrificial lambs."

"We've got intel there are key people here. We have other units searching other parts of this complex. If they're here, we'll find them."

Returning down the stairs, they searched the rooms on the lower level. The women's clothing was in one of those rooms. Once the five ladies could dress, they smiled.

"I feel human again. What now?"

"We get you out of here."

Cautiously exiting the building, they moved toward the hole in the fence. Hurrying the freed captives beyond the fence, the troop moved them to the extraction point. At that point, it was only an hour since the incursion had begun.

Sitting together in a small stand of trees, they waited until a second of the teams arrived with more captives in tow. Wesley was in this group. He went straight to Lily.

"I'm glad you're unscathed. We had a tester moment. The guards were Asian and tried to fight us. We had to take them out as they wouldn't surrender. Fortunately, it didn't require using weapons. Our CIA agents fought them hand-to-hand. We freed ten souls, but not the prime characters we're looking for."

"That sounds like what we encountered. We surprised some North Korean guards, so we didn't need to kill them. Did you find the women in their underclothes?"

"As a matter of fact, we did. I didn't ask about…well, you know. If that happened, I wasn't going to embarrass them. They can discuss it with professionals at the debrief."

The next arriving group had a larger group of captives. Patty Baymill led this team. She had facial injuries, and others in the team had bandages from wounds.

Patty spoke to Lily and Donna. "We entered one of the larger buildings after we found several smaller buildings empty. The element of surprise helped to an extent as there was a large guard contingent. We overpowered the night guards, but that involved some weapons discharges. The sleeping soldiers awoke and tried to mount a defense. Their weapons weren't in the sleeping area, so we had the advantage. Even with that, it was a difficult engagement. Once the officers went down, the troops surrendered. Then we could search for any captives. As you can see, we found over fifty people. They were in pretty rough shape. The women…"

"Were the women partially clad?"

"Is that what you found too?"

"Yeah, these guards are a bunch of pervs."

"Listen, as we exited, I heard sounds of action going on with our fourth group."

"Do you want to go back in after them?"

"I'm leaning that way."

"Okay, we can leave a few people here to guard them. The choppers should be here very soon."

Patty and Lily gathered teams and they raced back to the base. The sounds of fighting led them straight to the fourth team. Racing inside their building, they were hard-pressed in a firefight, outnumbered and in trouble. The appearance of reinforcements changed the sure defeat into a battle turning in their favor. Miniguns were a huge equalizer as Andy and Joe sprayed the enemy positions. As enemy troops dropped, the resistance faltered, and soon the allies were able to conquer the foe.

Moving quickly through the building, they found the remaining captives huddled together in fear. At last, they found the one US senator at that site. She was not injured in the fight but was in poor shape from the abusive captors. Again, it was necessary to locate the clothing of the women before they could leave the base.

By the time they got to the rally point, the choppers had landed. Loading the civilians first for the flight to safety, the allied troops formed a defensive perimeter to guard against potential enemy reinforcements. Eventually everybody was in the air flying northward. It was comforting to see fighter jets cruise in from above to protect them.

As they neared the Canadian border, two enemy MIGs approached behind them; however, they were two against twenty USAF fighters, so they turned aside quickly. Once into Canadian air space, the passengers visibly relaxed. Landing soon afterward, the grateful freed captives walked to waiting trucks, which took them to a nearby camp for American refugees.

The military personnel went straight to a debriefing about the operation and their observances and impressions. It seemed a miracle there had been no allied casualties, only bumps, bruises, and minor cuts.

Patty and Lily took the lead in answering questions. The commandant, a Canadian colonel, spoke.

"You did well. What did you find down there?"

Lily answered, "They were poorly prepared. It seemed like they had just arrived, but the prisoners said they were there for many months, at least six. The guards we saw were Asian, possibly North Korean. The only pursuit after we took off were two MIGs late. They were outnumbered and broke off near the border. My thought is we had a one-time easy win. I'll guarantee word will spread fast, and they'll shore things up in the future."

"I agree with that." He turned his head toward Patty.

She added, "They seemed to treat the prisoners differently, by sex. The men got the crap beat out of them, poorly fed, and kept in poor shape, while the women were kept in their underclothes. We didn't ask about the obvious, but probably there was abuse involved. The administration has been getting markedly worse by the day with women's treatment. Humiliating and debasing the women definitely would fit into the misogynistic and inhumane nature of those vile leaders. I understand abortions are now a capital offense. Women are now guilty for being raped, while the rapists have no consequences. I wonder what the avid evangelical supporters of this administration think now? The mantra they bought was an administration for the people. They've discovered that actually it's the people for use by the administration, or I should say misuse."

Lily asked, "The senator we rescued, how is she? Was she able to provide any useful intel?"

"She's going to need time to recover. Not only was she subjected to the deprivation of food, she was also molested. We have counselors helping her. She appears to be the only female captive that was physically tortured at this base. For a bright, accomplished woman like her to go through this is appalling."

"I heard tell that now the White House is pondering quarantining women during their periods as it's now considered unseemly to menstruate. Apparently, we're supposed to be ashamed of our natural bodily functions. Dear Leader is losing his marbles, going farther off the deep end in a hurry."

"It wouldn't surprise me. He's made so many sneering remarks about women in the past. Nothing he says or does surprises me any longer. *Misogyny* is a word he doesn't understand but is proud of nonetheless."

The ladies chuckled.

"It may not surprise you that he's brought in Saudi experts to guide him about the treatment and proper place of women in any society. No rights, no vote, no say in their lives, vassals at the whim of men, it's predictable from that crowd."

"It's just another step toward installing a completely totalitarian country. He really thinks they're insulated from consequences. I guess we'll find out if he's right. With the way the entire country has collapsed financially, I suspect it will be in a short duration for that answer to become crystal clear to the supporters of the regime. As I see it, about the only option they have is to go down in flames whether now or later, but that's just my opinion."

"I truly hope to do something about this…personally."

"I can't disagree."

The session took several hours as every unit member was questioned for their observations, impressions, and suggestions. It served as an emotional release as much as a strategy session for those in attendance. Afterward, they walked outside to find the unit members informally gathered.

"What's up, boss?" Wesley asked.

"A lot of questions," Lily replied. "With all of the intellectual resources we've devoted to the problem figuring what's behind the curtain, it's still a puzzle. I'd say even without knowing who's ultimately responsible, we've got our hands full with what and who we do know. I'm of the opinion the unknown bad guys used our own natural failings to build on top of it, a separate misguided national agenda. Why anybody would want total anarchy and the breakdown of any civilized society, I can't imagine. However, that seems to be an ongoing element in play."

Joe muttered, "My weapon is getting anxious to see some more action."

Everybody chuckled.

"No worries, Joe. I anticipate another mission in the very near future. I haven't heard that from anybody. It's just a gut feeling."

CHAPTER 11

As the unit walked out of the building after the meeting, Gamal made a beeline for Lily. Hussain was with him.

"Hi, Gamal, what's up?"

"Do you think we will have more of these excursions into enemy grounds?"

"Yes, of course. We don't intend to leave the USA to those deficit people to use as their playpen. Why do you ask?"

"I'm here because of you and only because of you. I wonder what my future will be. I'm not an American. I have no rights here. It's the same for Hussain."

"We won't let anything bad happen to you guys while you're here."

"I don't doubt your intentions. It's other people who have power that worry us. We're not men they want coming to America."

Donna spoke. "You'll always be welcome with us. It may be that we can get you into the military in some capacity. You've certainly proved your courage and your value."

"Is this true, Lily? Is it possible?"

"What I can say is we'll do everything possible to be sure you're taken care of. That can go in a lot of directions."

"I understand. If I'm sent back home now, I'll be seen as an American vassal. I think my outcome would not be good. My life there would be a short one."

Patty walked over.

"The president just pardoned everybody in the nation, so he's emptied out all jails. Those criminals are roaming around in packs terrorizing the populace that's still there. Anything goes in his 'perfect America.'"

Donna replied, "Wow, I guess there is no bottom to his warped-ass urges. He's sitting safe in the White House surrounded by Russian T-72 tanks and Kremlin soldiers along with a cabal of other foreign right-wing troops. He really intends to utterly destroy the USA. I think he aspires to get the Hero of the Soviet Union medal."

Patty continued, "There has been a new flood of refugees trying to cross the borders out of the USA. Now those folks that rejoiced in throwing us down are seeing the fruits of their labors. No food, no safety, no education for the kids who are in danger if they go outside, it's a living nightmare."

Lily asked, "Are they being allowed into Canada and Mexico?"

"There are huge crowds waiting back there stuck at both borders. The only advantage to them at this point is the criminals won't attack them within range of our border weapons and air cover. The foreign troops assigned to the border have backed way off. We show no mercy to their depredations. We're even providing food to feed the refugees across the border. Isn't it ironic the bigots and supremacists that tormented refugees are now in that same category seeking handouts from the same people they hassled?"

"It is ironic. Maybe, in a way, it's justice being served. What goes around comes around, even for the powerful."

"Amen, sister."

A caravan of vehicles entered the compound bearing Canadian flags and decals. Parking at the headquarters building, a number of military officers and civilian officials went into the building. Lily and Patty headed that way out of curiosity.

Lily commented, "I could be wrong, but I think the Canadian Prime minister was among those civilians."

"I wonder why she'd be here? We're not exactly the center of transplanted US power."

"I don't know."

Guards were stationed at the doors. Lily walked up. "Hi, John, what's going on?"

"We got a call from them about an impromptu meeting. I don't know what it's concerning. Our brass is in there, so I guess we'll find out once they're done."

"I can't imagine it would be about good news."

"I can't disagree."

John paused a moment, listening to his earpiece.

"Ladies, I just got word to send you in to this meeting."

"Okay." Lily looked at Patty before they entered the building and went to join the discussions.

Canadian soldiers were at the door. They saluted Patty.

Walking into the room, all eyes turned toward them. Lily felt self-conscious.

The prime minister spoke. "Welcome, ladies. Thank you for coming on short notice. We'd like to discuss a matter with you. Recently, our joint forces have been monitoring events in the USA, but in addition to that, we're also trying to watch developments around the globe. There have been some disturbing events that are confusing and I'd say very dangerous, like uprisings in unexpected places, Muslim populations in both China and Russia that have struck at government facilities and forces. These are significant enough strikes to cause casualties and damages far beyond what we could have expected from those sources. We'd been going on the assumption that Russia and China were spearheading this invasion of the USA, but apparently these is another player, or players, out there also taking action. All of our suspicions about the current American administration being puppets of that plot could still be true, but what this latest change means going forward, we can't say. Do you feel confident in your ISI men that we can get believable information from them to help understand the full situation and to help plan our next steps?"

Patty and Lily looked at each other. Patty spoke. "We've spent considerable time with them both in combat and then fleeing for our lives across the globe later without any problems. Where their ultimate loyalties lie, I can only guess. What do you say, Lily?"

"I agree. I don't want to give a blanket statement clearing them as a possible threat, but I agree they've been trustworthy and useful so far within our unit. If they would know about Muslim developments now, with having been away with us for such a time period, I wonder."

"That makes sense... However, I feel it's worth talking with them. I would like for you to sit in on that discussion to ascertain the truth and value of any facts they provide. We need good intel."

"Certainly, ma'am. We'd be happy to help."

"Thank you. We have a few things to discuss beforehand, but perhaps you can come back with them in an hour?"

Lily replied, "Can I suggest bringing along Gamal? He's been a great help for me gauging things involving Muslims. I realize he's young, but he I would trust implicitly. His judgment always seems to be spot on."

"That's fine. We'll see you back here shortly."

Walking away, Patty and Lily were silent for a time before speaking.

Patty asked, "Do you have any thoughts about this latest development?'

"I feel like the PM does. We need more information to be able to make intelligent choices. I would trust Gamal, but he came from a village as a young man. He would have no high-level source of information to give us. Our ISI friends might know more, but it could be the attacks from the Muslim forces are a late development they have no knowledge about."

"I guess we'll find out."

Entering their quarters, Donna had convened all the unit members.

"I figured you would have things to tell us," she advised. She nodded to Patty.

"You're right, Donna," Patty answered. "I want to let you know what we were told. There have been attacks by Muslim military forces in a number of places, including China and Russia. I believe they aren't necessarily State sponsored troops, rather more like insurgents. These are significant attacks, which would seem to say they have powerful backers. Going against those two countries takes much more than built-up rage against oppressors. It takes resources and an understanding there will be ongoing support from those background sponsors. Lily?"

"We'd like to ask our Muslim members if you can provide any insight to help us make some decisions? We realize you've been out of that theatre serving with us, but perhaps you got some inkling of plans before you left?"

Gamal spoke. "I know nothing. I would never have heard about such things in my small village."

Hassan Aboud answered, "There were rumors of rumblings in the Arab world, but nothing concrete. There have always been rumors of Muslim uprisings. As you say, it has been much time since I was in our office though. Did you see anything in Mossad, Ari?"

"It's the same as with you. Rumors were too insubstantial for us to take any investigative actions."

Mohamed and Abdul shrugged their shoulders. "There were no plans of this type we were made aware of. Honestly, what was happening in the tribal areas isn't always clear. If there were people plotting these kinds of large-scale attacks, we don't know. It's curious who would back such ventures against major powers? There seems far too much risk for open confrontations. Who would have the resources needed to abuse major powers?"

"To answer that question, we've only got speculation and hypothesis. I'd rule out this American administration for obvious reasons. They're hosting all the countries who are our prime enemies."

Gamal spoke. "I know I'm the youngest and the least qualified to speak, but perhaps there is a different player in this game. There are individuals of great wealth and power in the world. If they banded together for reasons I don't know, could they pull strings to make these contrary things happen?"

Lily smiled at him. "At this point, we can't afford to discount any possibility. Thank you, Gamal."

Gamal continued. "I've heard your Western adage, 'Everybody has a price.'"

"Sadly, that's true. If they could buy their way into the security services of countries…"

Patty commented, "There could be traitors on both sides of this situation. Information integrity would be questionable at best and possibly altogether worthless. It would explain a lot about how the enemy dogged us during our harrowing escape. What the motive was, I'm still unclear. There is so much we don't know, starting with trying to ascertain who are the players."

Ari and Hassan had been eavesdropping nearby. They both walked over.

Hassan spoke. "Don't misunderstand me when I say you Americans tend to work from your prejudices and preconceived notions. Although there is a threat from Muslims, we aren't the ultimate boogeyman. There are no Muslim entities capable of an attack on this scale. Working in coordination with someone else is a possibility, but no Muslim nation would perpetuate such actions with no chance of winning in the end. Do you see what I'm saying?"

Ari added. "Israel has a greater risk being surrounded by Muslim enemies, but the primary attack came here against America. When we first started this operation back in the Middle East, it jumped out at me that we were the target, this little unit. It made no sense. I think you're correct that there are other players in the background, powerful players. Even now, though there is considerable turmoil in the Middle East, Israel has experienced no attacks, and what fighting is happening is mostly the Shia versus Sunni rivalries."

Patty replied, "I can't disagree."

Lily spoke. "All of that is true, but it remains, what do we do? I don't think any of us can tolerate this situation any longer. A raid like that last one we did accomplished so little, was it worth it? Granted, we spared some folks having a bad time, but we need to accomplish much more than that, in my opinion."

Patty replied, "I think higher-ups are trying to formulate a grand strategy, however, there are so many unanswered questions it's not a simple solution. We have a great deal of power with the migration across the border of the bulk of US armed forces, but making an all-out assault on our homeland doesn't make sense to me at this point. We can cause a great deal of damage, but to what end? Do any of us want to see our personal homes flattened?"

Wesley joined the conversation. "What's apparent to me is there is no going back after what's happened. Those people who tied themselves to this administration sold their souls. Even with the corruption and the treason, they will stubbornly defend their side into their graves. It isn't just in the USA. That schism has developed in all of the Western countries. People in my hometown in England are telling me very disturbing things. The evil in people is being energized and emboldened. Families are staying indoors because the people out on the street may look to take advantage of the weak and the innocent. Crimes of opportunity. It's a dark time."

Lily spoke. "I want to say that's above my pay grade, which is passing the buck and the responsibility up the chain, but I can't be naive. I think we all need to contribute in whatever way we can. Giving our ideas can strike a spark, possibly."

Andy and Joe wandered over and smiled at Lily. She eyed them curiously.

Andy answered her last comment. "Ideas are fine, but Joe and I prefer the hammer when it comes to facing any foes."

That evoked laughter across the entire room.

Donna replied, "Monkey see, monkey do." It caused longer and louder laughter.

Lily glanced at Patty, their boss. She was laughing the loudest of all. Neither Joe nor Andy was fazed by being the butt of the joke from their teammates. Rather, they continued to eye Lily appreciatively. Being superb physical specimens and good-looking guys, it did cause her to react enough she turned her face away. After all, it had been a very long time since she'd been home with her husband.

With turning her head, she saw Gamal nearby observing the exchange. He had a pinched expression of jealousy. There were elements of human emotions she hadn't banked on in play here.

Donna noticed it all and leaned over to her. "Are these knuckle-draggers bothering you?"

"No, of course not. It's an unusual situation. Pent-up emotions are understandable."

"Are you talking about your emotions? They seemed to get to you this time. I've not seen that before."

"It doesn't bother me."

"Right, I saw your face flush red. Are there—"

"Donna, let's drop this. What I noticed more was Gamal. He looked to be jealous. That struck me as odd."

"Does that surprise you? Everybody knows he worships you. He's a young, impressionable dude. You're the fantasy of his life at this point, probably his first love."

Lily shook her head with a wry smile. "If that's true, it's the last thing I need. We've got real problems to deal with. Let's talk about that instead of silly things."

"Okay, but understand, who you are evokes people, a lot of people. Do you think Sheik Rahman focuses on you for some ideological thing? Don't you remember the African dictator who fixated on that past woman US Secretary of State, Rice was her last name, I think? He had all sorts of photos of her. It's out there. You have no idea what's going on inside somebody's head."

Lily could think of no response.

"Lily, you've got to factor in these weird possibilities."

A messenger came over to Lily.

"Ma'am, you need to gather your unit. You're being dispatched back south of the border again. Please come with me to the command room to get the intel and your orders."

"Lead the way." She gestured to Patty as they passed by. Patty joined them.

"What's up, Lily?"

"Apparently we're going to hear new intel and to get orders on a new mission."

"Do you know where we're going?"

"I don't."

"Having a mission this quickly concerns me. Although I'm curious what intel they got, you know me, Lily. I like planning everything down to the tee. If this is a hurried, ill-conceived plan, I will have something to say."

"Good, I agree with you. We'll find out soon enough."

Arriving back at the headquarters building, they walked inside. Considerable officers were already present, both American and Canadian. More people filed in until the room was full to near overflowing. Lily and Patty sat down in the middle of a row as most seats were already taken.

A Canadian general stepped to the podium.

"Thank you all for coming again on such short notice. We're getting intel suddenly and rapidly. The PM has left for other engagements, but she left me with her instructions. A joint Canadian and US computer team monitoring the web has found what could be a focal point for these messages that we haven't deciphered. It's in the central USA in your state of Missouri. What or who is there, if they're guarded, if they're the head of the snake, we'll need to determine that on-site. I realize it is incredibly dangerous, especially with foreign troops being on alert after our prior raid. I'll allow anybody who wants to bow out to do so with no recriminations."

None in attendance said a word.

"Okay…Lily, I realize we're putting a lot on your team, but you're as competent and prepared a unit as we have. What do you say?"

"We'll do it, sir. Does anybody want out?"

Her unit members chuckled.

"There's your answer, sir."

"Good, we'll get you set up as soon as possible. Get some chow and get a little sleep. It will be a night departure."

"Yes, sir."

"By the way, we're going to have a number of units set up all across the border areas from the Atlantic to the Pacific ready to jump in as needed. However, you realize there would be a time element before they could come to your rescue. We don't feel we can send a massive force at this time. It may happen in the near future, but there are a great many unknowns."

"Understood, we'll handle the assignment, no matter what we find."

"I don't need to say be very careful, but I'm saying it anyway."

"Thank you, sir. Do we have any idea what their air asset situation is? That worries me more than anything on the ground at this point."

"There are elements of enemy air assets flying in to US air bases, but we still have a huge advantage in the skies. They can't divert major numbers of their air corps due to the troubles and attacks within their own borders. Thus far, China seems to be getting the worse of it. That is why you don't see any Chinese troops and planes. They kept them at home."

"Interesting."

"At any rate, I'll let you go. If we get any new intel, you'll be the first to know."

The unit members walked out of the meeting together, going back to the barracks before they went to the mess hall. For as serious was their near future, they were relaxed and somewhat buoyant. Truly, this very diverse group was as cohesive as a family with their difficult shared experiences.

Gamal looked at the glop a server placed on his tray.

He looked at Lily with concern. Whispering, he asked, "What is this?"

She chuckled. "I have no idea. Welcome to the US military food service."

Donna laughed out, standing behind Lily. "Don't worry, Gamal. You won't die from eating it. You may get some neurological issues, like a facial tic or something."

Gamal looked truly distressed.

"Donna, come on. He doesn't get your humor."

Donna continued to smirk and snicker.

They barely finished the meal before a messenger came looking for Lily and Patty.

"The general said they're moving up your departure time, you're leaving in two hours."

"What changed?"

"I don't know."

While the crew went to gather their gear, Lily headed for headquarters.

The young secretary smiled when she came in the office.

"Hello, ma'am. I see you got the message?"

"I did. I'm wondering what else I need to know?"

"I'm sorry the general had to leave. What little I know was there was some development where you're going. I think they plan to call you on your flight south to explain. By the way, you're going to be joined by two people on this mission. Johnston Beauregard and Jane Lucien. They're from the computer teams researching these hackers."

"Are they field trained?"

"Not to my knowledge. I believe the reason they're being included is if we find this person, we want to jump into their computer to access the data before it gets deleted."

"Do they know what to expect from a potential firefight?"

"Probably not."

"That's great. Who signed off on it?"

"I'm told it came from the top."

"Hmph."

"They'll meet you at the plane."

"That doesn't give me much time to ready them for the mission. I don't need them freezing up from fear in the middle of some dicey encounter."

"I'm sorry, I'm just the messenger."

Lily turned and walked away perturbed. When she returned to her unit, all faces looked at her scowling facial expression.

"Well, I was told we have two new members for this mission, Johnston Beauregard and Jane Lucien. They're computer people sent to analyze the computer if we catch this main hacker, and no, they're not field trained."

Joe spoke. "This has all the makings of a cluster——."

"No argument here. We'll need to get them up to speed during the flight."

Patty asked. "Have they ever parachuted?"

"I don't know, but I suspect not."

"Whose idea was this?"

"Unknown. Probably some genius."

Andy spoke. "Whoopie! I can hardly wait. If they break their ankles in the jump, I'll carry the girl. Joe can carry the guy."

Joe replied, "No way, I'll leave that honor for Donna."

Donna grimaced. "—— you, Joe."

Lily asked, "Is everybody packed up and ready to go?"

Joe replied, "You know we were born ready."

"Hoo-rah!"

Lily and Patty laughed. The non-SEALs had all joined in the macho shout, and that included the Muslim members. Gamal and Hussain had happy smiles.

Hussain shouted, "Hussain the SEAL!" Everyone laughed at that.

Gamal asked, "What is this word —— that you use?"

Lily replied, "Pay no attention, it's not a word you need know or use. Remember who's doing the talking with that."

Lily's phone rang. "This is Lily." She listened for a time before hanging up. "I was just advised the foreign troops patrolling around the country have been facing resistance from the criminal elements and also from the right-wing groups. As near as they can tell, it isn't USA nationalistic fervor. Rather, it is more like turf wars. Whether we'll land in the middle of something like that, I can't say. It won't be our job to take sides in a fight between those two opponents."

Wesley asked, "Do we trust the accuracy of this intel?"

"My opinion, a lot less than before this quantum shift in the world happened. Regardless, it's the task we've been given, so we do our best. We've made it through all our scrapes up to now."

Wesley added, "I don't feel reassured."

"Duly noted. Gather up, folks, and let's head over to the plane."

Walking slowly together to the airfield, as they approached the assigned plane, they saw the two new members waiting. Johnston was a tall, gangly, nerdish-looking man with large round glasses. Jane was short, petite, attractive, but very young looking. Her long brown hair hung free.

Steve Sawyer muttered, "I guess the high school reunion party is over."

"Quiet," Lily whispered as they approached.

Jane smiled broadly. She took a step up to Lily. "I know I look young. I'm actually twenty-two. I graduated early from Harvard. Johnston graduated from Texas."

"Welcome. Can you tell us what training you've had, if any?"

"It happens both of us have jumped from aircraft, if that helps."

"It does, although this will be your first time landing in a combat zone."

"We're open to whatever orders you have for us."

"Okay, we'll talk on the flight. We'd like to know more about where we're going, what is leading us there, and what to expect?"

Jane looked at Johnston.

"I hope I can explain this properly. Johnston and I have narrowed in on a location in Missouri. Whoever is there is very skillful at covering their tracks, but we're very skillful too. To an extent, I guess you could say we're speculating, but in our business, certainty is very fleeting. This is basically our best guess. As far as what is there, like guards, I would expect there will be. This person has managed to amass a worldwide movement and potentially has vast assets accumulated both in money and men. I'm talking about assets like on the scale of a nation."

"Good to know. When you say a worldwide movement, I don't understand how people can get behind such a negative plan. Destroying civilized societies makes no sense. How can they believe lawlessness is a good thing?"

"I agree it makes no sense, but there is a resonance amongst disenfranchised groups along with the ever-present anarchists that has gained momentum. They're so busy being against, they really never consider what to be for. I do think those people who chose to stay behind have gotten a strong dose of reality. Crime is running rampant in the open and is basically unchecked. The foreign soldiers have no interest or incentive to keep the peace and protect the people. They're often the prime instigators of evil."

They started to file onto the plane. As always, the equipment was already loaded.

Patty and Lily flanked the two computer specialists as they took seats.

Jane sat between Lily and Johnston. She leaned around him to talk to Patty.

"So you're a SEAL?"

"I am."

"That's very impressive to me. I don't think of women as SEALs."

"It's not an easy path and not meant for everybody. Women can do anything if we're given the chance."

"I like that. I didn't really think of it that way. Maybe I should expand my aspirations."

"Find what you're good at and what you love and put everything into it."

"I will."

Lily commented, "You may already be in your area of strength. Finding your sweet spot within it might be your test."

"I do like computers. That's very true, and I do get a lot of pleasure when I unravel the schemes of an opponent. They really do think they're the only smart people around. They're wrong." She laughed; Lily smiled.

"Lily, so you're married? Is that a problem with what you do?"

"It's a situation that can be challenging, and it takes a lot of managing. I'm lucky I've got a great husband and two super kids. Being separated like this is…awful. I'm not sure where they are right now."

"I'm sure they're safe somewhere here in Canada. We got masses of people across the border before everything was shut down. However, there was such a massive glut of displaced humanity, it's been impossible to catalog them all promptly. The same is true down in Mexico. Speaking of Mexico, they've been remarkably magnanimous toward an American people that have been patently unfair to them over the centuries. You don't hear from them that Americans are murderers and rapists and the women are breeders and all that racist crap that we did."

"The American nation has plenty to feel ashamed about. It's depressing how shallow we've been. People allowed those mischaracterizations to flourish because that is how they want it to be. Racism is far more embedded in some people because they don't want to change. It's easy for the majority folks to write it off as stupid people at work, but ask minority folk what it's like to spend their lives in the gunsights trying to cope. Can you imagine having to tell your children the police aren't to be trusted? I can't."

Patty looked at Lily with a sad face.

"I'm sorry, Patty. I got off-message on a tangent."

"Lily, every one of us in this plane agrees with you."

"Back to this mission, Jane, we hope for a quick in and out, but our experience is if something can go wrong, it will. We'll protect you as best we can, but prepare yourself for some unpleasant surprises. If we find this person, you need to work really efficiently. For example, if you find on their computer some ongoing operation, you need to shut it down before they can accomplish their evil intentions. We can take their records and equipment away with us, but there could be ongoing assaults in progress that need to be addressed quickly. Do you understand?"

"Completely. I understand how serious the threat is. Remember, I've been studying and trying to unravel it from the start. If I can have a hand in pulling their plug, I'm all for it. Trust me when I say, Johnston and I are very good at what we do, possibly the best. We won't let you down."

"We trust you. I'm just trying to help you understand what's ahead. I doubt you've been in a combat situation before."

"That's true. We've always been safe, far away from the troubles. We're willing to do our part though. You guys have shouldered too much of the burden in the past. Sharing with you in taking chances, we need to pull our weight. I can't imagine what it was like for you on the run one step ahead of death in the Middle East and Africa. It frightens me even just thinking about it."

"It wasn't fun. Are you guys comfortable carrying sidearms? Have you fired a weapon before?"

"We both have, but I can't say I'm particularly proficient. The first time I fired a handgun, the recoil came back, and the gun popped me in the forehead. It hurt."

Lily and Patty chuckled, along with the others of the team within hearing range.

"Don't worry about it. Your weapon is only for emergencies to protect your life. We all had our own embarrassments at our beginnings too. We'll do the fighting."

"Thank you. We probably seem pretty lame to you guys."

"Not at all. None of us could do what you do with your computers. We're duly impressed with you. What you do is the most important step we can take to counter this dire threat to civilization."

"I hope it's not too late. Whomever is there, they have a long reach."

"At any rate, again, if we run into combat, don't get involved unless absolutely necessary. Things can happen quickly, and we can't have you blocking a shot we need to make in a hurry."

"We've got it, ma'am."

"You'll be fine. Trust us to protect you."

"We will."

Already the sky was dark as they cruised southward, gradually angling slightly southwest. There was no sign of enemy aircraft or ground antiaircraft fire.

Wesley eyed Lily. When he caught her attention, he smiled and flashed a thumbs-up sign. She smiled and nodded to him.

Her focus sharpened, as it always did, when she prepared mentally for an engagement.

Lily glanced at Jane, who was glassy eyed. The plane started to drop in altitude.

The pilot came on. "Ten minutes."

A red light came on, and the back hatch opened. The team stood. Lily felt Jane's hand touch her.

Looking back, she tried to reassure her. "You've jumped before. We'll be all around you. Just relax."

"Right." Now Jane looked rattled.

Patty was behind her. She patted her on the shoulder. "We've got you surrounded."

Jane tried to smile.

Walking to the opening in single files, they readied for the drop.

The red light blinked, and the members moved out. Lily leaped, and then Patty pushed Jane out and quickly followed her. She heard

Jane yelp. Fortunately, she had no trouble with her chute opening. After that, it was merely a matter of getting her onto the ground without breaking a leg. Johnston managed to drop successfully when they landed and gathered together to form up and begin the mission.

Although it was night, it was still very dangerous. Moving into a town even with so many people gone, there were still dogs to bark and late-night folk moving about. It wasn't 2:00 a.m. yet, so the bars weren't closed.

Slinking along in two columns, one on each side of the street, they headed for the address they'd been given. It was about half a mile they needed to trek without being detected. A car whirled around a street corner up ahead careening about, loud music blaring as the people in the car raced down the street, the last thing the team needed. Dropping down and back to avoid discovery, the car raced by, but the damage was down. Lights came on in several houses along the way, and some dogs started to bark.

Waiting for a short time, the teams slowly resumed their approach but very cautiously. Making best time was very difficult. They had to drop down again as a front door opened ahead, and a man stepped outside on his porch to look around. He had on a robe. Instead of going back in the house, he decided to smoke a cigarette.

It was nerve-racking being forced to wait. Lily pondered sending a man to take care of the issue but wisely waited it out. Eventually the man went back into his house, and the team resumed moving ahead.

On the left, they approached the address in question. This was an older neighborhood, and the modest wood-frame homes were not lavish by any stretch of the imagination.

Patty pulled up beside Lily as they knelt down, casing the house and those homes around it.

Patty whispered, "A good hideout for somebody looking to avoid attention. If they have vast resources, you'd never know it here. What are you thinking?"

"I can't get it out of my mind this could be a setup. If we tip our hand and strike, and they somehow leaked false intel, they might be able to identify our sources. Our felon could be in one of the surrounding houses or in a different state altogether. Something doesn't feel right to me."

"I hear you. You're right. This house could be one big booby trap."

CHAPTER 12

"We can't sit here all night. Let's go, but not with a full attack mode. We leave people watching all these other houses. I'd like to avoid a firefight if possible. No need for civilian casualties if we can avoid it."

"That may not be in the cards. If that target house is rigged, we activate whatever defenses they have here, and it may trigger reinforcements."

"Agreed. Our computer friends stay out of sight while we take care of business."

Lily signaled Donna, who crept up to her side. "We need to ferret out any traps. Will you, Joe, and Andy very carefully enter the target house and the houses on each side of it? We have no idea if there are hidden dangers, so be very careful."

"You've got it."

Lily and Patty watched nervously as their dear comrades slunk forward to take the initial risks.

Each approached a side door into the various houses. Carefully negotiating the door locks, they disappeared into the houses.

For a short time, the team waited outside, anxiously hoping for the best. It was the house to the left that Joe entered where suddenly an interior light came on, and they heard a muffled shot. Suddenly there were numerous shots.

Patty raced into the side door of that house followed by Ari, Ron, Wesley, and Steve. Lily was surrounded by Grace, Hassan,

Gamal, Mohamed, Abdul, and Hussain in case something developed in the other houses. The two computer nerds stayed hidden.

The weapons fire increased, which caused lights to come on in houses all along the block.

Lights came on in the suspect house as well as the other neighboring house. Fortunately, there was no gunfire there.

People started appearing on their porches, weapons in hand. Mostly it was hunting rifles and shotguns.

"What's going on?" one of the men shouted from down the street.

Ignoring the shout, Lily moved, followed by her team members, and went into the suspect house. They found nobody present and went down into the basement. Donna was there, eyeing a large computer array. Lights were blinking on the computers as they functioned on automatic.

She looked at Lily. "I don't know if this is what we're looking for."

Lily sent Ari outside to hustle in Jane and Johnston. They hurried to the computer system, eyeing it expertly.

Jane exclaimed, "The camera is on. This is a trap. Somebody somewhere else is watching us."

Jane started typing on the keyboard when suddenly, the screen blinked out and then was replaced by a skull-and-crossbones symbol and then the sound of laughter.

"Let's move, folks, get out of this house in a hurry."

They raced outside, barely avoiding the large explosion in the basement.

The gun battles next door ended in the meantime. There had been some thuggish rough-neck types living there. They were subdued to end the fight. None of them survived.

Joe had been wounded in the encounter along with Ron and Wesley. None of them were life-threatening injuries, fortunately.

Deploying in a defensive array as neighbors sprinted down the street brandishing their weapons, the man who'd initially shouted at them spoke.

"Who are you people? Why did you blow up that empty house?"

Lily decided to talk to him. "We're a special forces team sent here to check that house for a dangerous traitor."

"Special forces for who? Are you from Washington?"

"Not anymore we aren't."

"Do you mean you're part of the US military that fled across the border?"

"Exactly. We've been trying to piece together this plot that's ruined our nation."

"Honestly, I voted for that bastard in the White House, but with everything that's happened since, I deeply regret it. I wish I'd left with everybody else."

"It's never too late to be a patriot. Can you tell me about this house, who lived there?"

"Nobody, but there was plenty of traffic. We figured out pretty quickly it was a ruse. There has been a lot of riff-raff move into the town, and we get foreign troops come through town periodically. It's strange. We're such a backwater, there is nothing here of interest to them. We've lost most of our young people, so we have no future. I doubt we could get away now."

"We hope to do something about that in the near future. We just don't want foreign entities to become entrenched to the point where we need to invade our own soil."

"Well, God bless you. Is there anything we can do? We've had enough of this rotten life." The other neighbors voiced their agreement.

"I'll leave a sat phone with you so you can get current intel to us, if you're agreeable."

"Sure."

"I think the person we suspect is the mastermind for this whole scheme is alerted now we're onto them. I think there may be a force coming here to find us. We can't stick around to protect you, so if they come and question you, play dumb. You heard the shots and the explosion but were afraid to come outside. I wish we could take you with us, but it's not possible at this time."

"Good luck and stay ahead of them. We look forward to becoming Americans again."

"We will, and thank you."

The unit hustled out of town into a nearby forest. While the unit members' wounds were addressed, Lily contacted Canada.

"It was a trap. There was a computer network in the basement but operating on remote. An explosion was triggered when we tried to access it, but we were away before anybody got badly hurt. We took three injuries in a firefight next door but no casualties. It was hard to tell if they were guarding the house or if they were just some thugs we stumbled onto."

"Did you encounter trouble in the town?"

"Not really, the remaining residents came out, but when they found out we were US forces, they quickly sided with us. I left a sat phone with a guy, Jim Harker. He was a former soldier and regretted not leaving during the migration. He agreed to give us onsite intel."

"Good, Lily, that will be helpful."

"Meanwhile, our elusive bad guy now knows we're after him. Do we stay here or head to the pickup site?"

"I'll get back with you shortly. Stay out of sight. Since you're down there, we'll see if we can salvage the incursion."

"What are your thoughts about the intel we got? Do you think we may have been fed a line of crap to try to take us out again? Somebody has been hunting us all over the globe."

"We will definitely look long and hard at that issue." The unit waited until she ended the call.

Donna asked, "What now?"

"For the moment, we wait. If there is some other place we can go since we're here, they'll let us know."

"When you asked if this was nothing but a setup ambush, what did they say?"

"They'll look at where the intel came from. It's hard to say if it is the same person who's been on our tails all along. How are you, wounded guys?"

"We'll live," Joe replied. "However, I don't like the vibe here so far. It's bad karma."

"All we can do is use great caution. This wasn't going to be easy. Whatever current sources we have for intel seems to be unreliable or compromised. We can't assume the old comfort level with what info we got from the agency."

"We know that, but we don't have to like it."

Johnston and Jane stood mute, observing the exchange with worried looks.

Lily smiled at them. "Don't worry about our little chats. Sometimes in this line of work, you need to vent a little steam."

"No problem," Jane muttered. "I understand your concerns completely. We're a part of this too."

"Eat a ration pack. We'll get a little sleep while we wait."

"I'm not sleepy, I'll stay up and keep watch," Donna said.

"I'll join you," Patty added.

The other team members reclined to get some rest after a munch. It was dark, so sleep wasn't far away for them.

Lily awoke later at dawn. Donna and Patty had been replaced by Joe and Andy on guard duty.

Team members were slowly rising, maintaining total silence. There was no sound from the nearby town other than one car driving in. The car passed through and kept going.

Donna muttered, "No welcome reception team from our foes. Perhaps they don't get up this early. I'm kinda disappointed. Putting more of them down seems like a pretty good plan to me."

Lily replied, "I very much doubt we're done with any fights on this trip."

Patty commented, "It jumps out at me there have been no authorities coming out to investigate."

"That matches up with our intel most police departments left the country, and the foreign forces don't do any policing. I am surprised we haven't seen any patrols. I sort of feel sorry for those towns-folk. They should have left with everybody else."

"Choices have consequences. I know I need to get new material rather than saying the same things."

Lily's phone rang.

"This is Lily."

She listened for a considerable time and then hung up.

The unit members gathered close.

"They traced back on the intel, and it appears we were duped."

"Who is vetting this stuff?" Joe was irked.

"They're trying to go through Canadian sources now. Hopefully it will improve the data."

"What do we do in the meantime?"

"There's a site on the West Coast that might bear fruit."

"So…that means what?"

"They're working on it."

"Are we supposed to stay here and have a picnic?"

Patty interjected, "Don't take it out on Lily, Joe."

"Sorry, I didn't mean anything against you, Lily. We put our lives on the line for this sketchy intel? That's what I'm mad at."

Lily answered, "No problem, Joe. We all feel the same way. That experience in Asia and Africa got my attention. I'm glad they don't seem to be zeroed in on us now."

She looked at Jane and Johnston. "What are your thoughts?"

They glanced at each other. Jane replied, "This target person has got to be not only smart but plugged in, even with the massive disruptions in the government. Who would be looked at by both sides as being favorable and trustworthy?"

"That's an excellent question. None of us could know that, but I'm going to pass it on to command, and they can check into it. Thank you, Jane."

Lily made the call, talking at length with joint command. The unit listened closely.

"In summary, it's a great idea from Jane, but nobody here could provide an answer. It's way above our pay grades. You guys that set the grand strategies need to research who you call and who you trust with the most critical data. Who do you trust to guide you? Who did you trust? To pull off the most calamitous events in human history on a worldwide scale, I imagine that would be a small pool of candidates. Somewhere in the world, this person is laughing at us, and we've had enough."

She listened for a time.

"We'll be waiting here until you give instructions, but remember, we're very vulnerable if we're discovered here."

The next day, the town received the arrival of a large patrol of foreign soldiers.

Donna was with Lily, eyeing the troops.

"Lily, they look like possibly North Koreans. They act brutal enough, slapping around the townsfolk. What do we do?"

"We can't really go to their rescue. Tipping off the enemy of our whereabouts will not work. Right now, they'll assume we left the area."

"I'm worried if this mastermind is plugged in with our headquarters, he'll soon know we didn't return to base, and the big chase starts up again."

"I've got that same worry. I plan to stay here for the moment, and we certainly don't want to be out during the daylight."

"It makes me sick seeing enemy troops driving around in US Army vehicles on US soil. How could it get like this?"

"I wish I had an answer."

"Why don't I call back headquarters and yank some chains?"

Lily laughed. "That is not a good idea, Donna."

"It would help make me feel better."

"I'm sure, but we don't need to add to our troubles. Let's see what they come up with."

Watching the enemy troops in action in the town, they conducted lengthy searches of all the houses in the town before they left. One truck stayed behind, and the soldiers started a search of the surrounding areas.

Donna and Lily slipped back deeper into the trees. The unit members were tense watching them search, automatically deploying into defensive arrays.

Lily whispered to them, "We do our utmost not to engage. Only fire if there is no other way."

It became more tense as two soldiers came walking toward them. They were looking down for signs but chatted as if convinced nobody would be here to find.

They stopped short of entering the tree line to have a smoke, talking idly. Staring back at the town and their truck, finally, they went back, leaving the team in safety. Another near miss.

After the enemy truck pulled away, the team relaxed.

Wesley said, "I've had enough of these scares to last a lifetime." Everybody chuckled.

"Amen to that," Ari exclaimed.

Out of the blue, Gamal mentioned, "I like these food packets."

That brought another laugh.

Donna replied, "Gamal, if you think rations are tasty, you need a lot of reeducating."

Gamal looked at the smirking faces of his fellow team members, confused.

Hussain spoke. "Gamal, I like them too. These Westerners haven't starved enough in their rich lives to understand our perspective. Getting food at all is never a guarantee where we live."

"You've got a point," Lily reflected. "We should count our blessings better."

Her phone rang.

"This is Lily."

She listened intently for a time. "Yes, ma'am, I understand."

After hanging up, she looked at the faces of the team, her team, which at this point was like family.

"There is no definitive proof that site in the west is our target, but they want to try it anyway."

"So how do we get there?" Wesley asked.

"This area is crawling with enemy troops and patrols. We're going to borrow local transportation and drive out of here, at least far enough we can establish a new landing zone for pickup."

She eyed the uniformly skeptical looks.

"Listen, I know this is not a great plan, but there aren't any good options. We make do, like we always have."

Ari commented, "I think I can speak for everybody when I say, we're worried that our good luck can't last forever. One of these days…well, I don't look forward to it."

"I understand completely. I feel the same way, but we're here, and we play the cards that are dealt."

"So what's our play?" Joe asked.

"We head back into that town and start there. Maybe there are vehicles that will serve our purposes. A lot of people fled, so there could be plenty of vehicles left behind."

"Okay. Gear up. Let's go."

Creeping cautiously forward, they reentered the town and went to the home of the former soldier.

"Hey, guys, I thought you were long gone. What's up?"

"Hi, I'm glad you weren't harmed by the enemy troops. We couldn't rush to your rescue without betraying our position for obvious reasons."

"We understand. Playing dumb seems to work well with our guests from across the sea."

"We need vehicles to drive west."

"No problem, there are plenty still around here. I worked at a car dealer, so I can get codes to cut keys for you."

"That would be great. We need to be on the road ASAP."

"Let's go up to the Chevy dealer. This won't take long."

"Thank you for helping us."

"I'm still an American citizen and a patriot. We want our country back. God bless you guys for taking the fight to them."

An hour later, keys in hand for three vehicles, the team loaded up their equipment and set out westward. With a local map, they avoided settled areas as much as possible driving on back roads. Progress was slow, but it couldn't be avoided.

Getting toward the western part of Missouri, skirting Kansas City wasn't easy. It was the main metropolis for both Missouri and Kansas and like a funnel for roads in the area. Additionally, the prairie flatlands ahead provided far less cover for a convoy trying to avoid notice.

"Listen, everybody," Lily explained when they pulled off for a quick meal. "We're going to need spacing between us so it doesn't seem like we're traveling together. We stay within sight in case of trouble. Any questions?" The troop simply nodded their heads.

At that point when they resumed, Lily decided to enter the expressway for faster travel. Maintaining separation as a defense against being discovered was a risk. However, getting out of the area was more important at that point in time.

A column of enemy troops passed them going the other direction. They drove US Army trucks, but they flew the flags of their home countries.

Lily stared at the sight, her gut roiling with anger. "Bastards," she muttered.

Pulling into a rest area was another risk. They needed gas, but there were enemy troops moving about. Still dressed in uniforms, most stayed in the vehicle. Those unit members dressed in civilian clothing, like Ari and Hassan, Wesley, etc., pumped the gas, and then went inside to purchase some food and water.

There was an incident when a soldier started to question Hassan. He smiled and glibly handled the conversation. That soldier watched him purchase supplies and then walked outside. Hassan sat down with Ari on a bench and ate a quick snack, chatting idly. Eventually the soldier walked back into the building.

Quickly hustling to the vehicles, they pulled away back onto the expressway.

"Scary," Wesley muttered as he got back into Lily's vehicle.

"It was. I really don't want a firefight anywhere with civilians around if we can avoid it."

They checked the rearview mirrors; there was no sign of pursuit.

"Did we get away?" Gamal asked.

Lily smiled. "It seems that way."

Traveling for many hours, Lily's phone rang.

"Yes, ma'am," she answered.

After ending the call, Lily explained. "We have a new landing zone up ahead. It will be in Colorado just across the state line. We still have a considerable distance to drive, so settle back, maybe try to nap."

Gamal fell asleep almost immediately. Lily's mind was whirring with thoughts about the mission and what to expect. It took time to clear her mind and doze off. When she awoke later, Gamal had slumped over onto her shoulder in his sleep.

He awoke when she did.

"Oh, I'm so sorry. I…eh…"

"Gamal, it's not a problem. Don't worry about unimportant things."

"Really?"

"Really."

"In my country, it wouldn't be proper being close against you like this."

"This isn't your country. We've all been close together right from the start. It can't be helped in the field. As I said, don't waste time worrying about unimportant things. We've got our hands full with the mission."

"It seems to me you're more worried about it this time?"

"I don't like having so many unknowns. Being fully prepared is part of having successes."

"I understand. I'm learning so much from this time spent with you. I know I keep saying the same things, but it's true. Thank you again for including me."

"Thank you for what you contribute."

They pulled off at a rest area to use the facilities and have a quick meal before returning to the road. This time the building was clear of enemy troops.

Traffic in this new America was far less populated than had been previously before the collapse of society. Between having most people gone and the fear of the remaining dangerous people to take the risk of traveling, the team passed enemy columns often but thus far without any problems. This time, however, a curious pair of soldiers watched them leave the building heading back to the vehicles.

They walked over toward the vehicles. Lily hand signaled her troops to act calm and nonchalant. As the soldiers came close, Lily stepped up along with Patty.

She smiled as she spoke. "Hello, gentlemen. How are you today?"

"Who are you? Show us your papers to be traveling."

The team members casually moved to claim some weapons.

"Sure, our papers are in the trunk. Please come."

The enemy soldiers eyed the team nervously, staying on the sidewalk.

"Is there a problem?" Lily asked.

"You get the papers and bring them here."

"Certainly."

Walking to the back and reaching into the trunk, she took a pistol with a silencer. Stepping around the car, in a single movement, the soldiers were hit by shots from several directions while team members quickly grabbed them to drag them to the rear to be tossed into the vehicles. Looking around, it didn't appear anybody had seen the fight.

Driving away quickly, they traveled to the next exit, got off onto the side street, and drove a short distance to a wooded area to drop the bodies out of sight. Returning quickly to the expressway heading again toward the landing zone, they paid close attention to what was behind them.

Patty spoke. "It won't be long before somebody will realize they have missing soldiers."

"All we can do is get to our destination as quickly as we can."

"If they put assets in the air, I don't know that we'll make it."

Lily took out her phone and called Canada.

"Ma'am, we may be compromised. We were forced to take out two enemy soldiers. We've still got probably five hours drive time before we get to the LZ."

She listened for a time.

"Yes, ma'am. Thank you."

She spoke to Patty. "They're going to assign air assets to intercede if enemy aircraft are dispatched. Meanwhile, we're going to pick up the pace. Honoring the speed limit to avoid notice doesn't matter now if they're out looking for us."

"Won't it take a while for friendlies to get here? Could they arrive in time to save us?"

"They've moved a carrier fleet off the California coast. Naval planes are closer and have gotten the assignment to cover us."

"What about Marines in that fleet?"

"They will make a drop also at this new California location. If there are enemy troops protecting this person, we'll have plenty of backup. We still can't be sure if this person is allied with the enemy or a separate player in events around the world."

"As long as we can take them out, I see that as a positive step for us."

"By the way, Russia has renamed a town after our president. I guess they see him as a good enough comrade to warrant their accolades. He's certainly done more for them than they could ever have done on their own. Also, uprisings have escalated virtually everywhere on the globe. That is part of the reason we haven't been flooded with more foreign troops. They're facing significant trouble at home. Canada and Mexico are doing better than most because with so many American armed forces present, they can quell troubles in a hurry. I told you they had already conscripted the cartel soldiers into the national army and absorbed the cartel money into the federal government. Problem solved. A lot of debts paid off and now a lot of safe streets as a result."

Patty chuckled. "Win-win. I like it."

Racing along the expressway, they covered miles but felt it was too slow, even with speeding.

Eventually, they crossed the state line into Colorado. Getting off the main expressway, they headed for the designated landing area. Arriving early ahead of their evening arrival time for the transport aircraft, they unloaded the equipment and waited.

Deploying in defensive formations was automatic for them after so much time together and with the stressful situations they'd faced.

Lily stood watching the skies for any signs of enemy aircraft. Donna walked over.

Lily spoke. "I'm amazed at how our young additions have adjusted to life in the unit and on the run. They've learned and followed our protocols flawlessly. I've told so many people out in the world you don't need a Western upbringing to be able to be competent and smart. Gamal, from a small village in the mountains, and then Hussain, from a Somali warlord camp, would have been the last candidates those people would expect could make this kind of progress."

"I can't disagree."

"I'm not saying they're at our level of skill, but they certainly haven't been detractions. They pull their weight and add to the team with their unique talents. Gamal is very insightful for a young guy. It is too bad people can't know about them."

"Maybe if we win in the end, something can be done about that."

"I really don't see how. Our missions are kept secret for good reasons. I can only think what we do for them would probably be something personal from the team members."

"I'm sure if you ask them, they'd wish to be allowed to stay in America, or I should say America as it was."

"You're probably right, Donna. I hope we can get back to the point that we want to stay in America."

Both women turned their heads at the sound of a helicopter approaching. It was too early to be allied aircraft. The unit had already covered the vehicles with brush and slunk out of sight.

The chopper was a large Russian combat chopper scanning the area. With the large side wings and heavy weaponry mounted under those wings, it was a scary sight. It didn't come directly over them as it was paralleling the highway. It made no turns or changes in flight path.

After it passed by, the members came back out.

Wesley walked over. "I think they missed us."

"I think so too, but I hope we're right. We need clear skies for when our people get here."

"Even if enemy aircraft come then, I'd put my money on us eliminating any threat."

Lily smiled. "That's optimistic, Wesley."

"I'm a glass-half-full kind of guy."

"I always liked that about you."

"Wow, was that a compliment? Lily Carson doesn't give out compliments. What's up with that?"

"Shut up." She chuckled.

"He's got a point," Donna chimed in, smirking.

Lily pointed her finger. "You shut up too."

Patty walked over. "We've got a couple of hours before dusk. Everybody is anxious to get going. They're all getting weapons ready."

"I'm ready to go too. This waiting around gets annoying. Making no progress is even more annoying."

"Hopefully this time we're finally heading to the right place so we can do something about it."

They heard the sound of considerable trucks out on the highway, like a significant convoy of troops was passing.

Grace Bailey joined them. "They've probably got an idea we're somewhere in the area. Our battle at the site of the trap would have set off their alarm bells."

"I agree," Lily replied. "However, I'm more convinced there is another player. I think the reason there was no quick response back in that town was we struck this other guy's ambush. The fact they didn't have a large defense there tells me it was only a means to determine how close we are. It would have been obvious the level of skill we dispatched. Therefore, it's a clue that we know about them."

Patty added, "I think this next step out west will be the acid test. I doubt we'll find another setup. I have a feeling we'll find the real thing, including a robust defense."

Joe had wandered over. "I'm fine with that."

"Meathead," Donna muttered.

"You're just as bad as the rest of us," he retorted.

"True." She laughed hilariously. They bumped fists.

Lily joined the team with checking and readying her weapons. Hussain and Gamal were sitting nearby, watching her and smiling. She nodded, and they waved back and smiled broadly. Walking over, she asked them, "What's got you guys so smiley?"

Gamal looked at Hussain, and they chuckled.

"Well?"

Hussain answered, "We…eh…"

Gamal cut in, "We're glad to finally have a showdown."

Lily replied, "A showdown won't necessarily be a fun event. We've been very lucky with too many close calls. Our opponents are shooting also. Any of us could go down at any time."

"I've been in shootings much of my life," Hussain replied. "I know how to handle battles."

"I know you've been in conflicts, but none of us should ever get complacent. I never want to lose any of my comrades, and now that includes you two."

"We like that about you. We'll protect you too. I think you don't understand you're important to us. We wouldn't be in America without you."

"I suspect this America isn't what you expected."

"We look to find this bad person who has caused this. America needs to become America again. The risk of our lives is worth it. This is how we both feel."

"Thank you for that. However, I suspect this isn't the whole reason you were smiling. I think there is something else."

They smirked. Gamal spoke. "You know we're young men. Sometimes we don't make sense or sometimes dream of other things."

Patty walked over. "I think our transportation is arriving early."

They heard the sound of choppers approaching.

CHAPTER 13

With the equipment ready, they loaded up and were soon airborne traveling westerly. It was a bumpy ride, both with going over the Rocky Mountains with the usual atmospherics there, plus the approach of a storm, which rocked the aircrafts wildly. It was harrowing and tested their stomachs to hold down their recent meals. Lily glanced at Hussain and Gamal. Both appeared distressed with the flight issues.

"We'll get through this, guys, hang in there."

They nodded, but the uncomfortable looks remained.

The chopper pilots ascended to try to get above the storm. It only partially worked as this was a massive weather front, and the mountains funneled strong drafts upward into their flight path. All they could manage was to slightly decrease the stressful ride.

As they gutted their way through the discomfort with difficulty, even for experienced paratroopers, it was disconcerting. Nobody uttered a sound as they held on grim-faced. The aircraft were rocked wildly, buffeted severely in trying to fight through the teeth of the storm. It was a test of the skill of the pilots to maintain control in the most trying circumstances.

Remarkably, none of the helicopters crashed traveling at a time no aircraft should have been aloft. It did aid them in that the enemy would not have anticipated flights through such weather. That aided their attempt at a surprise attack.

The storm did slow their forward progress, causing them to approach the suspect area much later than scheduled. Their allies, Marines from the fleet, were already waiting at the landing site. It pleased everybody there were far more troops than anticipated, a veritable army.

Lily and Patty hurried over to greet the Marine commander.

"Hi, I'm Patty with the SEALs, and this is Lily from the agency, or maybe I should say the former agency. I can't you tell how happy we are to see you came in force. We have no idea what we'll face."

"Hello, I'm Captain John Grant. We're glad to be here. Sitting on the sidelines as that lunatic in the White House decimates our country has been intolerable. Did you hear the latest?"

Lily asked, "What now?"

"He declared this is no longer the USA, it's the USSA, the United Soviet States of America."

"What! I can't believe this."

"They got a decree from the Duma back in Mother Russia mandating the new structure for American society. Of course, the current rubber stamp legislature approved it on a voice vote. Russian troops were stationed inside the building watching who voted and how they voted."

"Those bastards."

"We have ground transportation here for the drive into this city."

"Good."

"We're loaded up and ready to leave whenever you are."

"Okay, we'll get our gear onto the vehicles. We're ready too. This may be the most important moment we'll ever have."

"Our rules of engagement are basically no mercy. Obviously, we won't go in wildly, guns blazing, shooting down innocent civilians, but as far as resistance, whether foreign troops or private armies and security forces, we will bury them. Do you agree?"

"We do. Remember, Captain, we've been chased around the globe, barely escaping with our lives. It's time to balance that ledger."

"We're on the same wavelength. Let's go get 'em."

The nearby Marines shouted loudly, "Hoorah!"

"Mount up!"

Troops loaded quickly into the waiting convoy of vehicles. Driving steadily down the hills to coastal areas, they entered an expressway heading southward. There was little traffic as it was after 1:00 a.m. Driving fast, they gained on a jeep, an enemy patrol vehicle. They were spotted by the enemy driver too late, so when the enemy tried to squeeze off rounds at them, an RPG round was already on its way to exploding their vehicle.

Passing the burning hulk, they stared. "I doubt they got off a call about us," Lily muttered. "We're not that far away from the target."

Once they entered the city, they were joined by helicopters covering their approach.

Traveling rapidly on the mostly empty streets, following the plan, the vehicles split up to make approaches from multiple directions. It became evident to Lily this wouldn't be like the trap in Missouri. Lights went on, and armed people flooded out of house onto the streets. From behind houses, armored vehicles appeared to join the defense.

"I think some of those are US military vehicles we left behind in the migration. We couldn't take everything when we left," Captain Grant explained.

The shooting started almost immediately. Lily's heart was thumping already. They waited only long enough to gauge the initial stages of the conflict and the positions of enemy troops.

Patty commented, "I really don't see any foreign troops among those guys. This is all in-country personnel."

"That makes me think we're at the right place. I think this is the hidden player we've been looking for."

"Finally."

Marines attacked from the east and west closing in on the defenders. Lily and Patty hustled with the team to prime spots to ensure good sniper perches to help cull the opposition. It was grisly work, but there was no alternative.

From the very start, the battle didn't go well for the bad guys. Initially, they gave a stiff fight and appeared to have military experience, but the ultimate outcome wasn't really ever in doubt. They were facing highly motivated, enraged, trained, and elite US military forces. This force was deadly efficient.

Surprising to Lily, they didn't show any sign of giving up the fight and surrendering. Consequently, it was a fight of attrition as the enemy ranks were steadily culled. Moving quickly toward the suspect house, Lily raced to keep up with Donna and Patty. Joe and Andy flanked them. The battle-ready Marines were not far away but were still locked in battle with the remaining defense forces, who were maintaining a delaying action.

"We need to get inside that house, right now!" Lily shouted. She was surprised to find Gamal on her right and Hussain on her left as they followed the SEALs up the steps to the front door. Crashing the door apart, they raced into the house. An elderly couple stood shaking in terror.

"On the floor!" Joe shouted.

The woman was crying, the husband ashen-faced.

"We must go!" Gamal shouted. He raced to a door that led down into a basement. The team followed.

The basement was full of banks of computer screens. A man sat typing on a terminal.

"Freeze!" Joe and Andy shouted simultaneously.

Grabbing the man, they yanked him out of his chair onto the cement floor with a hard thud, more like a splat of adipose.

"Wow, a four-hundred-pound fat guy in his parents' basement. Who would have thought?"

Jane and Johnston were quick to jump into the seats to get into the computer. Both typed furiously, saving data the heavy man had just started trying to delete. He'd failed as they got to him faster than he thought possible.

Both of the specialists said "Wow" over and over again.

Patty walked over with Lily to look at the screens. Their experts were working so fast it was hard to understand and follow their work.

"What did you find?" Lily asked.

Jane replied tersely, "We can't talk yet. We need to finish this fast."

Marines streamed down the stairs. Lily and Patty turned to Captain Grant.

Lily asked, "Is it over out there?"

"Yes, we only got a few of them to give up and surrender. There were many ex-military folks, but a lot of them are ex-cons. They were well paid so that is where their loyalty went. So this is the guy?"

"We believe so. I think our people managed to salvage much if not all of the data on his systems. As you can see, they're working feverishly, so I gather we struck gold."

They glanced at that man, facedown on his belly, his hands trussed up. It struck Lily that he was staring at her.

They walked over. She spoke to Andy and Joe. "Sit him up."

"I'm Lily Carson."

"I know who you are."

"What's your name?"

"Jason, Jason Jaye."

"How do you know me?"

"You don't remember. I met you a number of years ago at a seminar you gave. You inspired me to apply at the agency."

"I never told anybody anything about the agency."

"I'm able to read between the lines."

"So you say you applied at the CIA?"

"I should have known what would happen. They rejected me. Fat people get no credence, no leeway, no respect. Well…how do you feel about me now?"

"What does that mean? I had nothing to do with your application. I don't know you. What do you mean, how do I feel now?"

"Ask your techs over there. They can explain what I accomplished. You should have supported me."

Jane stopped typing and came over. "I can't believe you've done this." Incensed, she was white-faced, aghast at what she'd seen.

"Tell us, please?" Lily asked.

"He set in motion a plan to destroy all governments everywhere. It didn't help the rest of us having this demented current president in the White House, but all countries are under siege with no exceptions as the Russians, Chinese, and other dictatorships are discovering. He was engineering total worldwide anarchy. Basically, taking everybody back to the stone age. There was a world full of the disenfranchised people ready to follow his lead. They think they're going to get their slice of the pie. Duh! The strong will always gobble up the weak. That will never change. What we are frantically doing, in addition to preserving the data, is to reverse his decrees and directives to the contrary forces in the world. I fear he has done damage that may not be reversed."

She looked at Jason directly. He smirked. "I suppose you expect me to congratulate your exploits. That is not going to happen. You're obviously an amoral person with no thought for the staggering deaths you've caused. Did you think your outcome would be some panacea for mankind? Is this your version of validation? You disgust me."

"I will never be forgotten. My name will live forever in history."

"Right up there with Adolf Hitler. We'll see how you enjoy the rest of your life living in a dark hole at some black site."

"Get him out of here," Captain Grant commanded. Marines picked him up roughly and basically dragged him up the stairs stumbling painfully all the way in their rough hands.

Jane returned to the computer terminal; Johnston was reading data on his screen.

Johnston spoke. "This was the other player you always suspected, Lily. He was effective breaking into secure systems, but he had help too. Hackers around the world see computer systems as a challenge to be conquered. In addition, he was able to resonate with disgruntled government employees too. Once he started getting key access, everything took off pretty fast. Whatever complaint somebody had, Jason exploited. He built a fairly vast network of confederates working toward his anti-goals. They weren't really for anything, just universally against. You can't really say this was a wake-up call. It went so far beyond that. Seeing the current state of this country, no functioning economy, no ready food supply, danger merely by going out your door, people getting killed rampantly, foreign flags flying everywhere, it's appalling. Adding in the rise of morally bankrupt people to power, it's a perfect storm. In order to regain control of the USA, or should I say, to take out the USSA, we've got a serious war ahead. I see no way around it. Enemy troops are entrenched on our soil now. That's an issue that will need to be addressed very soon."

Lily answered, "I understand."

Jane added, "They had actually issued orders to various armies and navies for many countries to start a new world war. I have no doubt nuclear weapons would have been used at some point in time."

"That is chilling."

"We remanded those orders, but whether it's too late, I guess we'll find out. I don't know how many rogue commanders there are out there across the globe acting out of control."

"Doubly chilling. I'll pass on this information to our command so they can take prompt action."

Gamal tapped Lily on the shoulder. "Do you think we will attack your White House?"

"I would hope that never happens. I will say there needs to be substantial changes in the country, in every country actually."

Lily walked up the stairs to go outside to make her call. Looking around, Marines were stationed everywhere. Curious neighbors cautiously came outside to see the aftermath of the huge battle. With rare exception, they were happy to see US Marines guarding their street.

Lily dialed command back in Canada.

"Sir, we've captured our culprit and secured the scene and all of his equipment. Our people are going through it now. He was into everybody and everything. We've remanded orders he gave to various armed forces from numerous countries. He's being flown to you right now. His parents don't seem to be a part of it. They're elderly and confused. Jane tells me that soon she can transmit to our computer system what's on his devices. Once we've extracted and sent every detail, we'll destroy the system and sever his network for good. One less bad guy in the world."

"That's very good, Lily. We needed some good news for a change. These are dark days, and endless frustrations take a toll. Now, I think we've finally turned the corner on this horror."

"Thank you, General. He's done significant damage. I hope we can repair and recover our old life, but it might be the supreme test of our generation."

"I can't disagree. We're going to monitor international events for a short time to see if your interventions have impacted the operations of the allies of this man. We won't wait long to take action to reclaim our country."

"That sounds good to me. Do you want us back in Canada?"

"For the moment, we're going to leave you in California along with the Marines. At the very least, we can pacify and reclaim one of our cities. It's a first step."

"Yes, sir. We'll be waiting for your further determinations. By the way, if we're confronted by foreign troops, what are our instructions, the rules of engagement?"

"I'd say, don't go looking for trouble yet. That will come soon enough, but definitely if they attack, don't hold back taking it to them. We'll deal with that kind of battle with overwhelming force. In the meantime, you will have appropriate air cover."

"Good, thank you, sir. I've got a team itching for action. I'll hold them back as best I can."

"Right now, our Navy owns the West Coast. We're working on aggressive plans for the very near future."

"Yes, sir."

"I've got to go to a meeting, but we'll keep in close contact, Lily. Thank you and your team for your vital service."

She was pleasantly surprised when the entire Marine contingent remained in the city to aid in the repatriation efforts. The local residents, those who'd stayed behind whether from loyalty to the old regime or those locked in place due to being unable to join the flight across the border into Mexico, came out astonished at the sudden massive battle in their city.

In another pleasant surprise, among the American residents, there were no issues and no resistance. Instead, people were genuinely grateful for a return of US forces.

A young mother walked up to Lily with her three young children.

"Excuse me, ma'am. We've been near to starving. There is no food anywhere. Can you help us?"

"We're combat troops, but I'm sure there will be prompt actions taken to remedy that problem as soon as we can fully secure the city."

"What went on here? What was that big battle?"

"I believe we found the man most singularly responsible for all that has happened to this country and all across the globe."

"Do you mean Gerald Perkins? What could he do? He was sort of antisocial, living at home with his parents. The parents were really nice people."

"That may be true, but Gerald was not. He had an ax to grind, and unfortunately, he had computer skills to wreak a great deal of havoc."

"We didn't know. It just seemed that suddenly everything was upside down, and the weird messaging from Washington was hard to follow. When everybody fled overnight, those of us that couldn't leave were left unprotected and in fear for our lives. Suddenly there were criminals boldly walking the streets doing terrible things. My husband was killed early on trying to protect us. I've been desperate for a while now. It's been so hard."

"I'm so sorry that happened to you. We're here now, so better days are ahead."

Lily glanced at her children. They were emaciated and listless. "Let's get some rations into you. It can tide you over until we can provide steady meals."

The woman's eyes teared up. "Thank you," she whispered, choking with emotion.

Unit members had seen and heard the entire conversation and quickly stepped up to share from their personal supplies. The little ones were finally able to smile as they ate healthy food at last.

Their mother gratefully took food but only after all her children had received nourishment. Lily personally gave her own food at which time she gave Lily a fierce hug.

The gesture gave Lily a warm feeling. Doing something benevolent was a nice change from constant battle with taking lives.

Lily's phone beeped with a text. It surprised her.

"Hey, we've had a push across the southern border from Mexico into California. The Army is driving north to retake San Diego. There has been another push to free El Paso."

"Finally," said Joe. "We should have started the war before now."

The group turned their heads at the sound of helicopters and planes approaching.

"They're ours," said Patty.

The flights went to a nearby airport. It was a sizeable landing of additional allied forces.

Within a day, the local police precinct offices were recovered and stocked with those same officers who'd fled with the bulk of the populace. Police cars were quickly on the streets, causing raucous celebrations as people finally felt safe to come out into the open. They were anxious to direct the officers to the criminal elements who'd mercilessly tormented them during the occupation.

As they secured the area, Lily found it surprising there were no foreign troops to be found anywhere in the city. What remained of the thugs and gangs were dispatched rapidly with the help of citizens guiding authorities to the culprit's lairs. Once again, the American flag flapped in the breeze wafting in off the Pacific Ocean.

A steady supply line was established from the fleet to aid in feeding the populace. For those who had been trapped here, it was a godsend, and for those who stayed because they believed in the old regime suddenly had no problems switching sides. The strong dose of reality with the heinous actions stemming from the White House changed their minds. Many fell all over themselves trying to prove their newfound loyalty to the country.

"I didn't know" was a common reply, as if they were now absolved. It was a statement that didn't fly with those trapped people who had endured the brunt of the abuse and privation.

Lily, Patty, and the other leaders agreed on their positions in the matter. They showed no patience with the worst of the perpetrators.

When Lily spoke with the first of the former regime supporters and heard that lame excuse, she replied, "We aren't the people who will make judgments about you. We're here to drive out the bad elements. You now have your own police department back, so you can take it up with them."

It solved one of the short-term issues, but there were many more to deal with.

More Marine units landed as using this city as a rally point, they moved out to the nearest towns and cities to continue the reclamation effort. That process went well as the locals were eager for the relevant safety of having American troops on the ground and in charge in the area.

The first serious battle occurred when they approached San Francisco. Asian enemy forces were using the city and harbor in their operations. Having the coast basically blockaded by the US Navy gave a great advantage to US ground forces closing in to engage enemy forces. At sea, naval forces faced attacks from enemy subs but repelled the assaults successfully. It resulted in fewer enemy subs left to plague American vessels.

The enemy wasn't willing to incur all-out war, so the number of vessels they committed were far short of the considerable American naval fleet in the area. To the south, Mexican naval vessels joined the effort to form an invincible shield down the entire West Coast. Enemy navies rapidly sailed for home.

There was too much turmoil back in their home countries to allow the enemy from sending significant numbers of ships.

It was a far better beginning to the war than many anticipated. The iffy motivation levels of the troops in the departing enemy ships mirrored the sagging motivation levels in their ground forces. Badly outnumbered and going against highly enraged American, Mexican, and Canadian armed forces was a guaranteed loss.

Most enemy commanders were looking for a way out. It wasn't rare as days went on that enemy forces petitioned for cease-fires and free returns out of the country. It was expedient to facilitate those departures rather than face further battles.

While Lily's original team remained occupied in the west, they got notice of the state of things elsewhere.

Lily shared the intel with her unit.

"Guys, our forces have been crossing in force from Canada and Mexico, and it's been very promising. What enemy troops wanted here is true everywhere. They all want to leave. The only place there is any significant resistance is the mid-Atlantic area. Those ardent supporters of the regime know what's coming for them. Facing charges of treason and the penalties that go with that has stiffened their backbones, so they're digging in. The Russian tank corps stationed at and around the capital have yet to stand down. It doesn't look good for them as their hastily installed Russian air defense systems are woefully inadequate to deal with the level of power we're using. They just have too little, and it's too late for them to have any chance of winning. I think they're also going to sue for a cease-fire. Mother Russia is exploding with battles everywhere in their country now, and they're forces here are needed to defend the homeland.

"Our West Coast is in good shape for us all the way up to the arctic. Russia isn't engaging with the Alaskan coast. The Central US has even less conflict, so once the East Coast matter is resolved, it will just be a mop-up operation. The only place we've encountered domestic resistance is in the South. The new army of the Confederacy has chosen to do battle. It's not going well for them either. Although there are large numbers of them, too many aren't soldiers, just ideologs with hunting rifles or shotguns. They have no air cover, no qualified leaders, and no plans. They were following the plan of all the bad guys joining together, so now when the neo-Nazis, skinheads, cartels, militias, and crime syndicates have dropped off table and they're left alone, the message is sinking in. Their dream of unchecked anarchist societies where they can give vent to their base urges is never going to happen. Consequences for their evil deeds are knocking on their doors, and they're getting scared. The prospect of going down in killing fields is dawning on them."

Joe spoke. "I assumed we'd be taking it to them. This is kind of a disappointment."

The unit members laughed.

"We'll still have plenty of work to do, but at least it doesn't seem the worst is going to happen. For a long time, I was fearful we were done as a country and as a people."

"What about…that guy in the White House?"

"If there ends up being a battle for Washington, it will be a shame. I wouldn't be surprised if he's willing to sacrifice any and all of his supporters. He is a spineless, weak person. You won't see him out front of a battle with a weapon in hand."

"I would like to be a part of that battle."

"Joe, I have no control over that."

"I know, Lily, it's just how I feel. All of this was so needless."

"I agree."

The collapse in remaining resistance occurred shockingly easily. Within a month, the Confederate army basically evaporated back into their homes. There were few significant battles. In their first confrontation with the returning US Army and Marines, it was a colossal mismatch and monumental setback as after a few shotgun blasts, most of the rebel "troops" turned and fled.

As far as Washington, the Russian forces stood down and agreed to leave boarding Russian ships for a rapid departure. The recalcitrant president dressed as a Russian soldier to slip away with his foreign friends, leaving his lackeys to hold the bag for the aftermath.

When they heard the news, Donna looked at Lily.

Lily muttered, "Do svidanya, comrade."

They laughed.

Moving to Russia wasn't the triumphal event he dreamed. He wasn't accorded the honors and accolades he craved as he took up residence in a plain apartment building small flat outside of Moscow to live as a nondescript, inconsequential man rather than a former world leader. His absconded fortune was quickly blocked from following him out of the country. His phone calls to the Kremlin weren't answered. It was a pitiful ending for a pitiful man. In spite of his efforts, the United Soviet States of America met a quick end, and the United States of America arose again. Equally shocking was that he alone fled the country, leaving his family behind to face his consequences. The former first lady was quick to seek alternatives for her companionship while she tried to skirt any residual liability, rapidly blaming her former spouse for all possible bad actions. "I knew nothing."

One of the former US political parties struggled with the weight of rampant complicit behavior during that dark period. Rather than severe punitive action, the other party chose to attempt a guarded compromise. It was a difficult prospect with plenty of bitter feelings. Those politicians who'd faced abuse and unjust imprisonment were hard-pressed to find forgiveness in their hearts. Shameful acts burned into their brains were not easily dismissed, and the urge for revenge was a strong one.

Calming the waters was a necessary goal, but accomplishing it was seemingly impossible. However, the populace had learned a lesson about unchecked power and the divisiveness of misinformation. One party no longer their avid base of mindless believers and sycophants. That power was gone.

At long last, Langley was reclaimed by the original CIA staff. Undoing their previous sabotage acts to protect the country by regaining defense capabilities was task number one. Entire teams were brought in to revamp their systems in light of Russian agents having access to national secrets and processes. Lily led her team back into the same conference room where they'd met originally on the precipice of the national tragedy. It was a much different atmosphere now.

On a personal level for Lily, parting with team members she'd come to cherish as family wasn't easy, but most of them were anxious to get back to their own families. When it came to Gamal and Hussain, both young men were sad and depressed they couldn't stay in America.

Gamal spoke. "I miss my family, but I find it so hard to face leaving you. I've become a man, thanks to you and the team. My former life as a villager seems meaningless and useless. My eyes have been opened in so many ways. I see possibilities here."

"That's not true. Your life could never be meaningless or useless. You can be a beacon there, a leader to show them a different way. Hating the West isn't the way to live your life."

His head was down.

Lily looked at Hussain. "For me, it's worse. Going back to Somalia, I'll be a traitor to the warlords, so I'll be dead soon."

"We're going to place you with friendly forces so you can fight for a better Somalia."

"In my country, there is no hope. I will do what I can, but my ending is assured."

"I'm not sure what to say to that."

"There is nothing you can say. I accept my fate. Think nothing more about it."

The SEALs walked over. Donna gave Lily a fierce hug. "Anytime you want to play with the big dogs, let me know. We can get you set up at SEAL boot camp."

Lily laughed. "No, thank you. I've had all of the training I want."

Wesley hugged her warmly also. "Oh, what could have been," he whispered into her ear.

"Goodbye," she replied.

Even the two ISI agents were surprisingly emotional in parting with team comrades. Lily accepted their hugs.

"I wish you well, guys. Maybe you can convince your friends we're okay people."

Abdul spoke. "We can tell them about our experiences with you, but with some, they believe what they wish, regardless of any facts to the contrary."

"I understand. Stay safe."

At long last, for the first time in what seemed like forever, Lily could go to her home. Walking in the door to see her family brought her tears of joy. The firm group hug of the four of them lasted for a long time. Afterward, she could hear their story about what they went through. Her daughter wouldn't leave her lap.

"Mommy, I missed you so much."

"I missed you too, darling. I'm so sorry you had to go through that."

"Daddy took care of us, but it was really scary."

"I know, honey. Your dad is somebody you can always depend on."

Her son came over to hug them both. "I knew we would make it in the end. Can you tell us what happened to you?"

"You know I can't talk about my work, but it was really scary for me also. Thank the living God it's over."

"What do we do now?"

"I brought rations home so we'd have food to eat. It will take a while before everything gets up and running again so we can go to the stores to shop."

"I wish it was just like before, with school and friends."

"It will be soon enough. We've been through the worst, so from here on, it will just get better, darlings."

"Good."

For Lily to be able to resume her role as a wife and mother was food for her soul.

"Jack, you were incredible protecting the family. I was so lucky to get you."

He snickered. "Well, being pulled out of my meeting in Europe to find out my wife is a tier-one operator was a little disconcerting, but I managed. I worried less about us because I was able to control our situation. What scared me was not knowing what was happening to you."

"I wanted to call you, but it would have put you into the gunsights of the enemy. It bothered me every single day I was away from you guys. There were times I just wished you were there to give me a hug. You know what it's like to be deployed."

"I do."

"Well, now we pick up the pieces and rebuild."

"I worry if we can rebuild after the travesty of this administration. All of the hatred and evil doing."

"I know what you're saying. All that we can do is go day by day. My hope is that all of the hatred and animosity this guy engendered can drain away, and people will embrace community again. They followed his rhetoric about his vision of a perfect world and once they got it, I think they've learned their lesson. I hope they learned anyway."

"Many of them probably have, but I suspect there is still a significant number of people who'd still like to burn down American society to be set free to wallow in their base instincts and uncontrolled urges. We dealt with some vile people while we were on the run. I hated that our children were exposed to such people. Thankfully, I kept us clear of any harm, but there were some iffy situations. The kids were deeply scared."

"Hearing that adds to my simmering anger. I can't help having this need for revenge. Getting past that has been a test for me."

"How was it parting with your team?"

"It was traumatic. We've been through so much, proved our value to each other, and dodged some very serious bullets. Our two young guys, one from the Middle East and the other from Africa, I hated I couldn't help them stay in the USA, especially our Somalian. He has no living family back in Somalia and will be hard-pressed to avoid the warlords looking for him for siding with us."

"That's terrible. I wish him the best."

"We'll see how long it takes to get a new government in place and to get our national defenses back up and running. I believe the efforts to sabotage agency systems to keep them out of enemy hands will take time to repair and replace. I'm sure that will be job one for me back at the agency. It will be preferable to running for our lives across the globe."

"Everything everywhere is chaos. In my business, it will take a long time to recover, if we can."

"At least we're back together. That's the first best thing for me."

"I agree."

"I'd say I can make us a great dinner, but there's not much available when it comes to rations packets."

They both chuckled and hugged.

The flag of the United States of America flew over the entire country once again. It was a symbol and a sign of one people pulling together to conquer the problems remaining from the national nightmare. Lily had peered at the American SEAL and the Latin phrase "E Pluribus Unum," out of many, one. She hoped that could happen. Going forward, being a mom again was a balm for her spirit as they aggressively tackled the rebuilding issues as a family and as a nation, and she tried to forget the harrowing chase across the globe.

At last, contrary elements were brought to heel, and the noble aims of a once-proud country resurfaced. No longer were there overt animosities along the southern borders as the genuine and decent treatment of American refugees by Mexico surprised people who'd harbored the worst feelings and treatments for that country and their people. Those prejudiced people who'd perpetrated the worst in humanity no longer were open and vocal about their reprehensible ways. They slunk back under their rocks and rotten logs, out of view, no longer tolerated by the masses of the people. However, hiding from prosecution for their crimes didn't spare them, as the newly reinstalled authorities were relentless in hunting them down.

A new day dawned for all of North America, like the clouds of darkness were finally parting. After all the turmoil, it was like a miracle.

The End

ABOUT THE AUTHOR

Dennis K. Hausker is a 1969 graduate of the Michigan State University, a Vietnam war veteran, married to his wife since 1968. She is a retired teacher, described as "warm and fuzzy" for her classes. Denny loves sports and travel and loves writing. His favorite author, Michael Crichton.

CPSIA information can be obtained
at www.ICGtesting.com
Printed in the USA
BVHW031143201221
624514BV00014B/63